Saleh
A Prince of Malaya

Saleh
A Prince of Malaya

SIR HUGH CLIFFORD

With an Introduction by
J. M. GULLICK

SINGAPORE
OXFORD UNIVERSITY PRESS
OXFORD NEW YORK
1989

Oxford University Press

Oxford New York Toronto
Delhi Bombay Calcutta Madras Karachi
Petaling Jaya Singapore Hong Kong Tokyo
Nairobi Dar es Salaam Cape Town
Melbourne Auckland
and associated companies in
Berlin Ibadan

Oxford is a trade mark of Oxford University Press

Introduction © *Oxford University Press Pte. Ltd. 1989*
First published as A Prince of Malaya *by Harper & Brothers Publishers, New York, 1926*
First issued as an Oxford University Press paperback, 1989

ISBN 0 19 588929 0

Printed in Malaysia by Peter Chong Printers Sdn. Bhd.
Published by Oxford University Press Pte. Ltd.,
Unit 221, Ubi Avenue 4, Singapore 1440

INTRODUCTION

THE central character, Raja Muhammad Saleh, is the son of the Malay ruler of the State here called Pelesu. The story covers a period of ten years around 1900, when Pelesu (a thin disguise for Pahang) has only recently come under British administration.

Saleh's boyhood is spent in the very traditional and privileged environment of a Malay royal household. Then, at the age of fourteen, he is sent off to England to be educated privately in the home of a clergyman at Winchester. After surviving the initial culture shock of this drastic transition, Saleh shows the enthusiasm of a convert in absorbing, so far as he can, English behaviour and attitudes. However, he has an uneasy feeling that beneath the friendly welcome given by his English contemporaries there lies a contemptuous rejection of him as an outsider and inferior. An encounter with an Indian girl who speaks with the vehemence of Asian nationalism, is followed by a painful episode in which Saleh overhears an English girl, to whom he is attracted, say that a proposal of marriage from him would be 'quite impossible' and 'an insult' (pp. 81–2). In the emotional breakdown which follows, Jack Norris, a British official on leave from Pelesu, succeeds in calming a deeply wounded and distressed young Malay.

The voyage back to Malaya is marred by another humiliation (p. 125). At the court of Pelesu he finds himself an outsider by reason of his English ways. His father snubs him brutally (p. 160) and his mother, who had hoped through Saleh to regain her lost primacy over a rival, is in despair (p. 166). His attachment to the colonial regime in Pelesu for training in administration is another fiasco since his education in England has done little to prepare him for work which he finds tedious.

British officials are briskly unsympathetic in their dealings with him.

He drifts into raffish idleness and falls under the influence of opponents of the regime. Thus Saleh becomes the titular leader of a hopeless revolt which ends with his death. Norris, the voice of Clifford himself, ends the book with 'May God forgive us for our sorry deeds and for our glorious intentions'.

The novel was written and published in two parts, as *Sally: A Study* (1904) and *Saleh: A Sequel* (1908). In 1925 Clifford wrote a note on a copy of the earlier part to explain its origin. Raja Alang Iskander, son of Sultan Idris of Perak, who had been a student in England since 1895,

... came to stay with his Father and me at the Hotel Cecil in June, 1902, the year of King Edward VIIth's Coronation. He had then for five years been living with the family of A. L. Smith, who was later the Master of Balliol College, Oxford. . . . Alang spoke Malay haltingly when he first joined us; but it came back quickly, and his last confidences to me were made in the vernacular the night before he sailed for Malaya, as he sat on my bed and wept (Wicks: 14).

On the basis of this episode, Clifford wrote Part 1 as a fictional study of the stress to which a Malay (Saleh) is subjected by an unwise decision to send him to be educated in England.

The final chapter (pp. 97–105) of Part 1 was intended to round off the story with a discussion, in which the well-meaning English tutor and his wife (Revd and Mrs Le Mesurier) remain optimistic that Saleh will retain much of the benefit of his up-bringing in their home. However, Norris (Clifford) predicts (p. 105) that at best Saleh will be saved by shedding his 'dual personality' (p. 132) and drugging himself with the 'animal joy', the empty pleasures of Malaya as a 'Land of Cockagne' (p. 105).

In 1904 Clifford did not intend to continue the story and wrote 'The End' at the foot of his manuscript of Part 1 (p. 105), before sending it for initial publication, in four instalments

(November 1903–February 1904) of *Blackwoods Magazine*. However, the printer substituted '(to be continued)' in place of 'The End' (Clifford 1908: 6). By the time this appeared in print, Clifford was at work in Trinidad, to which he had been transferred most reluctantly in 1903. (The 1904 book has an anguished preface and a rather poor poem about his enforced removal from further service in Malaya.) Moreover, the Colonial Office had extracted from him a qualified undertaking to wind up his prolific writing about Malaya (Gailey: 41).

However, Clifford's readers were not satisfied. Some of them reproached him with 'a vile practical joke' over the words '(to be continued)'. Others said that he had ended the story abruptly just as 'it was at last about to become interesting'. He was also accused of lacking the courage to carry his theme through to its conclusion. He justified himself saying, 'I have for Raja Saleh a very warm corner in my heart and I doubt my ability to make others feel for him that measure of forgiveness which is the child of complete comprehension' (Clifford 1908: 6–7). However, he was not a man to refuse a challenge and so, when the crisis which had brought him to Trinidad eased in 1906, he wrote the whole of Part 2 in a month (August 1906). This, like Part 1, first appeared in *Blackwoods Magazine* in instalments (May–August 1908) and was almost immediately republished as a book entitled *Saleh: A Sequel*.

The two parts, with the omission of an opening chapter by which the original Part 2 picked up the story from Part 1, were combined as *A Prince of Malaya*, and republished, with a new preface, in America in 1926. This book is a reprint of that combined American edition of both parts.

Unlike so many of Clifford's short stories, this novel is not based on a real-life episode or figure thinly disguised. There was no historical model for Saleh. Hence the reader can take the book as fiction, albeit set in an historical context, and enjoy a well-constructed narrative, with vivid description and, on the whole, subtle characterization. However, those who are also interested in Clifford's mode of depicting his times in Malaya may find a good deal more beneath the surface.

As an example of that method, Norris's first encounter with Saleh in England leads him to recall the ceremonies of Saleh's birth (pp. 8–12). Clifford had been present at similar ceremonies for the newly born Raja Alang Iskander (Stockwell 1980: 25). Saleh, after years in England, encounters an initial difficulty in speaking Malay with Norris (p. 7) like that which Clifford had noted when he met Raja Alang Iskander in 1902. Even if a character in a story is not *closely* modelled on a real person, Clifford builds into the fictional picture touches of the model or experience which he has in mind.

Mrs A. L. Smith, who may well have been the model for Mrs Le Mesurier, wrote at length of Raja Alang Iskander's five years in her family circle (Smith: 145–6, 163–5). From this source, we can observe the actual events in which Clifford found the raw material which he reshaped to make Part 1. It was Clifford, on leave in 1896, who introduced Raja Alang Iskander to the Smith household, 'with some pomp and circumstance', emphasizing that his 'future position might one day be important'. Clifford's vehement condemnation in these pages of the education of a young Malay in England may, to some extent, reflect his regret that he was partially instrumental in making one such arrangement.

At this time, A. L. Smith was a tutor at Balliol, who accepted resident pupils, English and occasionally 'Oriental', to coach them for entry to an Oxford college. Smith was a talented academic, an enthusiast for undergraduate sporting activities, a sympathetic teacher but also impatient with those who could not profit from his help, active in many outside fields. He does not much resemble Le Mesurier in the book (p. 28). Mrs Smith noted that by 1902 the young Malay, who was known in the family as 'Alang', 'was thoroughly at home in our family and a great favourite, companionable and intelligent but ... I used to think that he was learning nothing in the sense of book-learning, I mean, but his character did develop'. There is nothing to suggest that he formed an attachment for any of the Smith daughters, of whom there were seven, or their friends, but their mama would not have told us anyway.

The arrival in England of Sultan Idris, his father, whom he had not seen during five or more formative years, led on, step by step, to the crisis described by Clifford in his note of 1925. The Sultan, escorted by Clifford, came down to Oxford and no doubt received a personal report from Smith on his pupil's lack of progress. Mrs Smith was 'engrossed' in the preparations for receiving the Sultan. Among other problems she had to get her husband 'properly garbed' (left to himself he retrieved his oldest suits from the pile set aside for jumble). A distinguished party had been invited to take lunch with the Sultan in the college hall, but he kept them waiting by withdrawing into a private room, and Clifford had to explain that 'H.H. was engaged in praying for us'. In due time the Sultan emerged in splendour with 'a huge diamond glittering in his headgear'. At the last moment it was realized that the Smiths' dog could not remain in the company of this eminent Muslim guest.

When the lunch, 'a grand affair', was over, the party withdrew to the Smiths' house, where the girls played tennis and sang to the Sultan, 'which H.H. seemed to enjoy'. Mrs Smith continues: 'But as I looked at him I rather trembled for Alang's future; he seemed divided by centuries from the standards of his father, so mysteriously had the atmosphere of an English home affected him.'

Tension between father and son reached crisis when the Sultan inspected the 'gorgeous uniform of white cloth embroidered with gold tigers across the front' which Iskander had imprudently allowed a London tailor to make for him to wear, when riding in his father's carriage in the Coronation procession.

In his displeasure, the Sultan decreed that Iskander's cousin, Raja Chulan, who was in the royal party, should take Iskander's place and ride in the procession.*

It was a crestfallen young Iskander who departed from Oxford 'one day, very sadly and reluctantly, like a small boy going off to his second term at school, when all the novelty is worn off and he knows the worst'. This was the prelude to the final emotional scene in Clifford's hotel bedroom on the eve of his departure to Malaya.

Raja Alang Iskander is certainly not the model for Saleh in Pelesu (in Part 2), and it would have been a grave error of taste if, in Part 1, Clifford had indicated any connection between the fictional Saleh and the real Iskander, son of his friend Sultan Idris. Hence the story of Alice Fairfax is a necessary contrivance to illustrate Clifford's point. On his return to Malaya, Iskander was for a time a rather feckless and extravagant young man, but he made a successful career for himself in the Police, acquired *gravitas*, and in time became Sultan of Perak (1918–38). In that capacity he was a leading champion of 'Malay rights', showing 'a quick fiery temper' (Yeo Kim Wah: 210). In 1924 he visited Mrs Smith, recently widowed, at Oxford and they went off to view A. L. Smith's grave. Her verdict on him is, 'I may say that no pupil has ever repaid us better for all the trouble we took with him.'

We will come shortly to other possible models for the presentation of Saleh's experiences in Pelesu. First, however, let us look at the sombre Pelesu (Pahang) background.

---

*The Sultan, who appeared at the 1903 Durbar in Kuala Lumpur wearing a military uniform with a cocked hat (Gullick 1987: 203), had no choice on this occasion. British protocol required Malay royalty who attended Coronations to appear in Malay national dress. Sultan Abdul Hamid of Kedah, who arrived intending to wear a military uniform at the 1911 Coronation, had to instruct a Savile Row tailor in the intricacies of making suitable Malay dress as a substitute (Sheppard: 20).

As Pelesu is undoubtedly Pahang it might be supposed that Sultan Ahmad of Pahang (r. 1863–1914) is the model for Saleh's father. There are some touches of Ahmad, as where Baker complains that the ruler is 'most uncommonly inaccessible' when required to attend to official routine business (p. 171). However, the differences are more striking still. Saleh's father is a fat, coarse, boorish man (pp. 14, 165). Sultan Ahmad, on the other hand, had 'handsome, clean-cut features' and also 'languor and grace and . . . quiet almost melancholy gentleness' (Clifford 1929: 180). Moreover, Clifford, who said that he had been admitted to Sultan Ahmad's 'intimate friendship' (1929: 179), would not have published so harsh a portrait of Ahmad in his lifetime, if ever. A clue to a different 'original' is found in the repeated references (pp. 11, 158) to the addiction of Saleh's father to 'an absurd assortment of bright colours' in his clothing. This was one of the distinctive features of Raja Yusuf, Regent and later Sultan of Perak (1876–87) when Clifford was there. Swettenham (1895: 163) says that Yusuf 'affected gay colours' and Clifford adds that Yusuf was 'a barbarous person of unspeakable manners and morals', and that, after his death (in 1887), he was known to his subjects as 'the late king, *God be merciful to him*' (Clifford 1929: 171).

In Saleh's mother Clifford depicts the typical situation of a first wife of a Malay ruler, who has lost her youthful good looks, and with them her place in her husband's affections. Saleh is 'the incarnation of a last hope' (p. 142) of restoring her fortunes but is destined to disappoint her. It would have been a breach of Malay decorum if Clifford ever penetrated to the women's quarters of the *istana* at Pekan, which he describes so vividly (p. 143). But Isabella Bird, not disqualified by her sex, gives a similar, if less sordid picture (Bird: 233), of the claustrophobic environment of a middle-aged royal wife in Selangor. We do not know if Clifford had a model for his portrait of this bedraggled, opium-sodden figure of a woman still under forty (pp. 147, 153), but it is one of the most powerful passages in the book.

Raja Pahlawan Indut, champion of the good (or wicked) days before the detested Nasareen intruded upon Pelesu, manipulates Saleh into leadership of the final revolt. In his description (p. 154), Clifford mentions that Indut had 'a particularly gentle voice and manner'. Elsewhere he says that the historical Raja Mahmud ('Raja Haji Hamid' in others of Clifford's stories) had 'the silkiest, most conciliatory manner of any Malay that I have ever known' (1927b: 16). In this book, too, there is a reference (p. 94) to Mahmud's presence in Pekan, as Clifford's companion. Raja Mahmud never led a revolt but the colonial regime found him an awkward, intransigent man, with a similar history of prowess as a warrior (Gullick 1987: 82). In the final passage of this book, dealing with the hopeless revolt, Clifford could draw on his knowledge of the semi-suicidal mood of the Pahang rebel leaders, of which he gave a chilling account elsewhere (Clifford 1898: 223–42). The attack on the police station (p. 233) and other episodes of the revolt are derived from different events in the protracted Pahang revolt. At various points (pp. 88, 231, 238, 251) Clifford introduces his concept of Malay *amuk*, on which there is a considerable literature and many different views (Gullick 1987: 240).

There are some excellent shorter character studies, such as Saleh's bumptious half-brother (p. 137) and the slave girl, Munah, to whom Saleh is briefly and disastrously married (pp. 178, 217–22). As always, Clifford finds space for Malay ceremonies, such as shaving the infant's head (p. 11) and a royal wedding (p. 220). Clifford's Malay fiction is a superb source-book of social history. By contrast, the Europeans do not come to life. The English girls who befriend and attract Saleh are insipid, sentimentalized lay-figures who inhabit a world which does not know the coarseness of Edwardian social life. The British administrators, too, are cut in cardboard, and lack depth.

The search for traces of historical background should not be pushed too far. The book is fiction, not history, and normal licence must be accorded to the author in presenting his theme in imaginative form. Saleh is totally uprooted at the age of fourteen from his Malay environment and is then exposed for five years to the effects of living in an alien society. Secondly, he returns to a Pelesu/Pahang which is still hardly touched by the cultural factors which have so much altered Saleh's outlook. In historical Pahang, as in fictional Pelesu, the pressure of newly imposed colonial rule erupted in armed revolt. However, none of Saleh's actual contemporaries of the period around 1900 were so comprehensively exposed to such abrupt and powerful pressures.

This stark exposure of conflict is characteristic of Clifford, who was a man of strong imagination and emotion. When, for example, he gave a lecture in 1899, entitled 'Life in the Malay Peninsula—as it was and is', his audience at the Royal Colonial Institute included Hugh Low and William Treacher, who had been in Malaya with him. In the discussion after the lecture both expressed, in guarded language, their sense that Clifford had given a highly-coloured picture. The Malays, said Low, were not 'an unamiable set of people'. Treacher advised the audience 'to be careful how you digest the exciting fare that has been presented to you' (Kratoska: 249, 251).

Pahang did not offer any suitable material on the experiences of Saleh as a civil servant. Perak, despite the markedly different environment, may have done, though not in connection with Iskander.* Writing in 1902–6, Clifford was not to know that

*Clifford was on friendly terms with Sultan Abu Bakar of Johor (r. 1863–95) (Stockwell 1980: 29) and must have known that the Sultan and several of his ministers had been educated at the Singapore school of Revd Benjamin Keasberry, as had some of the Kedah bureaucrats of this period (Makepeace *et al.* 1: 448). Sultan Abu Bakar's private secretary was 'a very clever Malay educated in England' (Thio: 108). But Clifford did not regard these states as comparable with the FMS (Clifford/Kratoska: 244).

Raja Alang Iskander, on his return to Perak, would find a very useful role as Assistant Commissioner of Police (1905–16). In this capacity Iskander 'entered wholeheartedly on his duties and toured the country repeatedly' (Morrah: 103) in marked contrast to Saleh's lack-lustre performance (pp. 192, 203).

However, it may be that Clifford's imagination had been stirred by what he had seen and later been told of the two sons of ex-Sultan Abdullah of Perak. When Sultan Abdullah was sent into exile in 1876, there was no obvious successor at that time. Raja (later Sultan) Idris had been too close to his deposed cousin (Gullick 1979: 118). So Hugh Low arranged that the unpopular Raja Yusuf, whom we have suggested was the model for Saleh's father, should be Regent of Perak. Meanwhile, Raja Mansur and Raja Chulan, the young sons of ex-Sultan Abdullah, were sent to be educated, first at the Raffles Institution in Singapore and then at the Malacca High School. Among the Perak aristocracy it was understood—and much debated—that one or other might in time become ruler (Sidhu: 130).

Isabella Bird in her book (Bird: 276) calls them 'two nice Malay boys' but in a private letter (Gullick 1979: 117) she gives a fuller picture:

They are 9 and 12 with monkey-like irrepressible faces. They never cease speaking and are very playful and witty but though a large sum is paid for their education at the house of an English schoolmaster at Malacca they speak atrocious pidgeon English *and never speak Malay* (emphasis supplied). They are never still for one instant, chattering, reading snatches from books, asking questions, turning somersaults, jumping on Mr Maxwell's shoulders, begging for dollars.

When Clifford first came to Perak in 1883 they were youths thirteen and sixteen years old. Both, like Saleh, were appointed to the state civil service but neither was satisfactory. Anderson described the elder, Raja Mansur, as 'an unmitigated black-guard' (Sidhu: 114).

Raja Chulan was not a success in the civil service, from which he retired in 1911, but in later life he was a distinguished and influential Malay 'elder statesman' (Sidhu: 114f), with whom Clifford on his return in 1927 resumed his personal friendship. Chulan, however, married a daughter of Sultan Idris and caused the latter much concern by pressing for recognition as a potential successor to the throne. Idris spoke very frankly to Ernest Birch in 1909 of his misgivings over the shortcomings of his ambitious son-in-law, and he would have had the opportunity of doing so during his long conversations with Clifford in London in 1902 (Clifford 1929: 191f).

Although he builds into his story elements of people whom he had known, Clifford's main purpose is more general—to expound his profound distrust of the impact of English education on the Malay ruling class. Saleh returns to Pelesu 'unfitted by training to be a Malay Raja, unfitted by nature to be an Englishman' (p. 242). He feels 'isolated, estranged and outcast' from his own people (p. 141). To the colonial regime, 'the denationalized Malay is the devil' (p. 167), a problem not a partner in their work. For the presentation of this basic theme, as a picture of a clash of cultures in the Malaya of his time, Clifford, in his preface, claims 'relentless accuracy'.

In the person of Le Mesurier, the kind English clergyman, we have a typical specimen of the teachers to whom Malay students (but not Iskander) were too often sent. In Kuala Lumpur, as Clifford may have known, the 'Raja School', established in 1890 for Malay youths of Saleh's type, was in the charge of a more ebullient but no less inefficient clerical tutor, Frank Haines, who taught 'moral values' but ignored the 'scholastic and vocational side' of his job (Stevenson: 151).

More than once (pp. 45, 97, 193) we learn of Saleh's lack of intellectual progress or interests, his 'colossal intellectual failures' (p. 44). Nowhere, however, does Clifford face the question of why five years' personal tuition was so unproductive.

He might well have argued, of course, that if Iskander made no progress as the pupil of so eminent a teacher as A. L. Smith, it must be assumed that *by its very nature* this education was bound to fail—and was indeed destructive.

In his foreword to *Saleh: A Sequel*, Clifford states this view:

Englishmen in Asia, at the bidding of Lord Macaulay, who in his turn was inspired by idolatrous worship of book-learning to be gotten in the schools, have been busily engaged during the past three or four decades in endeavouring to impose on their Oriental brethren education of a purely Occidental type. They have ignored the fact that the genius of Asia differs from that of Europe in kind rather than degree. They have failed to see that the education of the East should proceed along lines adapted to its special character, suited to its peculiar bent, following in logical sequence the trend of its natural development, which in turn is the result of uncounted centuries of transmitted tendency and inherited sentiment and tradition. Instead they have endeavoured to force the Oriental mind out of the channels in which it should have run its appointed course, and to divert it into canals of its own fashioning.

The results are with us now in what is euphemistically called the 'Unrest' in India; but the end is not yet.

There was once a man named Frankenstein (Clifford 1908: vii–ix).

Nowhere in his fiction or his other writing does Clifford, so far as I know, describe the system of education which would have been 'suited to the peculiar bent' of Malay culture and tradition. He gave tepid praise to Malay vernacular education in village schools: 'The effect of education on the Malay is, undoubtedly to make him at once a more law abiding and more useful member of society; and the extraordinary ignorance of the Pahang natives ... makes the duty of education all the more imperative in our case' (AR Pahang 1896). He also recognized the beneficial effect of widening the horizons of the Malay ruling class, noting that every one of the Pahang leaders who had attended the first Durbar of FMS Rulers at Kuala

Kangsar in Perak had 'gained some enlargement of his ideas, some desire to see similar improvements effected in his own neighbourhood' (AR Pahang 1897).

Both he and Swettenham praised Sultan Idris as a paragon of the 'enlightened' Malay ruler, who kept his traditional place but shared their aspirations (Clifford 1929: 193; Swettenham/ Kratoska: 187, and Swettenham 1948: 343). Swettenham went as far as proposing for the Malay aristocrat a system of education which would 'revive his interest in the best of his traditions' (Swettenham/Kratoska: 186).

The modern reader may recall that education in Malaya is now based on the dominant use of the Malay language (*Bahasa Malaysia*) as the medium of instruction. This, however, is not what late Victorian imperialists had in mind. As it happened, both Clifford and Swettenham had left Malaya before the early twentieth century 'new era' (Stevenson: Chap. 5) in Malay education began and they had no perceptible influence on it. These reforms were the major achievement of R. J. Wilkinson, during his all too brief period (1903–6) as FMS Inspector of Schools. Wilkinson, as much as Clifford, recognized that 'the effacing of the old social landmarks brought about a demoralisation' but continued—on a more positive note—that 'it should be the object of public instruction to combat' that situation (Wilkinson 1902: 686).

We do not know what view, if any, Clifford took of the two most important innovations of the Wilkinson era. The first was the foundation in 1905 of the Malay College at Kuala Kangsar. Swettenham, in the last months of his governorship had vetoed the original scheme put forward by Rodger (Stevenson: 177). Wilkinson had the utmost difficulty in securing the grudging acquiescence of the next Governor (Anderson) to an initial three-year experiment on a small scale. However, Sultan Idris, unlike the European colonial hierarchy, was sufficiently enlightened to see the merits of a school specially designed for

'the racial idiosyncrasies of the Malays' (Stevenson: 182) and
gave it his active and influential support. Clifford might have
found its ethos and organization, derived from the English public
school model, alien to his taste. However, it survived the initial
scepticism and became a flourishing Anglo-Malay hybrid
institution.

Wilkinson's other legacy was the series of *Papers on Malay
Subjects* (Wilkinson/Burns) and his effective efforts to revitalize
Malay education generally, thus stemming the demoralization—
'the old torturing doubt anent the inherent weakness . . . of his
race' which Clifford imputes to Saleh (p. 187).

In his romantic and at times emotional fashion, however,
Clifford was dedicated to the preservation of Malay society,
purged of its aristocratic excesses. He really did not want to
induce changes, even if 'suited to the peculiar bent' of the
Malay character. Allen (1964), in his penetrating examination
of the philosophy of Clifford and Swettenham in their attitude
to the Malays, was led to conclude that when Clifford returned
to Malaya in 1927 after a long absence he was beset by 'his
deep personal fear that the country should have been altered
beyond recognition' and that this factor may have led to his
mental breakdown. Already, in his 1926 preface to this book,
Clifford writes of the 'vast revolutions' which he had not then
seen with his own eyes.

In this book, Clifford begins to confront, though he offers no
solution to, the dilemma inherent in his view of Malay society
under colonial rule. He does not have occasion to expound in
these pages the sincere, if romantic, view of the Malay peasantry, which he had expressed elsewhere. In his 1899 lecture,
for example, he had praised their 'great and large-hearted
kindness' to each other, their 'chaste and honourable lives'
(Clifford/Kratoska: 241). He had written stories on this theme,
such as 'A Daughter of the Muhammadans' on the devotion of a
young wife to her husband afflicted with leprosy (Clifford

1899: 139; 1927: 127). For the peasants, the economic and social benefits of colonial rule, spiced with a judicious amount of simple education would safeguard 'a very Garden of Eden in these Malayan lands'. But he added that 'the serpent, in the form of the dominant classes, [must have] been excluded from the demesne' (Clifford/Kratoska: 241).

However, the exclusion from the demesne of Malay government of the unruly members of the upper class deprived them of the 'romance' and the 'freedom' of the old way of life 'leaving in their stead only the dirt, the squalor, and the unloveliness' (p. 169). 'Men loafed and sauntered through their lives, but now they lacked the frequent tonic of warfare' (p. 174). In fact, 'The tawdry shell, the valueless husk, had been left to the Malay by the Englishman; but the soul which it had once sheltered, the soul which had given to it meaning and force and value, had been reft from it' (p. 177). Official reports suggest that this is a faithful picture of the loss of morale at the court of Sultan Ahmad in the early 1890s and goes to explain the upsurge of revolt, limited as it was, in Pahang.

In his own despair, Saleh condemns a 'usurpation by white men who were infidels . . . of the inalienable right and heritage' of the Malay ruling class (p. 182). This is the backward-looking nationalism of the frustrated Malay ruling class, to which Islam lends a sharper edge.

The book presents Islam in a low key. Clifford had pursued the Pahang rebels into Terengganu, where the celebrated divine, Ungku Sayid of Paloh, 'had preached holy war to them' (Clifford 1895/1961: 45). However, Raja Haji Abdullah, the Islamic leader summoned by Indut to his aid in Pelesu, shows himself a 'prudent soul' possessing 'the rare virtue of patience'. He works on the feelings of Saleh as a Muslim but takes no part in the revolt (pp. 156, 228, 244). Elsewhere, Clifford had written that 'the Pahang Malay, in his unregenerate state, thinks chiefly of deeds of arms . . . he is at once ignorant, irreligious, and unintellectual' (Clifford 1897: 17). It is a historical fact that loss of power rather than the spirit of the *jihad* was the driving force of the Pahang rebellion.

Clifford, and also Swettenham, were much more concerned over the threat posed by anti-European Asian nationalism arising from an unwise policy, as they saw it, of English language education, 'an idolatrous worship of book-learning'. In this book, the Indian princess is a voice (p. 52f) rather than a personality, depicted in a fashion which reveals Clifford's lack of sympathy. It was not apparent in 1900 that Western education of a traditional élite, castigated by Clifford, would in the fullness of time produce from that élite the effective leadership of Malay nationalism (Roff: Chap. 7). Clifford's rejection, root and branch, of English education is based on his assertion that 'The genius of Asia differs from that of Europe in kind rather than in degree' (Clifford 1908: vii).

'A hybrid creation of two opposed and clashing civilisations' was the worst solution of all (p. 169). At one point (p. 196), Clifford argues that the Malays, as much as the Europeans, wish to 'keep their blood untainted . . . *the question of inferiority or superiority does not enter into the matter*'. However, whenever there is a comparison of *mores*, such as punctuality (p. 33), sexuality (p. 65), stoicism (p. 88), self-improvement (p. 102), spirituality (p. 105), and energy (p. 213), it puts the European on a higher plane. Even Norris opines that Saleh's English education has only made him 'as near an approximation to a decent white man *as a Malay can be*' (p. 99) and back in Pelesu Saleh is perceived to be '*dropping back* more and more into a Malay' (p. 216) (emphasis supplied). Throughout his writing on Malaya, Clifford shows much admiration and sympathy for Malay character, indulging in 'Rousseauesque eulogies on the virtues of the Malay villager in his "natural state"' (Stevenson: 9). But, like Kipling, he was a man of his time, viewing the world from a conscious position of assumed superiority.

Because this is a novel of ideas, as well as of events and characters, it tests Clifford's ability as an author to the full. It has been said that Clifford reveals 'two major weaknesses as a writer ... his general inability to present conversations realistically ... and his problems with regard to character development' (Gailey: 36–7). The latter may be dismissed as a constraint incidental to the short story, which was the form in which much of Clifford's work was written. In a short snapshot of a single episode it is hardly possible to show a character in the process of change. But in this short novel the developing character of Saleh himself passes from the naïve enthusiasm of his student days in England to the embittered, despairing leadership of the final revolt.

As Gailey recognizes (Gailey: 36), Clifford wrote his dialogue in accordance with the English literary style of his period. Where he depicts a conversation in Malay, as in the opening conversation between Norris and Saleh (p. 6), he uses a special convention of his own—archaic words of address and the occasional Malay word interposed. Dialogue of any kind must by its nature become different when it is represented by the written word (Sweeney 1987). Clifford's dialogue is at its best when depicting confrontation, as in Saleh's first appearance at his father's court (pp. 158–66) or the frosty conversation when he meets his European superior, Baker, for the first time (pp. 170–3). In many contexts, he sidesteps the problem by indirect statements of what was said, such as the gradual conversion of Saleh to their way of thinking by the persistent duo of Raja Pahlawan Indut and Raja Haji Abdullah (pp. 178, 229). Taking it as a whole, the dialogue of the book moves the story forward and develops the situation and the character studies, as it should, though a reviewer in the *Manchester Guardian* found it 'a shade declamatory'.

Publication in two parts, divided by an interval of four years, deprived the book of the full impact which, as an entity, it commands. Moreover, Part 1, in book form, was published as only one of a collection of stories, among which some others, notably 'Rachel' and 'The Flight of the Jungle Folk', were found no less striking. Then again, Part 1 ends (p. 105) with what a reviewer (in the *Court Journal*) called 'a strange sense of doubt'. Finally, Part 1 appeared soon after Clifford's major historical work, *Further India*, which assured him of critical attention for all which he wrote at that time, but also tended to distract attention from it.

The reviews of Part 1 were numerous and, almost without exception, favourable though hardly profound. Most reviewers summarized the story and rated it vivid fiction, with some relevance to 'one of the hardest problems of the British Empire' (*Birmingham Post*), i.e. education in the colonies. One of the most interesting, and one of the few signed, reviews was by J. H. Lobban in *The Bookman*. Lobban contrasted the 'radiant tropical sunshine' of Clifford's perception of Malaya as a background, with the 'sombre and sad' note of Saleh's story. He also concluded that 'Mr Clifford's instinct has led him to stop precisely at the right moment'. That view, however, as we have seen, was unusual and did not prevail.

When Part 2 appeared in 1908, Clifford was very much a rising star as a colonial proconsul, and he was about to marry a celebrated lady author, but the interruption in his literary output since 1904 had caused some decline in literary interest in his work. There were fewer reviews, and many of them were in Commonwealth, not English, journals. The forceful denunciation of English language education in India in the Preface, quoted above, attracted notice. But one reviewer (*Cape Times*) queried whether these were 'deeper themes than the story-teller can be expected to treat adequately'. The stark detail of Pelesu and of Saleh's decline proved, as Clifford had feared, strong meat for those who did not share his knowledge. The *Manchester Guardian* reviewer, echoing the comments made on Clifford's 1899 lecture, said that it must be exaggerated. The 1926 American reprint, since it was not new material, does not seem to have attracted attention.

To the modern reader, however, who seeks to understand Clifford's book in its context, one may commend it as fascinating social history, to be pondered with due appreciation of the author's idiosyncratic views on Malay society, which he knew remarkably well and interpreted according to his own lights, being a gifted and imaginative British colonial administrator of his period.

Essex   J. M. GULLICK
January 1989

REFERENCES

Books and Articles

Allen, J. de V., 'Two Imperialists: A Study of Sir Frank Swettenham and Sir Hugh Clifford', *JMBRAS*, 37(1), 1964.

Bird, I. L. (Mrs Bishop), *The Golden Chersonese and the Way Thither*, London, Murray, 1883; reprinted Kuala Lumpur, Oxford University Press, 1967 and 1980.

Clifford, H. C., *In Court and Kampong, Being Tales and Sketches of Native Life in the Malay Peninsula*, London, Grant Richards, 1897.

_____ *Studies in Brown Humanity being Scrawls and Smudges in Sepia, White and Yellow*, London, Grant Richards, 1898.

_____ *In a Corner of Asia being Tales and Impressions of Men and Things in the Malay Peninsula*, London, Fisher Unwin, 1899.

_____ *Further India—being the story of exploration from the earliest times in Burma, Malaya, Siam and Indo-China*, London, Lawrence and Bullen, 1904.

_____ 'Sally', *Blackwoods Magazine*, November 1903–February 1904: republished in *Sally: A Study and other Tales of the Outskirts*, London, Blackwood, 1904.

_____ *Saleh: A Sequel*, London, Blackwood, 1908.

_____ *A Prince of Malaya*, New York, Harper, 1926 (reprint of 1904 and 1908 stories cited above).

_____ *The Further Side of Silence*, New York, Doubleday, Page & Co., 1927a.

_____ Autobiographical preface to *In Court and Kampong* etc., London, Richards, 1927 edition (originally published in 1897). (1927b)

_____ *Bushwhacking and Other Asiatic Tales and Memories*, New York, Harper, 1929.

_____ 'Report: Expedition to Trengganu and Kelantan', *JMBRAS*, 34(1), 1961; originally printed for Colonial Office use in 1895; reprinted Kuala Lumpur, Government Press, 1936.

_____ 'Life in the Malay Peninsula: As It Was and Is', in P. H. Kratoska (ed.), *Honourable Intentions*, reprinted from the *Proceedings of the Royal Colonial Institute*, 1899.

Gailey, H. A., *Clifford: Imperial Proconsul*, London, Collins, 1982.

Gullick, J. M., 'Isabella Bird's Visit to Malaya: A Centenary Tribute', *JMBRAS*, 52(2), 1979.

____ *Malay Society in the Late Nineteenth Century: The Beginnings of Change*, Singapore, Oxford University Press, 1987.

Kratoska, P. H. (ed.), *Honourable Intentions: Talks on the British Empire in South-East Asia Delivered at the Royal Colonial Institute 1874–1928*, Singapore, Oxford University Press, 1983; reprinted from the *Proceedings of the Royal Colonial Institute*, 1899.

Makepeace, W., Brooke, G. E., and Braddell, R. St. J. (eds.), *One Hundred Years of Singapore being some Account of the Capital of the Straits Settlements ... to the 6th February 1919*, London, John Murray, 1921.

Morrah, P., 'The History of the Malayan Police', *JMBRAS*, 36(2), 1963.

Roff, W. R., *The Origins of Malay Nationalism*, New Haven, Yale University Press, 1967.

Sheppard, M., *Tunku: A Pictorial Biography 1903–1957*, Petaling Jaya, Malaysia, Pelanduk Publications, 1984.

Sidhu, J. S., *Administration in the Federated Malay States 1896–1920*, Kuala Lumpur, Oxford University Press, 1980.

Smith, M. L., *Arthur Lionel Smith, Master of Balliol (1916–1924)— A Biography and some Reminiscences by his Wife*, London, John Murray, 1928.

Stevenson, R., *Cultivators and Administrators: British Educational Policy towards the Malays 1875–1906*, Kuala Lumpur, Oxford University Press, 1975.

Stockwell, A. J., 'Sir Hugh Clifford in Malaya 1927–29—*Pinang pulang ka-tampok*', *JMBRAS*, 53(2), 1980.

Sweeney, P. L. A., *A Full Hearing: Orality and Literacy in the Malay World*, Berkeley, University of California Press, 1987.

Swettenham, F. A., *Malay Sketches*, London, John Lane Bodley Head, 1895.

____ *British Malaya: An Account of the Origin and Progress of British Influence in Malaya*, London, John Lane Bodley Head, 1907 (revised editions 1929 and 1948, London, Allen & Unwin).

_____ 'British Rule in Malaya', in P. H. Kratoska (ed.), *Honourable Intentions*, reprinted from the *Proceedings of the Royal Colonial Institute*, 1896.

Thio, E., *British Policy in the Malay Peninsula*, Vol 1: *The Southern and Central States*, Kuala Lumpur and Singapore, University of Malaya Press, 1969.

Wicks, P. C., 'The Malayan Novels of Sir Hugh Clifford', *Malaya in History*, 27, 1984.

Wilkinson, R. J., 'The Education of Asiatics', *Special Reports on Educational Subjects*, Cmd. 835, Vol. 8, 1902.

_____ (author and series ed.), *Papers on Malay Subjects*, Kuala Lumpur, Government Press, 1907–1911; selection reprinted, P. L. Burns (ed.), Kuala Lumpur, Oxford University Press, 1971 (and individual papers reprinted at various dates).

Yeo Kim Wah, *The Politics of Decentralization: Colonial Controversy in Malaya 1920–1929*, Kuala Lumpur, Oxford University Press, 1982.

Periodicals

Birmingham Post, 18 November 1904.
The Bookman, December 1904.
The Cape Times, 15 January 1909.
The Court Journal, 19 November 1904.
Manchester Guardian, 16 November 1904 and 25 November 1908.

Archive Sources

Annual Report Straits Settlements 1956–7 (Keasberry's school). Straits Settlements Despatches of 1 September 1909 (Kedah bureaucracy) and 10 January 1911 (Chulan's civil service career). Letters of 24 March (E. W. Birch) and 17 April 1909 (Anderson) (character of Rajas Mansur and Chulan) in CO 273/355. Letters of 6 November 1909 and 8 September 1910 in CO 273/351 and 352 about two Kedah students (one a son of the Sultan) at Oxford and Malvern.

ACKNOWLEDGEMENTS

I am much indebted to Mr H. C. Holmes, grandson of Sir Hugh Clifford, for the loan of the relevant volumes of the Clifford Papers in his possession, and to Dr P. C. Wicks whose study (listed above) enabled me to discover the connection between Raja Alang Iskander and the origin of this novel. Both have kindly read and commented on earlier drafts of this Introduction but the responsibility for it in published form is entirely mine.

The passage from Isabella Bird's letter is reproduced by permission of John Murray, London.

FOREWORD

This book was written more than twenty years ago and, now that for the first time it is making its appearance in a single volume, I have not attempted to rewrite or to revise it. To do so would have meant throwing the whole picture out of focus, for the tragedy of Saleh and the fashion in which it is here related alike belong to a period which has passed away. The last two decades have witnessed vaster revolutions in fact and in idea than have been packed into any corresponding space of time in recorded history; and in no directions have greater transformations been worked than in the moral and material progress of Malaya and in the attitude of thoughtful Europeans toward racial questions in the East. Yet both the one and the other, as they actually were during the closing years of the nineteenth century, are depicted in this book with relentless accuracy; and since they were the elements which, in combination, resulted in the catastrophe of which poor Saleh was the victim, the story must stand as it was originally written if historical fidelity to the time when the events occurred which are here recorded is to be preserved.

Joining the civil service of Malaya in 1883, at an unusually early age, it so chanced that for the best part of the two decades that followed I was stationed in some of the more remote and primitive districts of the Malayan Peninsula and, to a degree unequalled by any of my brother officers, lived among the people in almost complete isolation from men of my own race. For nearly two years I was posted at the court of a

Malayan Sultan of the old school, whose autocratic
methods had not yet been subjected to any extraneous
interference; and I was thus afforded an insight,
rarely vouchsafed to a European, of the eccentricities
and excesses of unfettered native rule. Having acquired the vernacular in much the same effortless manner in which a child learns a foreign language; living
for long periods in native huts, on native diet and in
the native fashion; and in familiar daily intercourse
with Malays of all classes, I emerged from the experience possessed of a very intimate knowledge of the
people, of their modes of thought and outlook upon
life, and imbued with a deep sympathy and affection
for them. Looking back upon those days, I reckon
them as among the happiest and most interesting of
my life; but the end of them found me a firm believer
in the necessity for the intervention of Great Britain
in Malaya which, in my own time, I had seen transform conditions bordering upon anarchy into those
appropriate to a peaceful, prosperous and contented
countryside. Even then, however, I was trying to
look at and judge our work from the Malayan, and not
exclusively from the European, point of view; and if,
in spite of this, there breathes through the pages of
this book a certain arrogant confidence in our ability
and our achievement, that too was bred of an unique,
first-hand experience of the clashing of a highly ad-
vanced with an ancient but very primitive civilization.

Hugh Clifford.

A PRINCE OF MALAYA

Part One

A PRINCE OF MALAYA

Chapter   *One*

"DIVE? I should think so!" said his host to Jack
Norris. "You just watch the little beggar dive!"
It was early morning, and the two men were stripping
for a swim on board one of the big house-boats which
lie eternally at their moorings on the right bank of the
river near Thames Ditton. The place was littered with
sweaters, towels, flannels, boat cushions, books, news-
papers, pipes, and the varied accumulations of rubbish
such as only a house-boat full of bachelors can collect
when it lacks even the feminine influence of a char-
woman. Without, seen through the wide oblong windows, the tawny waters ran cool and inviting under
the glad sunshine of a bright summer morning. From
a spring-board rigged in the bows men from time to
time took running headers; in the middle of the narrow
fairway five or six heads were bobbing, while arms and
legs in number to correspond splashed gallantly. The
cheery clamor of the bathers carried far over the water.

Presently another head broke through the surface of
the river some twenty yards upstream—a head to which
the wet hair clung sleek and black as the fur of an
otter—and from it came a cry of defiance, the tone of
which was somehow strangely familiar as it smote upon
Jack Norris's ears. The swimmers answered the challenge with discordant chorus, and began to splash up
against the current, with straining arms and legs, in
the direction of the man who had uttered it. The
latter waited until his pursuers had nearly surrounded
him, were almost upon him, and then dived neatly,

leaving barely so much as a ripple behind him. Two or three men went down headlong in pursuit, to reappear in a minute or so, baffled and panting. A moment later, first one and then another were drawn under, with gurgles and splutterings of protest, by an invisible hand that had gripped them by the heels. With renewed splutterings each in turn came to the surface, laughing and shouting, breathing forth threats of instant retribution. Dashing the water from their eyes, they looked around, vainly seeking for some sign of their antagonist's whereabouts, calling upon him by name the while with humorous mock-wrath.

"Sally!" they cried. "Sally, you young ruffian! Sally! Sally! Sally, you villain! We'll pay you out properly when we catch you!"

Again the head, with its close covering of straight limp hair, came to the surface, far down river this time, and well out of the reach of its pursuers. Again that queer challenging cry came from it, and set Norris tingling with old memories suddenly awakened.

"Why, he is a Malay!" he exclaimed. "No one but a Malay ever used that lilting whoop. It is the sôrak —their war-cry!"

"Of course he is a Malay," said the part owner of the house-boat. "He is Sally, you know—a Malay boss of sorts. We all knew him when we were at Winchester. He is being educated in England privately, not at the school; but he is an awfully decent little chap, and was very pally with a lot of us."

Jack Norris stepped out on to the bows, and stood for a minute in his bathing-pants, looking across the river. The Englishmen had abandoned the hopeless chase, and the little Malay was swimming back to them, breasting the current with the unmistakable long overhand stroke of his people. The sight, and the echo of the cry which still rang in his ears, brought back to Norris suddenly the memory of many a swim in the glorious rivers of the Malay Peninsula; and for a space the banks around him, with their fringe of moored house-boats and floating stages, the trim towing-path opposite skirting the tall brick wall, and the great shapeless pile of Hampton Court Palace, its windowpanes winking in the sunlight, its ruddy bulk surmounted by grotesque chimney-stacks, picked out with white masonry and set with grinning gargoyles, were rolled back. He seemed once more to be standing on the beak of a Malayan *prâhu*, with an olive-green tide of waters surging past him, and spreading away and away to the marvelous tangles of forest that stood, more than half a mile apart, hedging the river on either flank. Then he braced himself and took a header from the bow, and the chill of the English stream smote him with a shock of surprise, for so complete had been the momentary illusion that he had expected to be greeted by the tepid waters of the East.

When he rose to the surface he found himself close to the man they called "Sally." His face—the boyish, hairless face of a young Malay—was turned towards him. The great, black, velvety, melancholy eyes of his race looked at Norris from their place in the flawless, olive-tinted skin in which they were set. The mouth, somewhat full, with mobile, sensitive lips that pouted slightly, had just that sweetness of expression that is most often seen in the face of a little child. The features were clean-cut, delicate, giving promise of more adaptability than strength of character: the whole effect was pretty and pleasing, for this was a Malay of rank and breeding, the offspring of men who for uncounted gen-

erations have had the fairest women of their land to
wife.

Mechanically Norris spoke in the vernacular.

"What is the news?" he asked, using the conventional
greeting.

"*Khabar baik!* The news is good!" the Malay
answered, speaking the words from sheer force of
habit, and he eyed Norris curiously with evident surprise. Then his face lighted up with a gleam of recognition, and his lips, parting in a grin, disclosed two even
rows of beautiful white teeth—teeth such as belong by
right to every Malay, did not the inexplicable fashion
of this people order them to be mutilated with the stone-
file and blackened by indelible pigment.

"*Ya Allah, Tûan Nori'!* It is thou!" he exclaimed.
The word or two of the vernacular, to which he
added the popular mispronunciation of Jack's name,
slipped from him unconsciously. An instant later he
corrected himself.

"Do you remember me?" he asked in English. "I
am Râja Saleh of Pĕlĕsu. I met you las' at Kâru."

He spoke his acquired language fluently, but with
a strong foreign intonation, lengthening the flat
English vowels and eliding the last of two final consonants. His words unlocked a forgotten chamber of
Jack's memory, and at once the boy himself, his
identity, his circumstances, and all connected with him,
were made so clear that Norris fell to wondering how
it had come to pass that, even for a moment, he had
failed to recognize him. Immediately the Englishman
and the Malay were busy interchanging news, the
former chatting volubly of men and places with
strange names, that surely had never before been
spoken on the bosom of the ancient Thames; the

latter listening and replying, but with a certain indifference and aloofness that were curious. Once
more, from force of habit, Norris spoke in the vernacular. Using the Malayan idiom like his own
mother tongue, he had never yet met a native who did
not prefer to converse with him in that language, or
who was completely at his best when employing the
white man's speech. The foreign tongue seems in
some subtle fashion to emphasize divergencies in taste
and character which the more familiar vernacular
mercifully hides. Iang-Mulia Râja Muhammad Saleh
bin Iang-Maha-Mulia Sultan Abubakar Maätham Shah
Iang-di-pĕr-Tûan Pĕlĕsu, however—to give his full
title to the youth who was known to his English
friends by the undistinguished name of "Sally"—had
not heard Malay spoken for years, and he seemed now
to shy away from it, as though it were not only unfamiliar, but also, in some sort, distressing to him. It
was only at a much later period of their intercourse
that Saleh came back to his Malayan tongue, and
found in it the only medium of expression with which
to convey to Jack an understanding of the feelings
that were in his heart.

Now, as the bathers dressed themselves on board the
house-boat—Saleh standing among them all in complete unconsciousness of the nakedness which would
have outraged the sense of decency of the meanest of
his subjects—Jack was busy piecing together all that
he could recollect concerning his past meetings with
the lad. So again the familiar surroundings of the
home-land faded, and were replaced by scenes that he
had looked upon, lived through, years before, and
thousands of miles away, on the banks of a mighty
Malayan river.

T HEY rose up singly—these scattered memories of incidents in which Saleh had played a part —lingered for a moment, and were gone; for the mind, when it wanders in retrospect, knows no trammels of space or time, and, flashing hither and thither at will, throws sudden gleams into the dark places with all the speed and the vividness of lightning. Thus, as in silence Norris dressed himself amid the hum of talk on board the house-boat, the trivial happenings of nearly a score of years were reviewed in less than half as many minutes, each picture rising before him clear-cut and complete to the last detail, glimmering for an instant ere it vanished to give room to another, just as a view cast by a magic lantern leaps whole and sudden out of the darkness, burns its impression upon our eyesight, and in a flash is blotted out.

Three big wooden houses, raised on piles above the untidy litter of a compound, connected each to each by narrow gangways roofed and walled; three high-pitched pyramids of thatch, the dried palm leaves rustling and lifting under the full beat of the noontide sun; a big brown river rolling by, with a dull murmur of sound, beyond the ten-foot fence of wattled bamboos which incloses in its lopsided square this palace of a native king. In the central house Jack Norris squats cross-legged, surrounded by a mob of expectant Malays of both sexes. The great barn-like apartment is bare, save for the *mĕngkûang*-palm mats spread upon the floor; and the bellying squares

of ceiling patchwork sagging from the rafters overhead, whence, near the center of the room, a big hammock also depends, swaying gently to and fro. Above
the hammock, in dingy contrast to glaring patterns of
the Manchester ceiling-cloths, an old casting-net,
whereof the soiled and rent meshes prove that it has
seen much service, hangs in an uneven oblong. It is a
barrier raised against the assaults of the *Pĕn-anggal*—
the Undone One—that fearful wraith of a woman who
has died in child-birth and who cherishes forever a
quenchless enmity towards little children. She, poor
wretch, wrenched terribly in twain, is doomed to flit
eternally through the night—a dreadful shape with
agonized woman's face, full breasts, and naught beside save only certain awful blood-stained streamers—
bringing a curse of destruction wherever she can win
an entry. But the gods, who suffer such things to be,
mercifully ordain that her onslaughts upon defenseless babes can only be made from above, and a dis-
carded casting-net dipped in magic water, it is well
known, will often stay and baffle her. Yet even now,
perchance, she may be lurking, unseen by impotent
human eyes, in the hammock itself, wherefore due
precaution must be taken ere the royal baby can be
safely laid to rest therein.

As the crowd sits watching, a grim figure strides
into the center of the room. It is that of an aged
woman, tall, erect, with a fierce mouth, wild eyes, and
a tumble of shaggy elf-locks making an unsightly
halo about her lean face, a woman dressed in the male
costume of a Malay warrior. It is Râja Anjang—the
witch of the blood royal—and at her coming a little
wave of tremor ripples over the faces of the Malay
onlookers. She is in a condition of trance—possessed

by her familiar demons: those unseeing eyes and
every rigid muscle in her big angular frame bear
witness to her uncanny state, and no man knows with
certainty what will befall while this inspired beldam
fills the stage. She wanders round and round the
hammock, moving with long masculine strides, mut-
tering fearfully words of a forgotten language which
none save the wizards know; and her elf-locks, stirring restlessly, seem to be lifted by winds which
should have no place in that still atmosphere. Then
stooping, she seizes suddenly upon a reluctant cat,
which the onlookers thrust within her reach, and
clutches the miauling creature to her flat breasts with
merciless grip. A chorus of minor witches squatting
on her right breaks into a wild chant of incantation,
while the devil-drums sob and pant in time to the
rhythm of the dirge. With her disengaged hand
Râja Anjang seizes the cord of the hammock and sets
it swinging in time to the chant, which grows momentarily wilder and wilder. The women who form
the chorus are rocking themselves backward and forward in a kind of hysteria of excitement; the hands
that smite the drums are raised between each stroke
high in the air with fingers wriggling rapidly in
frantic gesticulation; the hair and the garments of
the hag by the hammock are agitated anew, as though
those unearthly breezes, which are yet unfelt by the
spectators, were raging mightily. When the weird
song is at its shrillest the cat is dropped into the sag
of the hammock, whence it scrambles quickly on to
the mat-covered floor. It is promptly recaptured by
those nearest to it, and the witch pounces upon it with
the spring of a tigress. Again, and yet a third time,
the unhappy beast is clutched to that comfortless

bosom, is dropped into the hammock, and at the last is suffered to make its escape, spitting and scratching with bared claws and humped back. A wild cry goes up from the mouths of all the Malays present, and is succeeded by a heavy silence. The witch sinks to the floor in a shapeless bundle, sweating profusely, and rocks to and fro with smothered moans and cries. Her struggle with the ghastly *Pen-anggal* has left her utterly spent. The close atmosphere of the room is heavy with the reek of incense.

A little pause ensues, the stillness of which is tense with the recent excitement, and then from the inner apartment a huddled procession of women makes its way, headed by the king himself, a great rolling figure clad in glaring colors. One of the women carries a tiny burden swaddled in cloth of gold, the upper folds of which, being presently drawn aside, reveal the existence of a minute head. With much state and ceremony the crown of this head is solemnly shaved, the invisible fluff shorn from it being reverently treasured, and when this operation has been performed the baby is at last placed in the hammock, whence all evil spirits have now departed for their new abode in the body of the miserable cat.

A priest in a green *jubah* and ample red turban, who has sat complacently watching the magic practices which are an abomination to the Prophet's Law, stands erect and recites a rolling Arabic prayer with breathless fluency, his audience sitting with hands on knees and curved palms uppermost, chiming in at intervals with long "Amîns!"

Then the spectators rise to their feet, and each in turn files past the hammock and looks down at the child as he drops a dollar or two into a basket placed convenient for the purpose. Jack Norris, as he stands gazing down at the infant, sees a small brick-red disk, with a slack, slowly moving mouth, a shapeless button of a nose, a skin all crumpled with puckers, and two big dull eyes made grotesque by enormous arched eyebrows traced with soot upon the wrinkled forehead. The rest of the baby is immobile in its lashing of swaddling-clothes and is imbedded deeply in a nest of gorgeous Malayan silks.

It is thus that Jack gets his first glimpse of the boy whom his English friends call "Sally."

It is late at night in the audience-hall of the king— a big bare room without ornament or furniture—and the monarch, nude to the waist, is squatting on a mat beside a Chinese gambling-cloth. Around him sit a number of his courtiers, and facing him are two yellow Chinamen in loose coats and trousers of shining black linen. In the center of the cloth there rests a little square box made of dull brass, and presently, at a sign from the king, one of the courtiers begins to draw upward with maddening slowness the outer cover, which fits very closely over the inner box. A dead silence reigns while all eyes are riveted upon the dice-box and the hand that lifts its cover. Little by little, a fraction of an inch at a time, the outer box is raised, the narrower column of brass within it being disclosed more and more, standing squarely on the mat. At last the cover is free of that which it has incased, and more slowly than ever the courtier proceeds to twist it round in such a fashion that presently a corner of the hidden die will be made visible. The gamblers are leaning forward now with straining eyes; they draw their breaths pantingly; and still the hand gripping the dice-box moves with incredible slowness. The notes and dollars are piled in little heaps all in one quarter of the mat. The obsequious courtiers have followed the inspiration of their king.

There is another second or two of tense excitement and expectation, and then a shout is raised—a shout which is discordant and angry, tingling with passionate disappointment—a shout with which are blent imprecations and fierce ejaculations of disgust—a shout which ends in a sound like a sob. The king's inspiration has failed him, and he and his courtiers, in consequence, are the poorer by many good silver dollars. It is the last *coup* of a disastrous evening, and the king who is a prudent soul withal, will have no more of it. The Chinamen gather up their gaming-gear and their winnings, and depart into the night. Their unemotional faces—faces "like wooden planks," as the Malay idiom has it—betray no consciousness of the obvious hatred which they inspire. They are quite indifferent to it, for the money is duly pouched, and they know that the justice-loving British Government, in the person of the Resident, sits mighty and impassive on the river's farther bank, and takes thought even for the property and the lives of the despised yellow man. A little naked boy, who has been sleeping fitfully with his head pillowed on a courtier's knee, rouses himself, puts on an enormous orange-colored cap a size too large for him (his only garment), lights a cigarette, and sits listening gravely to the hum of talk about him—talk of all that might have been had chance proved less fickle. He is Râja Saleh, the king's baby son.

Jack Norris, who has been watching the play with such patience as he can command, sees that his time has come at last. He has visited the palace in order to have speech with the king concerning some of that shameless monarch's most glaring misdemeanors—matters connected with an abducted wife, an aggrieved husband, and a pack of motherless bairns—a squalid tragedy, in which the king has played the part of an ignoble Mephistopheles. The culprit is curiously insensitive. His feelings, overlaid by many strata of ruffianism and self-content, are things which have to be dug for. He knows now what has brought Norris to his hall, but he evinces no desire that the humiliating discussion about to take place should be conducted in private. In a sense he is somewhat proud of his achievement, for it is not every man of his years who can be a devastating *roué* as he, and he enters with gusto into a lurid account of his indiscretions, making display of an unfettered coarseness of speech and thought, while the little angel-faced boy, his son, sits at his side looking preternaturally wise. It is not the first time that the child has been privileged to listen to an exposition of his father's crude notions concerning morality and seemliness of conduct. It is Jack, not the king or his people, who is irked by the boy's presence, and finds the ugly discussion doubly degrading while those big sad eyes are fixed upon him. To the Malays the innocence of childhood makes no appeal, to them there is nothing incongruous in the subject of the talk and its baby audience. But duty may not be shirked; the matter must be threshed out, and before such listeners as the king may select; wherefore ignoble passions, and the wanton cruelties born of them, are freely canvassed for an hour and more. The discussion, as all who take part in it know well, is only a form, but it is deemed to be necessary

in order to salve the royal self-esteem and render
possible the king's inevitable surrender to a power
greater than his own.

When at last the end is reached, sweetmeats of unspeakable nastiness are served, the king, little Râja
Saleh, and Norris eating from the same tray, while
the courtiers range themselves around others in the
order of their precedence and rank. The child pecks
at the unwholesome stuff with the *blasé* indifference
bred of long familiarity and the absence of any attempt to restrain his appetites, and all the while his
grave looks are fixed upon the white man.

"Why dost thou not wear a hat, Tûan?" he inquires,
suddenly, gazing with open disapproval at Norris's
bare head.

"I follow my custom, little one."

"And thou wearest boots—even in the king's hall!"

"That too is my custom; moreover, it prevents my
feet from being bruised by stones on the way."

"I wore boots once, Tûan," says the child, proudly.
"Shoes of gold cunningly fashioned. That was on
the day when for the first time I trod upon the earth.
There was a great feast that day because of my boots."

"Men do not think it necessary to feast whenever I
put on my boots, nor can I afford to have them fashioned of gold. Did they hurt thy feet, little brother?"

"Yes," says the child, thoughtfully. "They hurt me
sore; but, Tûan, they were beautiful to behold. Do
thy boots hurt thee?"

"No, my boots are soft and comfortable. Thou
shouldst wear boots like mine, little one."

"So will I. Thou, Tûan, are doubtless wealthy.
Thou shalt send to Singapura and purchase boots for
me. Thou wilt send, wilt thou not, Tûan, for I desire

greatly to possess them?" He drops his little head on one side with so insinuating an air that he is altogether irresistible.

"Thou shalt have thy boots, little one, never fear," says Jack.

"Listen, you people," cries the child, exultantly, to the assembled courtiers. "The Tûan is sending to Singapura to purchase boots, yellow and comely. Armed with them, how gallantly shall I kick! *O Ma'!* there'll be many children with sore stomachs in the king's compound the day I don them!" and he laughs in joyful anticipation.

"There is no need to teach young tiger cubs how to use their claws," says an old man, admiringly, quoting a native proverb and the king leads the laughter.

"If thou makest any such use of thy boots thou shalt lose them," says Norris; "and now I must take my leave of the king."

"And wilt thou take the woman with thee?" inquires the child. "That will surely anger my father. When I am big I will take all the women I choose and use them villainously—ay, and keep them, too, if so I wish!"

"There is no need to teach young tiger whelps how to prey!" cackles the old man again, and once more it is the king who leads the applause.

Other pictures flit across Norris's memory. Days upon the river with boat and casting-net, or when the natives of the countryside muster to help drag the great *rĕlap*-cord downstream for miles, driving shoals of frightened fish before it, to be caught at last in cunning mazes of bamboo stakes. Days in the fruit orchards, when all the court goes a-picnicking and the boys gather in little groups to feast gluttonously while they talk knowingly of war and daggers and women. Days in the jungle, when the king and his people go forth to gather flowers, mounted on huge clay-colored elephants. And in every picture Saleh fills a space, always cutting a pretty figure; always gayly clad in delicate silks; always having as his right the best of everything that is going; always pampered and petted, flattered and adulated; always taught that his whims are. above aught else, that his desires are given him to satisfy, not to restrain; always applauded most loudly for his naughtiest deeds and sayings.

Then the recollection recurs of a day in the palace cockpit when Saleh's bird is mishandled by its *juâra*— its keeper—and the young prince in a fury of anger seizes a billet of wood which chances to be lying near at hand and deals the culprit a sounding blow upon the head. There is, unknown to Saleh, a long rusty nail in the billet, and the *juâra* is carried away, a limp burden, with blood streaming down a face gone suddenly gray beneath the brown skin. When Norris comes upon the scene the little râja is weeping passionately in a paroxysm of grief and self-hatred, which in his father's eyes is unmanly and far more reprehensible than the crime which is its occasion.

The memory of a later day comes next—the day which is the end of childhood for Râja Saleh. There has been much feasting and high revelry for weeks in the palace on the river's bank, culminating in rude horse-play on the yellow sandbank below the high fence, when all the world has been unmercifully soused with water, so that the gorgeous silk raiment of the feasters is drenched and ruined. Late that afternoon little Saleh is circumcised by the palace *mûdin,* and so enters at last upon man's estate. Immediately on his recovery he should celebrate his emancipation according to the custom of his people, by taking to himself a wife, or at any rate a concubine or two; but this lad, born and bred up in the villainous atmosphere of a Malayan court, has come into the world at an age of many changes. Hitherto the presence of the white men in the land has affected him but little, but now the alien folk step in and demand to have a hand in the ordering of his destiny. A year or two earlier, when the future seemed still so distant that pledges given concerning it could not affect the comfort of the present, the king had consented to the lad being sent to Europe to be educated. Now he repents him of this promise bitterly; but the Resident stands firm, and in spite of the boy himself and the frantic ravings of the palace women, he will not suffer the word, once passed, to be recalled.

It is a forlorn little figure that stands on the deck of the P. & O. steamer which has just slipped its moorings from the wharf at Singapore, with the keening of the knot of Malays which has come to bid him Godspeed wailing in his ears and with no friend in all the world save the European officer who is to see him safely to his destination. He is bound for that mysterious country concerning which naught is known save that it lies somewhere in that vague quarter which is called "above the wind." The ship moves away with an impassivity, a calmness at once cruel and inexorable. The boy feels himself to be a thing of torn and bleeding roots plucked wantonly from the soil in which they have won a hold. The consciousness of his helplessness, his impotence, crushes him; he watches his fatherland being drawn away and away from him with eyes wide with despair. What time, in the palace on the banks of the great river—the palace made suddenly so very empty—a woman weeps and laments with tears frantic and unrestrained, throwing herself prone upon her sleeping-mat, biting at the flock pillows and tearing her hair savagely, because her son has been taken from her by the infidels. His going robs her of the sole love of her dreary life, slips the last tie that binds her to her lord and master, who has long treated her with neglect and has lavished his smiles and his gifts upon younger and fairer rivals. How vast a work of kindness and of love must the white man do, in exile and bitter travail, to win enough of gratitude, from those they rule and serve, to outweigh the hatred they have inspired in that one broken woman's heart!

Chapter   Three

TO little Saleh, now some fourteen years of age,
that voyage across the trackless seas was in the
beginning a sort of dreadful nightmare. During the
first few days all other emotions were forgotten in
the compelling agonies of seasickness, and the boy
went through the successive stages of the malady,
fearing at the outset that he was like to die and later
that no such good fortune awaited him. By the time
the vessel reached Ceylon, however, he had found his
sea legs, and was able to give his undivided attention
to his mental miseries.

The first sight of the coast, with its clusters of
nodding palms and its shroud of vivid greenery, comforted him a little; for here, at any rate, was land,
friendly land covered with forest and fruit-groves
such as he had always known, not the vast emptiness
of the sea. Colombo itself, too, brought some measure
of consolation; for there were Malays here in fair
numbers, men with whom he could converse in his
own tongue, albeit they spoke a widely divergent
dialect, whereas on board the ship, since he as yet had
no English, he was to all intents and purposes dumb.
The white man in whose charge he was traveling
spoke Malay fluently, but Saleh, who had known him
hitherto only as a high official, regarded him with
awe, and gave him none of his shy confidence. A
further acquaintance with Colombo, however, ended
by increasing the gnawing homesickness from which
the lad was suffering. His only conception of the
whole round earth was as one vast tangle of forest
through which the big rivers crawled seaward, where-

fore, to him, the dissimilarity of Ceylon to the Malay Peninsula was more striking than its resemblance. The place was, in a disquieting fashion, reminiscent of his fatherland—a land of shadows filled with the echoes of distant voices; but it was to the boy only a mocking reflection of the reality, and its points of difference jarred on him like discordant notes. On every side, it seemed to him, he was met by sorry distortions of familiar scenes. It was as though he looked upon his home in a bad dream, and beheld it mockingly deformed and misshapen. He went back to the ship with a heart heavy as lead.

The vessel, her coal-bunkers replenished, put to sea once more, and began to thrust her nose into the boisterous waters of the Indian Ocean. The dreary interminable days, their monotony unbroken by the smallest happenings, trailed one after the other in slow procession; and Saleh, who did not care to read turgid Malay verse and was too shy to talk much with the only man on board who understood his language, learned for the first time what is meant by solitude and weariness of spirit. Each dull hour heaped up the burden that was crushing him. He was in the grip of a grinding home-sickness—a yearning so acute that it was as agonizing as an aching tooth, forcing itself upon his attention insistently, maddening him with a pain which yet lacked the relief of expression, and haunting his very slumbers. He longed with un-speakable intensity for all familiar things—the faces that he knew, even though they belonged to men and women for whom he cared nothing; for the sound of his mother tongue spoken with the native accent; for the scenes, the color, the very atmosphere of his home; for the trivial things of every day, so little valued

when they were his, which hitherto had made up life
for him. The depression, inseparable from lack of
occupation or interest, deepened the gloom of the
nostalgia, which darkened his days; but the emotion
that throughout oppressed him most sorely was fear
—blank, unreasoning fear. The immensity of the world
was a new fact which had been flashed upon his intelligence suddenly, had been revealed to him abruptly
with no course of preparation to soften the shock. It
smote now upon his understanding, numbing, cowing
him. He, who hitherto had never wandered more than
a dozen miles from the village in which he had been
born, who had lived in a land whose every inhabitant
was known to him, found himself now adrift upon the
bosom of a boundless sea, with countless eyes, he
fancied, glaring at him with a cruel glitter from those
restless waters, and the dome of the unpitying heavens
arching over him. On board the ship he was in the
midst of strangers, men who were not only un-
acquainted with him but belonged to a different race,
followed strange customs, professed an alien faith.
From time to time some unfamiliar port was touched
at—the blinding, burnt-brick mound of Aden, un-
softened by so much as a single blade of grass and
peopled by naked negroes who resembled Jins; the
white-hot sand-sweeps of Suez, where blue-clad
Arabs, with scarred faces, lived among strange beasts
of burden the like of which Saleh had never seen—
camels and asses; and later still the European seaport
towns, with their deafening roar of traffic and steam-
cranes, where white men dwelt in numbers past all
counting. These new lands terrified Saleh and caused
him to feel outcast beyond redemption; for every
step of the way, every turn of the churning screw,

bore him farther and farther from the folk he loved
and the only corner of the earth that was dear to
him. It seemed to him that he was the merest atom,
a thing infinitely minute, lost past all recovery in
limitless space. A sense of that awful vastness—
which somehow was interwoven with a sudden perception of the real meaning of eternity—came upon
the boy, shaking him with an abject terror. The idea,
to his unaccustomed mind, was so immense that the
sheer effort required to assimilate it set his brain
reeling, tottering. And constantly the haunting question obtruded itself. "How shall I ever find a way
back again across this uncharted wilderness?" At
that thought a cold despair would seize him and he
would fall to prowling about the ship like a caged
beast, his eyes wearing a hunted look, while he endured agonies that were doubly bitter because he had
no one in whom to confide his fears. So, when the
night came, he would sob himself to sleep and, tossing
restlessly upon his mattress when forgetfulness at
last had come, would call by name upon his mother
and upon others whom he loved, as men in heavy grief
murmur in dreams the names of dear ones who are
dead and gone.

The utter monotony of a long sea voyage to one unaccustomed to travel spins out the days in such
interminable wise that at the end of a fortnight one is
tempted to believe that more than half of life has been
passed in the belly of a ship. All the events of our
normal existence become faint and shadowy memories
—things that belong to some half-forgotten, unreal,
former state of being; things that have little practical
value or significance. The world is narrowed down to
the limits of the ship, its inhabitants to the number

of the men and women who journey in her. There
seems to be no special reason why anything should
occur to break the dead sameness of the days: it would
appear to be quite natural were the voyage to continue to the end of time interminable in its dull
routine, its regularity, its idleness. And this, too, was
Saleh's experience. With the passing of the third
week his native land became something incredibly
remote: the men and women who dwelt there little
more than moving shadow-shapes that came and went
vaguely amid the haze of memory. The natural adaptability of the boy, and, it may be, something of the
innate philosophy and patience of the Malay and the
Muhammadan, came to his rescue. He had settled
down insensibly into the life of the ship so completely
that he might have been a part of her; and though the
present manner of his existence brought him no active
happiness, he had found contentment of a dull vege-
table sort that had in it nothing of irritation, expectation, or hope. He was picking up a little English,
too—learning it as a child learns, unconsciously and
without effort—and he had all a child's delight in
making display of his new acquirement. He had
grown almost callous to the awful conception of the
immensity of God's universe, to the humiliating sense
of his own insignificance. These facts had lost their
power to terrify and appall. Nor did it now seem to
him to matter greatly if, after all, the land of his birth
and all that it held had sunk beneath the skyline past
the possibility of rediscovery. People were kind to
him, and the inertia of his race caused him to shrink
from the thought of the huge expenditure of energy
which a return to the Malay Peninsula would entail.
The conviction was upon him that he could never

again bring himself to undertake another voyage like
that which he was now making, yet this no longer
filled him with terror or with despair. He had reached
the condition which in his own tongue is called *kâleh*
—a state of blank torpor and indifference, incomprehensible to the average European, that, holding all
things of little worth, lulls the senses as with opium
fumes.

Wherefore it came to pass that the end of his
journey found Saleh with roots firmly fixed in the life
of the ship, parting from it and from the new friends
whom he had made with intense discontent; but it
found him also weaned already from his own people,
for whom in the beginning he had sorrowed so
grievously.

Chapter   Four

SALEH'S first impressions of the white man's
country remained later in his mind as a confused
and fearful memory. The size, the dingy ugliness,
the noise, the hurry of London combined to awe him;
the great towering buildings, blackened with smoke,
the blurred jumble of their roofs and chimney-stacks
half emerged in the gray mirk, stood around him in
serried ranks, hemming him in, stifling him; the color-
less sodden sky, lowering above them, seemed to bear
him to the ground through its sheer weight; the
danger of instant annihilation, with which at every
crossing of the streets the mighty traffic threatened
him, set him shaking with an ague of terror; but most
of all the frightful isolation, of which the seas of
strange faces made him conscious, clutched at his
heart-strings with a grip that was chill and paralyzing.
The immensity of the universe had cowed him once;
now it was the glimpse he had gotten of the unsuspected multitude of humanity—unnumbered folk who
had no thought or care for him—that robbed him of
breath. He had never yet felt so utterly lost as now
with these packed streams of unknown men and
women drifting past him. All his days he had been
an object of consideration, the son of a king, with
willing subjects ready at his beck and call. He had
never walked a yard without a tail of idle pages trail-
ing after him. Now he believed himself to be drown-
ing in an ocean of human beings, yet overwhelmed by
an appalling solitude.

A drive in a hansom through the throng of vehicles
set his heart in his mouth, his hand clutching vainly

at the arm of the man who sat beside him; the fearful
speed of trains that rushed along the labyrinths of
lines kept him in momentary expectation of catastrophe; but worse still were the crowds of Europeans
that stared at and jostled him in the streets—men of
an alien race of pallid, unnatural color, with intent
busy faces and hard eyes. Saleh felt much as a white
child might feel who was suddenly set down in the
midst of vast mobs of gibbering negroes. He was convinced that the blended horror and fear with which
his strange surroundings inspired him would last forever; that he could never become used to an environment so dreadful, so appalling; and all the while his
very soul was aching with longing for the soft moist
climate, the sunshine, and the lavish greenery of the
Malayan land. The bitter nostalgia revived with all
its ancient force, but his craving now was for inanimate rather than for animate things—for the familiar
places in which his days had been passed, not for the
men and women, his friends and kindred, who had
already become mere shadow-phantoms to his memory.
And still his every suffering was made doubly hard
because it was endured in secret and in silence.

After a busy week in London Saleh was sent to Winchester, where a home had been found for him in an
English family. This severed the very last link that
still connected him with the old life, for the officer
who had brought him to England left him on the platform at Waterloo, after handing him over to the
charge of a magnificent-looking personage who, the
boy thought, must surely be one of the great ones of
the earth. He was surprised when this brass-bound
potentate pocketed five shillings with apparent satisfaction and addressed him as "Sir"; but in this strange

land everything was puzzling, and Saleh despaired of ever getting a grip upon the bewildering customs of the white men. He would have resisted this sudden transfer of himself from the care of a man whom he knew to that of a total stranger, but he was past the power of resistance or protest. He was completely cowed, as a young horse is cowed by an alien environment, and with the innate fatalism of his people he set himself to endure all that might befall with patience and philosophy, which only added to his trouble, since it drove it inward, denying it the relief of expression.

At Winchester the boy was passed on to an immensely tall, upright, grave-faced clergyman, whose stiff black clothes and gaunt, clean-shaven face depressed the lad with gloomy forebodings. It was as though this man were an ogre—the grim custodian of the prison in which he was to be pent. All the passionate love of personal liberty, bred of the free life in the forest lived by uncounted generations of his forbears, awoke in Saleh, filling him with resentment against all the world, with savage impotent rage, with the instinct of fight, with a sullen desire to hurt some one, anyone, because he himself was quivering with despair and fear and pain. When the clergyman held a hand towards him, the boy shrank back, his gums bared for the moment in something like a snarl, his whole body tingling with blended anger and terror, his muscles braced for flight or for self-defense. His new friend looking down upon him through grave, preoccupied eyes, noted nothing of the lad's discomfiture, and as he shook him by the hand, patted him on the back, and gave him kindly welcome, he was happily unconscious of the fact that the little brown creature before him was longing for a dagger with which to stab!

Next, after a short drive in a cab, from the windows of which Saleh saw the effigy of a big black swan, that he decided must be some unclean idol of the white folk, he found himself standing very ill at ease just within the doorway of an English drawing-room. It was the first place of the kind that he had ever seen, and its smallness, its strangely low ceiling, the quantity of furniture, the endless knicknacks and ornaments, seemed to him to be things unnatural, barbarous, stifling. He felt as a wild thing may do when it finds itself in a trap. The narrowness of the confined space set him gasping; he looked about him with furtive eyes, seeking some means of escape.

The room seemed to him to be packed with people, for Mrs. Le Mesurier, the clergyman's wife, was seated beside a tea-table with her family about her. There were three girls with their hair down their backs and a boy, all of whom stared at the stranger with eyes made round by curiosity.

Mrs. Le Mesurier rose from her chair and came towards him, holding out both her hands in greeting. Saleh noticed that she moved as no Malayan woman ever yet moved, with a graceful sweeping carriage that had still the spring of youth in it, and that her eyes were soft and kind. Her thick dark hair fell low upon a broad forehead, parting in two glossy waves; her cheeks had a delicate tinge of pink, that seemed a blemish in Saleh's eyes, for he was accustomed to the even pallor of his own womenkind. Just as at Colombo it had been the dissimilarities rather than the resemblances that had arrested his attention, so now it was the points in which Mrs. Le Mesurier

failed to conform to the standard set by her sisters
in Malaya that at first struck Saleh's eye, yet as she
came towards him she appeared to him to be a figure
vaguely, elusively familiar, like something seen for
an instant in a state of previous existence fitfully remembered. The little feet so daintily shod, the pretty
undulating gait, the gentle *frou-frou* of her garments
as she moved, the soft delicate hands with their pink
palms and slender nervous fingers, outstretched in
greeting, the thoughtful eyes whose gaze was bent
upon him, all were quite foreign to his experience of
women—of the women whom he had known; and yet
. . . and yet, there exhaled from her a subtle air of
femininity, of tenderness, of he knew not what, that
reminded him irresistibly of his mother. No two
human beings could be more unlike, wider apart,
could differ more completely in their habit of thought,
in outlook upon life, in mental grasp, in opinion, or in
sympathy—in all things they resembled one another
as little as did their outer seeming, yet to Saleh they
were strangely, indescribably alike; for, though he
knew it not, it was the maternity which these women
shared in common that forged between them a subtle
link that made them akin. He did not reason or
speculate about it then or later, but he was conscious
of it, felt it in the very marrow of his bones, and as
his hands met her warm clasp his misery was tempered
for him suddenly, and something of peace was restored to him. Thenceforth I think Saleh was a little
less lonely and outcast in the heart of this strange
world into which he had been thrust so ruthlessly.

Chapter Five

"WHY are you crying? Only babies cry."

"Go away!"

> " 'Baby, baby bunting!
> Father's gone a-hunting;
> Mother's gone to get a skin
> To wrap the baby bunting in!' "

"Go away! Damn you! I hate you!"

"Oh, you naughty, shocking boy!" cried Miss Mabel Le Mesurier, *ætat* thirteen, throwing back her mass of ruddy golden hair with a shake of her pretty head. "How dare you say such wicked words! Where do you suppose that you will go when you die if you swear like that? If I were to tell father he would whip you."

"No, he wouldn't," said Saleh, savagely.

"Yes, he would."

"He wouldn't dare, because I should kill him," said Saleh, with the calmness of utter conviction, while the tears still stood upon his face.

"You couldn't kill my dad if you tried ever so; he is much too big and strong and brave, so there; but he would beat you worse than anything if he heard the awful wicked things you say."

"Go away! I hate you!"

"I shan't go away. This is my garden-house, not yours. I shall stay here just as long as I like. You are a horrid little savage blackamoor, that's what you are, or you wouldn't be so dreadfully rude and wicked."

"I'm not rude and wicked and a blackamoor," cried

[31]

poor Saleh, throwing his arms across the little rustic table before him and sinking his head face downward between them. "I'm unhappy, and I hate everybody, and I wish I was dead." His shoulders heaved with a fresh paroxysm of sobs.

Mabel stood looking at him thoughtfully, biting at the corner of her blue pinafore the while. She was a tender-hearted little woman, and she had come there to comfort, not to aggravate, Saleh's sorrows. She had only given way to her natural instinct when she had derided his unmanly tears. She had not intended to hurt him wantonly. Now she stepped nearer to him and laid a tiny grubby hand upon his shoulder. He shook it off with an irritable shrug, but she declined to take offense.

"Don't cry, Sally. Dear Sally, don't cry," she whispered. "Tell me what's the matter. Why do you hate everyone, and why do you say such naughty, wicked things?"

For a time Saleh strove sullenly to repel her advances; but her persistency and his own craving for sympathy at last prevailed; so presently he found himself telling her, brokenly, inarticulately, for the strange tongue still fettered his thought, the story of his misery. To the little girl more than half of what he said was unintelligible, for the things that most irked this Oriental boy were to her matters of course, to which custom had inured her from babyhood. Also Saleh, apart from the difficulty he experienced in giving form to his ideas, discovered that it was one thing to be acutely conscious of a sensation, and a wholly different matter to describe that feeling in words. But the little girl with the ready sympathy that belongs to womenkind, even to womenkind in the bud, listened to his halting explanations and made no sign when she failed to follow the meaning which they were intended to convey, while Saleh was aware of a sensible alleviation of his trouble, merely because he had met with some one who was willing to listen to him kindly, some one of whom he was not shy.

The sharp pangs of homesickness had become numbed into a dull ache; the awful fear with which this world of white men had at first inspired him had passed away; in his new home he was treated with kindness, and he no longer felt it necessary to stand on the defensive, no longer had the panic-stricken sensations of a trapped animal. None the less, his surroundings were utterly uncongenial to him. Their iron regularity oppressed him. The household was as punctual as a nicely adjusted piece of clockwork, and he, who had never been taught the value of time, chafed at the extravagant importance which the Le Mesuriers attached to never being so much as a minute late for meals, play, or lessons. Then discipline— another thing entirely new to him—had come to the ordering of his days. Each hour was ear-marked for the special use to which it was to be put. To Saleh this was the veriest tyranny—the tyranny of the slave-driver—and he felt himself to be covered with ignominy because he was obliged to submit to it. Then, too, this world of the white men seemed to be ruled by ideas, abstractions, which previously had had no meaning to him. Mr. Le Mesurier was perpetually putting his son George, and Saleh with him, upon their "honor" to do this, that, or the other, and George would turn upon Saleh, calling him a "cad" with the bitterest contempt, if he sought to break through the impalpable barriers thus arbitrarily set up. Saleh, who in common with most Malays had a keen desire to stand well in the estimation of his fellows, did not want to be looked upon as a "cad," but he could not for the life of him understand why Mr. Le Mesurier, of whose general wisdom he was profoundly convinced, had the wanton folly to put trust in anyone. Then also he had made the acquaintance of another obscure thing called "Duty." He was constantly being told that it was his duty to do this or that; or it was declared that duty required of him that he should abstain from doing something upon which his heart was set. Here was a notion which as yet was altogether beyond his powers of comprehension; but the children about him accepted it as a matter of course and were obviously ill at ease and out of conceit with themselves when they succumbed to the temptation to sin against its precepts. Those other abstractions, "Right" and "Wrong," were a perpetual puzzle to him. In his own country he had been used to hear of things that were *pâtut* or *ta'pâtut*—fitting or not fitting—but they had been largely questions of good or bad taste, matters of opinion dependent upon the point of view of the individual. Among white men, however, Saleh discovered, to his astonishment, that they were hard-and-fast categories into which actions were divided past all possibility of debate, and the simple answer, "It would not be right," sufficed in most cases to deter his new comrades from participating in the most tempting pleasures. Once again, for the life of him, he could not understand it. When he had suggested to George that indulgence in a certain vice—a vice for which in his father's court men and women mainly lived—would relieve the tedium of their studies, the English boy had looked upon him with horror, had

threatened to "knock his head off" if he talked like
that again, and had shown him with true British blunt-
ness how unfathomable was his disgust.

Honor, duty, morality—straitening things which
seemed to clog the feet of liberty, as Saleh had always
understood it—had come upon him suddenly, new
ideas difficult to assimilate, and in their own fashion
more numbing to the brain, more paralyzing, more appalling than those other revelations, the vastness of
the universe and the multitude of humanity, had been.
Then, too, the life in which he found himself was
strenuous, earnest, instinct with a restless energy that
jarred upon his indolent nature. It seemed to him as
though he had been transported to some lofty moun-
tain-top, and were called upon, without preparation,
to breathe the rarefied atmosphere of the upper airs.
He stood there morally panting, gasping—moving
with acute discomfort on a plane too high for him.
He longed for the denser atmosphere of his fatherland, and he despaired of ever becoming habituated to
that which seemingly was natural, congenial to those
with whom he now associated. As to ever winning to
a real understanding of the extraordinary points of
view of these people, that obviously was a patent
impossibility.

Beyond this there were half a hundred minor
matters which appealed to Saleh as incongruous. His
manhood was offended, revolted, by the position
occupied among white folk by the women. Even
after weeks of use, his meals were a humiliation to
him because Mrs. Le Mesurier and her daughters sat
at table. Even his own mother would not have
dreamed of taking such a liberty with her son. The
service rendered by the maidservants was natural

enough, but it hurt his pride and his self-respect to
find that he was expected to give way to the daughters
of the house in everything, that he was chidden if he
neglected to offer to carry a cloak for a lady, if he did
not run willingly on trifling errands for Mrs. Le
Mesurier, if he was not active in forestalling the wants
of her and of her daughters. From the moment of their
first meeting Mrs. Le Mesurier, by her grace and kindness, had won his heart; but still, to his thinking, she
was but a woman—a being of inferior clay to the
material from which he was fashioned—and he was
irked by a system that made of her a central pivot
round which the household revolved. This unquestionably was *ta'pâtut*—not fitting—yet apparently it
offended the sense of propriety of no one save himself. The absence of all forms, too, struck him as
barbarous. All his life he had been hedged about by
ritual. Those who had spoken to him had described
themselves as *pâtek*—thy slave; for was he not the
son of a king? But here all ceremony was dropped,
and, shorn of his titles, he found himself answering
to the name of "Sally," and being scoffed at and
mocked because "Sally" was in England a woman's
name. George, the young barbarian, even called him
"Aunt Sally" at times, and once at a fair had gravely
introduced him to a dilapidated cockshy, which he declared must be one of his near relatives, a hideous idol
of the white men at which certain savage creatures
were engaged in throwing missiles with grotesque
antics and an outrageous uproar. It was when he
next was addressed as "Aunt Sally" that he had first
tried to fight George, and, finding that the attempt
was a failure (for what could a man do who had no
knife ready to his hand?) had retired to the arbor in

tears. "Chaff," as George would have called it, was again something foreign to Saleh's experience. To him it was simply a rudeness, a brutality—not fitting.

As much of all this as his mental and linguistic limitations could make articulate he now sobbed out to Mabel, omitting only all reference to his disapproval of the undue exaltation of her sex, for Malays are not devoid of a certain instinctive tact. His trouble was of a nature too complex to be readily comprehended by his little listener; but, fortunately for mankind, a woman's sympathy is not always dependent upon her understanding, and Mabel, knowing he was very unhappy, without inquiring too closely into the causes, patted his shoulder and whispered words of consolation into his ear.

"Don't cry, Saleh dear," she said. "We all like you very much, and you are going to live with us for a long time, and be very happy, too, when you get used to us. You mustn't mind George. He is a boy, you know, and boys are like that. He is always trying to get a rise out of all of us. He likes you very much, too, really. He was only saying the other day how beautifully you swim and how clever you are in the gym. He says you can do things on the bar at the first try which it takes English boys years and years to learn. He only calls you 'Aunt Sally' for fun, just as he calls me 'Furze-bush' when I have had my hair in curl-papers."

Saleh shuddered at the recollection. His taste, molded by the lank, sleek oil-dressed heads of his own womenkind, was grievously offended by the sight of curls.

"And you called me a blackamoor," he said, sulkily.

"I'm sorry, Sally."

"You white people are so . . . so proud. You think many things of yourself, but we Malays have beaten you. The English soldiers ran like stags when we ambushed them during the war in Pĕlĕsu."

"They didn't!" cried the little girl, indignantly.

"Yes, they did. They ran and ran, and our people ran after them and shot them and shouted. I have often heard people talk of it!"

"English soldiers are very brave," said Mabel, with proud conviction.

"They are not as brave as the Malays, and they ran away," said Saleh, doggedly.

"I don't believe it," cried Mabel. "Besides, we won, didn't we?"

Saleh was silent.

"You called me a blackamoor," he said, presently, returning with resentment to his earlier accusation.

"I know I did, and I was a *beast,*" said Mabel, generously. "And Sally, I'm sorry—ever so sorry—and I'll never do it again; but you mustn't say that English soldiers ran away, because they never do, you know."

"But they did," objected Saleh.

"O Sally, Sally, you'll make me quarrel with you, after all!" cried Mabel piteously. "And I do want to be friends."

"I cannot be frien's with people who calls me blackamoor," said Saleh, looking at her and softening ever so little.

"But I won't. And I do like you, Sally, and when you are unhappy don't go away and cry by yourself. Come and tell me all about it, and I'll comfort you. I can help you in a lot of ways, if you'll let me. I know heaps and heaps of things. And I won't tell that you said such wicked words, only promise that you won't go on hating us, and that you won't mind George, and that you will come to me when you have the blues."

She spoke very earnestly, with her kind little hand still resting on the boy's coat sleeve and with her bright eyes shining. She was to Saleh like a being from another world, possessed of nothing in common with the women-folk of his own race. Her kindness spoke to him in his desolation, took him by the hand to lead his faltering steps through the darkness in which he was engulfed; and in that moment, I think, he began to understand why in our land the accident of sex causes women to be held in such deep reverence.

During the twelvemonth that followed—the painful first year in which Saleh was finding his level and fitting in as best he might with the circumstances of his alien surroundings—Mabel's friendship and encouragement, Mabel's advice, admonitions, guidance, made the rough path smooth and laid many a high hill low for him. Also it was through the child's eyes, though she was wholly unconscious of it, that this little outlier obtained his first glimpse of the kindness, the sanctity, and the exquisite purity of English family life. It was indeed a serene and wholesome atmosphere that his exotic lungs were made to breathe; but Saleh, the adaptable, learned at last to inhale it, not only with ease and comfort, but with keen pleasure, taking an active pride in living up to the high standard which, having begun by depressing and bewildering him, ended by awaking his appreciation, enchaining his sympathies, and kindling his enthusiasm.

The boy's pliable nature had been taken in time; its

upward tendencies had been stimulated, given room
for development. He had caught the health-giving
spirit of the honest English home life in which his
days were spent, and, chameleon-like, he lost the color
absorbed from his environment in Malaya, assuming
in its place the duller, more permanent character tints
of the British youngster. Only, by force of contrast,
the newer ideal was seen more clearly, was aimed at
more persistently, more consciously, with a keener
desire to attain to it. Thenceforth, till very near the
end of his sojourn in England, the denationalization
of Râja Saleh was a completed fact. The Malayan
shell was there, more or less intact; a mist of nebulous
memories, hovering somewhere in the background of
his mind, told of a Malayan past; but within the lad
the Malayan soul lay dead, or slumbering, and in
its stead had been born the soul of a clean-minded,
honest-thinking, self-respecting Englishman, possessed of many of the virtues and not a few of the
limitations of its kind.

The work which the white men in their wisdom had
set themselves to do had now presumably been accomplished in triumphant fashion, with all the thoroughness, the uncompromising completeness, which belongs to white men's work. Starting with the axiom
that civilization—that is to say, the civilization of the
Englishman of the twentieth century—is a blessing,
they had brought all its forces to bear upon the defenseless Saleh. They had concerned themselves only
with the immediate achievement—the difficult experiment of which Saleh was the victim; they had made
no attempt to forecast results, to pry into the future,
to forsee in what manner their action would be like
to affect the lad himself and his individual happiness.

A high standard of civilization, with its exalted moral code and nobler ideals, was in itself a blessing, a happiness. That was the theory—a beautiful theory —and it was for Saleh, since the opportunity had been thrust upon him, to work it out in practice. Even the omniscience and the omnipotence of the white men have their limitations.

Chapter   *Six*

THE end of the fifth year of his exile in Europe found Saleh a very different being from the little, scared, half-savage boy who had been thrust, like a trapped animal, into Mrs. Le Mesurier's drawing-room. Regular hours, quantities of good, plain, English food, plenty of open air and violent exercise at all seasons and in all weathers, had wrought a great improvement in his physique. He was small of stature, judged by English standards, as are most men of his race; but his beautifully built frame was spare, and hard, and active. Each limb was developed to the full, every muscle stood out in a rounded cord beneath the glossy skin. The blood ran warm under cheeks of which the olive tint was hardly more dusky than that of a Neapolitan; his hair, which of old had been so stiff and straight that it had resolutely declined to allow itself to be parted in the European fashion, was now silky and abundant, and, for all its blackness, grew with a slight wave in it, as an Englishman's hair should grow. His great dark eyes were clear and bright, lighting up readily with facile merriment, although there still lurked in them, when his face was in repose, that soft and dreamy melancholy which ever seems to me to speak of the dumb agony of a race doomed to early extinction.

Saleh had always been a pretty boy, and his beard-less face still caused him to appear incredibly youth-ful; but now, at nineteen years of age, he was more completely a man than any of the English youngsters with whom his days were passed. Also he was hand-some—not with the soft, foreign, almost feline beauty

that distinguishes so many Orientals, but with good
looks of a sturdier cast, bred of clean-cut features,
manly independence, and self-respect, which approximate far more nearly to English standards of taste.
The discipline to which he had been subjected, to
which he had resigned himself as to one of the inevitable facts of life, had not succeeded in eradicating
all the natural indolence of his character. He was
still "slack," incurably "slack," more especially whenever anything in the nature of an intellectual effort
was demanded of him; but he was not alone in this,
for the failing was shared by many of his English
comrades. In games, however, this weakness did not
show itself, for the sporting instincts of his race came
to his rescue. He pulled a good oar, for one of his
size and weight; he was a pretty bat and the neatest
of fielders; his activity and dexterity stood him in
good stead at Association football and at hockey; he
was a beautiful gymnast, and as a swimmer no one in
his set could touch him. That peculiar form of discipline which is best taught by games, in which a man
plays for the side, not for his own hand, had helped
to strengthen his character, and he owed far more
than he knew to the constant exercise which, demand-
ing so much of his energies, left little over to tempt
him to less wholesome things. In this direction, too,
climate doubtless aided him, climate and the whole
tone of the family of which he had become a member,
for Saleh had fitted into the new life so perfectly that
he now seemed to have no individuality apart from it.

Moreover, his whole outlook had undergone a
change and women had ceased to be regarded by him
as inferior beings, mere playthings given to their
master, Man, for his amusement. He had lived with

the Le Mesurier girls as brother and sister; Mrs. Le Mesurier had come to be his mother in everything but fact; and the girls with whom he from time to time associated were often his superiors in education and intelligence, and all now commanded his respect simply by reason of their sex. Five years before this mental attitude towards women would have seemed to him the veriest topsy-turvidom, but now it appealed to him as a matter of course. The change had come about so gradually, was the result of such daily accretions of experience, that he was conscious of no alteration in his point of view. It seemed to him that he had always thought of these matters as he thought of them now; and when he danced with a pretty girl— and he danced quite beautifully—his pleasure was as natural and as little sullied by unholy dreams as that of any right-minded English lad.

And with all this Saleh was thoroughly, if unconsciously, happy. He loved his adopted family dearly, without troubling to ask himself why he loved them; he reveled in the games; he delighted in balls and parties; he was without a care in the world, for his intellectual failures, which were indeed colossal, did not greatly trouble him. Also, during the first five years of his life in England he had no ambitions, no aspirations that were not easily satisfied by a success in the playing-fields or the gym, while his adoption into the family and social circle of the Le Mesuriers had been so complete that he had forgotten that he was divided from them by the accident of color.

Saleh had been transformed into an Englishman, and had himself accepted the fact of his inner transformation so unreservedly that to him it stood in need of no demonstration. His simple paganism, which

only by an excess of courtesy could be called Muhammadanism, had been scrupulously respected. It
formed no part of the white men's scheme that the lad
should abandon the faith of his fathers, wherefore,
loyally observing the letter of the bond, the Le
Mesuriers had carefully abstained from making any
attempt to convert their charge to Christianity. Had
they been minded to effect this change, it is probable
that they would have encountered little difficulty; but
as matters stood, Saleh's opinions concerning things
spiritual—if indeed he entertained any—had been
suffered to take care of themselves. None the less,
the sincerely religious atmosphere of the household
had made a deep impression upon his sensitive and
receptive mind; it had given him new standards, new
ideals, and, all unknown to him, had become a prime
factor in the regulation of his conduct. He detested
reading, hating the mere laborious drudgery of it, and
the Bible is a stout volume. He was neither expected
nor invited to study it, and, save under compulsion, it
was not his custom to study anything. Even if he had
been made to enter that great treasure-house of
Oriental wisdom, however, he was at this time too
little given to introspection to have made any personal
application to himself of aught that he would have
found therein. The text which propounds that grim
question, "Can the Ethiopian change his skin, or the
leopard his spots?" would have held for him no special
augury. The bitter meaning of those taunting words
was to be revealed to him in all its bearings in days
which as yet were hidden by the merciful mystery of
the future.

O F that fugue of distracting discords, which in the end was fated to bring to Saleh a dreary enlightenment, the first jarring note was struck, I think, by the little Princess.

The holidays of his fifth summer in England were spent by him on a visit to a friend, an old Wykehamist, whose people lived in a riverside house near Richmond. Saleh was quite contented to remain where he was, and had he been left to himself he would have declined the invitation unreservedly. Mr. Le Mesurier, however, thought that it would be good for him to be severed for a time from the support of his "home" surroundings and to be thus forced to stand alone. He therefore insisted upon an acceptance being sent, and in due course Saleh reluctantly followed his letter.

Harry Fairfax, the friend in question, had become very intimate with the Le Mesuriers, and had learned to look upon Saleh as a member of the family. Also he liked him for himself, and thought that it would be rather a "lark" to introduce the little stranger to his own people. His father and mother were a quiet, elderly pair, still wholly wrapped up in each other, who watched the bewildering doings of their offspring with a mild surprise without attempting to influence or control them. If Harry had expressed his intention of inviting Muck-a-Muck, the noble savage himself, to stay at Crosslands, Mr. and Mrs. Fairfax would have supposed that such was the fashion of the present day and would have raised no objection. Their daughters, Alice and Sibyl, who were also allowed to

do in all things very much as they pleased, thought
that their brother's proposal promised some amusement, and they were prepared to pay almost any price
for the rare privilege of his company at home. Therefore the prospect of Saleh's visit displeased nobody
except Saleh himself.

Just at first he was uncomfortably conscious of the
fact that Fairfax's relations—more especially the two
girls—eyed him with a certain curiosity, as a being
new to their inexperience. Living under the same
roof in daily intercourse with women, between whom
and himself there subsisted no such brother and sister
familiarity as that to which life with the Le Mesuriers
had accustomed him, brought with it a measure of
embarrassment. It made him shy, self-conscious, con-
strained—all things from which hitherto his simplicity
had kept him singularly free—and yet in some way it
was pleasurable, stimulating, even exciting. These
latter sensations were realized more fully later, when
the first strangeness of his new environment had to
some extent worn off; but at the beginning of his
visit Saleh felt himself to be divided from the Fairfaxes by an impalpable barrier. Its nature and cause
he did not attempt to analyze; only he was dimly
aware of its existence, and an unwonted feeling of
loneliness, of isolation, came upon him. Instinct told
him, hinted to him, that he was regarded as in some
sort an alien, a curiosity, and this made him sore and
angry, not with others, but with himself. It was as
though he had suddenly been revealed to himself in
a new light—had been made conscious of some unsuspected, unreal, yet inherent inferiority in his
nature which differentiated him from the rest of
humanity. He would rather have died than have

shaped such a thought in words; for the moment he shirked allowing it to take even nebulous form in the back of his mind—in his most secret self-communings; but none the less an uneasy restlessness was bred in him by these disquieting, vague, and, as he forced himself to believe, groundless suspicions. For some days, therefore, he shunned the companionship of his new friends, seeking refuge from them and from the shadowy fancies that troubled him in solitary rambles. These led him mostly into Richmond Park, for the big expanse of comparatively wild woodland held for him a curious fascination. Though he had almost ceased to remember it, Saleh was forest-bred, and he, to whom by right of birth belongs the freedom of the jungle, is driven by instinct to the woods and thickets when the craving for consolation is upon him. The old park, with its network of metaled roads, its tame deer and fearless rabbits nibbling the grass undisturbed by groups of Londoners picnicking noisily within a few yards of them, was but a poor substitute for the magnificent, untouched forests of Malaya. Even here, however, there were hollow places filled with tangles of underwood or mounds of brambles sheltered by which it was possible for Saleh to fancy himself very far removed from the hurrying life around him; and here, too, the huge gnarled trunks of oak and elm were silent comrades whose neighborhood consoled him with a sense of companionship and peace.

It was in Richmond Park that Saleh first saw the little Princess—a figure more exotic than his own—clad in a crimson frock, with a coquettish feather springing saucily from a toque of the same brilliant color. She passed quite close to him where he lay among the bracken, a dog whip in her little hand, and five great hounds of a breed unknown to Saleh, with long coats of white and silver gray, lean, fierce heads, sharp muzzles, and savage eyes. The girl's hair was black, as only the hair of an Asiatic woman can be; her clear pale skin was swarthy; her features—the straight, low forehead, the hooked nose with nostrils curving outward, the full lips, the rounded but slightly retreating chin—were strongly Semitic in cast; her eyes—the big, sloe-black, elliptical eyes of the daughter of northern India—were veiled and dreamy in repose under the heavy arches of eyebrow. She was of smaller stature than are most European girls, and her trim figure had ever so little a tendency to thickness; but her hands and feet were exquisite things, diminutive in size and most delicately formed, although at the bases of her almond-shaped finger nails tiny smudges of a faint dusky blue betrayed the Eastern blood. She looked at the youngster lounging on the grass, and passed him by with a toss of her little head.

After that Saleh saw her frequently, always clad in crimson or scarlet—for the love of colors crude and gay was innate in her—always chaperoned by those five great hounds, over whom she seemed to exercise a tyrannical ascendancy. The incongruity of this Oriental child and her surroundings began by piquing Saleh's curiosity, though it was significant of the extent to which he had identified himself with the people of his adoption that the little Princess, who, as a fellow-Asiatic, and one of his own color, should surely have been felt to be akin to him, seemed to him a being outlandish, fantastic, *bizarre*—infinitely more alien than were any of the English girls with whom he was wont to associate. Her beauty—for the little Jewish-looking lady with her marvelous eyes, the heavy arched eyebrows, and the wealth of blue-black hair, had her full share of good looks—made no appeal to him, even repelled him a little, just as the pink-and-white loveliness of Englishwomen had repelled him five years earlier. His taste had altered with the rest of him, and to-day he was as insular in the narrow range of his appreciation as any British-born youngster in the set to which he belonged. He had no desire to make the little Princess's acquaintance, for the sight of her was, in a manner, terrifying to him. It seemed to cross the *t's*, to dot the *i's* of his half-formed fears, to make his vague suspicions more haunting and less nebulous, to add to the restless uneasiness of which he was already the prey. Somehow or another that crudely tinted exotic figure moving so incongruously across the quiet English landscape, conveyed to him a hint that emphasized the falseness of the position which he himself occupied, and forced upon him an explanation of all that had troubled him since he came to stay with the Fairfaxes—the true explanation to which he still strove to shut his eyes. It was as though he had caught sight of himself horribly caricatured and distorted in a misshapen mirror, and instinctively he turned his head away, refusing to look at an ugly vision which was fraught for him with so much of pain and of humiliation.

O N the occasion of their third chance meeting the little Princess stopped and spoke to Saleh. He was lying in the bracken, as usual, idle of body, yet trying to keep his mind from digging too deeply into the enigmas that fretted him, and she halted in front of him, her dog whip in her hand, her great hounds grouped around her, and looked down upon him with a sort of haughty scorn in her eyes.

"Who are you, you little black boy?" she asked, insolently.

With the instinct of courtesy which the past five years had bred in him, Saleh sprang to his feet and stood before her, hat in hand. He felt himself to be insulted, outraged by the girl's rude words, but her sex rendered him defenseless. This, again, was the fruit of his English training.

"I am Râja Saleh," he said, speaking with the strong foreign accent of which he was blissfully unconscious. "My father is the Sultan of Pelesu."

"And where is Pĕlĕsu, pray?" asked the girl, her lips curling scornfully. "I have never heard of Pĕlĕsu."

Unlike Saleh, she spoke her adopted language perfectly, yet with that slight lengthening of the vowels and over-precise enunciation of the consonants which, when accompanied with a fluty falsetto voice, proclaims the "Chee-Chee" to the Anglo-Indian with uncompromising distinctness.

"Pĕlĕsu is a state—a very large state—in the Malay Peninsula," answered Saleh, sulkily.

The little Princess tossed her head and laughed. "Oh, that savage place!" she said. "I knew your father could not be one of the great princes of India, or I should have heard of him. I," she added, proudly —"I am a daughter of the great House of Baram Singh. We are Rajputs. We are descended without a break in our line from Alexander the Great, who went to the East that he might find the spot where the sun rises. My people have been kings for hundreds and hundreds of years."

"So have mine," cried Saleh. "And we too are descended from Alexander!" He spoke in all good faith, for every sprig of Malayan royalty, in common with the members of many princely houses in Asia, claims the proud distinction of the same mythical ancestry; but the little Princess laughed contemptuously at such preposterous pretensions.

"It is in the books—the Malay books. I have read it," said Saleh, feebly.

"There are plenty of lies in the books," rejoined the little Princess, sententiously. "But our chronicles are true. They are ever so old, and all the world knows about our descent. My people were kings for thousands and thousands of years!"

"And aren't they kings any longer?" inquired Saleh, innocently.

This time the little Princess bent upon him a look of scornful pity that was withering.

"Have you learned *no* history, you little black boy?" she asked.

"Oh yes," said Saleh, with the ineradicable childishness of his race, and anxious, too, to display his knowledge. "I know a lot of history, about Julius Cæsar, and William the Conqueror, and Clive, and Warren

Hastings, and Oliver Cromwell, the wicked regicide, and Marie Antoinette and . . . and . . . Sir Stamford Raffles . . . and ——"

"Oh, all that stuff!" she interrupted. "That is nothing; but the story of the House of Baram Singh is real history. The English robbed us!"

"I don't believe it," cried Saleh, bluntly, his loyalty getting the better of his acquired courtesy.

"Then that just shows what a stupid, ignorant little boy you must be!" she retorted. "Everybody who knows any thing knows what bandits these English are. They talk a great deal about right and wrong, and about injustice and justice; they are always sending poor people to prison for little thefts; but they make me sick—these English—they are such robbers! They were running wild in their horrid wet woods, naked and shivering under their blue paint, when my ancestors were civilized men and mighty kings. They were just miserable savages; and now, for all their prating about virtue, if men steal big enough things—a crown, a kingdom—they account it no crime, they think it glorious. Oh, they are such hypocrites and liars! I hate them! hate them!"

She ceased her tirade from sheer lack of breath, and stood there in the summer sunlight, quivering with rage. She would not have dreamed of speaking thus to any European; but, despite all her pride of race, this little brown boy did not seem to matter, simply because the accident of his color brought with it a certain sense of kinship. Also, she felt, all right-thinking Orientals must share the opinions to which she gave such uncompromising expression.

To Saleh, the denationalized, however, her words were the rankest blasphemy. To him the very fire of

her emotions was repellent because—because it was
un-English! This unexpected encounter with a point
of view so diametrically opposed to that which he had
assimilated through his training, sympathies, and asso-
ciates, smote him with a shock of horrified surprise.
The limitations of his imagination had so far pre-
vented him from so much as guessing that there might
be more than one side even to the question of
England's vast reformatory work in Asia, and his
Malayan memories had become too blurred and distant
for them to afford him any assistance in this direction.
Therefore the railings of the little Princess were in
the nature of an ugly revelation which, while it made
the fool's paradise in which he had been living so
contentedly totter to its foundations, outraged him
by laying sacrilegious hands on much which he had
learned to regard as holy. For the moment he was
dumb, and had no words at his command to oppose to
the bitter flood of the girl's rhetoric.

"And the English hate us, too," she went on, presently. "They hate us because they fear us. Some day
we shall drive them out of India, and my people will
go back and reign as before in their own land!"

"That is nonsense!" cried Saleh, with utter conviction. "You could never turn us out. We are much too
strong, and have got a footing there that nothing will
ever shake."

"That shows how little you know," she retorted.
"It will be done easily. We will outcaste them. We
will make it a sin for anyone, be he Hindu or Muhammadan, to supply the *Melch* with food or water. They
will try to force our folk to give way; they will call
out their soldiers; they will behave as they did in '57
—like the savages they are at bottom; but it will be

of no use. When it is their religions that inspire them, our people in India will die in thousands rather than sin at the bidding of the English. They have proved it in the past. It is the spirit of religion—not the accident of creed—which will unify our peoples, that will give them the power to die, but never to submit. The English will resist, for they are stubborn; but in the end they will have to go and India will be ours once more. It can be done; I have heard my people speak of it, and some day we will do it!"

The dark blood dyed her pale cheeks to a deeper hue; her eyes, which had lost their dreamy melancholy, flashed as she gazed into vacancy like some tiny savage prophetess; her words poured from her, tingling with excitement, thrilling with the sincerity of her emotion, and Saleh stood before her, carried away in spite of himself by the contagion of her enthusiasm, but horrified at the picture which her words conjured up, and filled suddenly with a great fear for his friends.

"I do not think like you," he said, hesitatingly, and even to his own ears his words sounded weak and stupid. "I like the English. They are my friends. They do a lot of good. They are kind people and are just in their dealings."

He was painfully aware of his lack of eloquence; the very strength of his feelings rendered him more than usually inarticulate. He was loyally eager to vindicate the honor of his friends—of the nation of his adoption; but he was conscious that he had neither the brains nor the words to argue successfully with the little spitfire before him.

"You *like* the English!" she cried. "You dare to say that you *like* them—you, an Asiatic, the son of

one of the many whom they have despoiled! Only
cowards like them, cowards who fawn, as dogs fawn,
upon the hand that beats them—thus!" And she
struck the hound which stood nearest to her a vicious
blow upon his muzzle with the handle of her whip.
The great beast, whimpering a little, cowered on the
ground at her feet, looking up at her uncomprehend-
ingly with his heavy, slavish dog's eyes. "You are
like him if you are fond of the English!" she cried,
and struck the cowering creature again with her little
cruel hand.

"Leave him alone! Don't be so cruel!" shouted
Saleh, quivering with anger. Five years earlier the
brutal treatment of any animal would have had no
power to move him, and his quick indignation at the
girl's maltreatment of her dog went far to prove how
utterly dead, or how completely lulled to sleep, was
the Malayan soul within him. Her words had disquieted, pained, tortured him; but now as he watched
her brutally punish an unoffending animal he felt
that he hated her.

"Ah!" she cried, triumphantly, "you do not 'like'
me when I am unjust to Rustam here, yet you praise
the English, who have done much worse things! They
hated my grandfather because he was a man and
fought them. They beat his armies because they were
ill-armed; they took his country from him, stealing
even his crown jewels, like the brigands they are; and
they carried him away to this horrible cold England
to die in exile! But he never ceased to hate them and
to show them the measure of his hate, and they
watched him always, because they were afraid of the
poor old man whom they had wronged, but whose
spirit they could never break!"

"I am sorry for him," said Saleh, "but perhaps there were reasons which you do not know. Perhaps his people were unhappy when he ruled them."

"That is the nonsense which the English hypocrites have taught you to talk," the girl replied, with infinite scorn. "If his people did not love him, why did they fight for him? Why did the English have to kill hundreds and hundreds of them before they could conquer his country? Answer me that."

"I do not know. I have not read about it," said Saleh, who found himself at more of a disadvantage than ever.

"And if you had read of it, it would be in English books, written for the English by Englishmen, and crammed with lies! They can always find an excuse to justify their wickedness, these English; but the truth—ah, that is different! Only we who have suffered know the truth!

"Listen, you little black boy. They tried to make my father different—to turn him into an Englishman. He became a Christian (it is bad to be anything but a Christian in this land), and we are all Christians now. But when we win back our country we shall be restored to caste.

"My grandfather had tried resistance all his life, and it had failed. My father pretended for a long time that he was a friend of the English, hoping that would better serve his purposes; but because he spent some paltry sums—for even in exile a king must live lavishly—the English, who had robbed us of everything, were very angry on account of his debts. Then he escaped—went to Russia; but the Russians are white men, too, and liars like the English. They made fair promises to him, but they never would *do* anything. They only wanted to make a tool of him. Then despair seized him and he came back here and made his peace with the English—outwardly. He was a broken man then. He used to sit all day with his head fallen forward upon his breast, his hands idle, doing nothing, only thinking, thinking, thinking— thinking of all that ought to have been his—and waiting for death. He died of a broken heart, my father, and it was the people whom you and other cowards 'like' who broke it! Oh, how I detest them; but still more I hate and despise black men like you who pretend to love them!"

She spoke with so fierce a passion that Saleh drew back from her, shocked and dismayed; outraged, too, for instinctively he was aware that the little Princess would never have dreamed of using such words to a white man, and Saleh desired above everything to be treated as an Englishman. Her action in addressing him at all, even more than the words which she had uttered, was to him an insult, a humiliation.

"I am not a coward and I do like the English. You must be a wicked girl to talk as you talk, and I don't believe what you say about the English is true. They are just people and very kind people." Once more the hopeless inadequacy of his words caused him to be smartingly conscious of his own intellectual impotence.

The little Princess only answered with a disgusted ejaculation, and, calling to her hounds to follow her, she left him with a look of blighting contempt and a toss of her pretty head.

Long after she had passed from his sight behind the trunks of the elms Saleh stood where she had left him, knee-deep in the bracken, jarred to the very marrow, confused, humiliated, and beset by vague doubts. During the whole interview his own inferiority had been borne in upon him with the force of a new discovery, for throughout she had spoken to him as though, because he was not white, he ranked no higher in her estimation than if he were one of her hounds. Coming precisely at the moment when for the first time his color was beginning to trouble him, the wound thus inflicted had eaten deep into his soul; but also, apart from the purely personal question, he had been offended by all that she had said against his friends. His was a nature formed for loyalty, and her abuse rankled. Moreover, her words had violated the integrity of that facile optimism which hitherto had led him to accept the world as he found it, subscribing without reserve to Pope's astonishing article of faith, that "whatever is, is right!" Now, in less than half an hour, his universe had been turned topsy-turvy before his eyes: white had been made to look like black, right like wrong. It was horrible, unnatural, and infinitely bewildering, for it made him feel as though he were being robbed of his dearest beliefs and were being left with nothing solid for his feet to rest upon.

As he turned homeward he tried, with the Malayan instinct that ever shuns the contemplation of aught that is distressing, to forget the little Princess and her dreadful charges; but, do what he would, the thought of her still clung to him as a hateful and haunting memory.

FROM that day onward Saleh abandoned his rambles in Richmond Park. He dreaded to meet the little Princess again and to be forced once more to listen to the bitter railings which had so disquieted him. Yet the story of the House of Baram Singh, as she had told it, still troubled him; for if she had spoken the truth, her people had been the victims of injustice and hardship and their history was a dreadful and inexplicable tragedy. He wished that he possessed a deeper knowledge of history and of affairs, for he felt dimly that there must be some explanation, something resembling a justification, for all that the English were stated to have done. Failing such knowledge, he was plunged in doubt, in uncertainty; he was a prey to uncomfortable suspicions suddenly aroused; he longed to be convinced that all was as it should be, but knew not where to turn in search of enlightenment. He could not bring himself to ask questions of the Fairfaxes, partly because he was reluctant to appear to be identifying himself with Asiatics as against white folk, to be ranging himself on the side of the lesser breed—partly because the memory of his interview with the little Princess set him wincing whenever he recalled it to mind. The incident had left behind it an impression as of something shameful, something upon which he must not suffer his thoughts to dwell, if the old serene and peaceful happiness and contentment with his lot were to be lured back again. Therefore it was with something of a shock that he heard the name of Baram Singh spoken one day at the Fairfax table.

"I see the Baram Singhs are still knocking about," Harry Fairfax remarked, suddenly.

"Oh yes," said Sibyl. "Princess Marie played hockey with us all this winter. She is a beautiful half-back."

"I remember her playing when I was at home at Christmas," said Harry. "She played an uncommonly good game, but she struck me as being a trifle vicious with her stick. I have a dent in my shin-bone the depth of a walnut-shell to remember her by."

"She dances beautifully," said Alice.

"I remember that, too, and, by the way, Fred Castle was awfully gone on her. Did it ever come to anything?"

"No," said Sibyl; "but I think his people were rather glad to get him away. He went out to India to join his regiment in March."

"Ah!" said Harry, ruminatingly, "that will cure him."

"But her brother, Prince Alexander, has been married since you were here."

"Yes, of course. Wasn't there a great row about it?"

"Dreadful. Her people were furious; they did everything they could to prevent it," said Sibyl, with the eager interest which so many display only when discussing the misfortunes of their friends.

"I suppose she thought it smart to be 'Princess Anything,' in spite of all drawbacks," suggested Harry.

"Yes, I suppose so," assented Sibyl; "but she has not got much out of it. Lots of people give her the cold shoulder, and I believe that she is not particularly *bien vue* even at Court."

"Serve her right!" said Harry.

"Oh, how *could* she!" ejaculated Alice, who had so

far been listening in silence. "She must have been a horrid girl!"

She gave a little shudder, and then suddenly, as her eyes lighted upon Saleh's attentive face, her delicate skin was dyed to her very forehead with a burning blush.

"Keep off the grass!" said Harry, and then he and Sibyl laughed, while Mr. and Mrs. Fairfax looked embarrassed, and Saleh glanced from one to the other in utter perplexity.

The words of the conversation were in themselves familiar, yet the meaning which they seemed to have conveyed to the rest of the party was something which Saleh felt that he had caught imperfectly. What concern of his could the family affairs of the Baram Singhs be supposed to be? Yet he was dimly aware that Alice's evident embarrassment had been caused by his presence, and the fact, which to him lacked all reason, was distressing. Once again he felt himself to be an alien; once more he was filled with anger against the little Princess, who seemed fated to bring upon him unmerited humiliation.

The memory of this trifling incident was soon effaced, however, by the unusual graciousness with which Alice treated him during the afternoon that followed. She was enthusiastic in her praise of his play at lawn-tennis, and repeatedly chose him as her partner. Later, when they went on the river after tea, she said kind things about his handling of his oar, and pointedly invited him to share her seat in the stern for the homeward row. She fancied that she had hurt his feelings, and was determined to make amends; but Saleh, who was conscious of no grievance against her, and consequently was expectant of no reparation, saw in her overtures only the natural expression of her personal liking for himself. Her approval and her graciousness warmed him with a glow which that of the Le Mesurier girls had never had the power to kindle. His proximity to her thrilled him, as he sat beside her, in a fashion that was new and wholly delightful, nor did it occur to him that her advances were somewhat more frank and open than such courtesies are apt to be between a girl and a man with whom she feels herself to be upon a footing of perfectly equality. To Alice, Saleh's nationality and color made him to all intents and purposes sexless. In her estimation he was not a man like other marriageable men, and she accordingly admitted him behind that barrier of reserve which is the girl's natural intrenchment against the aggression of the male besieger.

Therefore, as the boat lolled down the Thames that evening through the fragrant summer gloaming, Alice went out of her way to be "nice" to Saleh, her desire to allay the pain of a wound thoughtlessly inflicted leading her, though she had no inkling of it, to work him a far more lasting injury.

THENCEFORTH Saleh marveled at the folly which had driven him to ramble alone in Richmond Park, and at the prodigality with which he had so wantonly wasted precious hours that might have been spent in Alice's company. His one desire now was to be near the girl, to watch the play of her dainty features, the grace of her every movement, to listen to her, to feel the thrill that shot through him when she spoke to him or smiled upon him. The remaining members of the Fairfax family had sunk in his estimation to the utter insignificance of shadows. They were to him of no sort of account, save as happy satellites that revolved round his star. For him a room was empty till Alice chanced to enter it; a game or a jaunt was unspeakably stupid and wearisome if she took no part in it; and Harry Fairfax cursed Saleh's "slackness" hourly, since the latter shirked every amusement that might take him away from the society of the girl.

Mr. Fairfax and his wife had never passed beyond the stage of being unable to see anything in the world except each other's faces, so that they were quite blind to what was happening. The young people of the household were not less obtuse. They liked their guest, and noted with a certain surprise how very like an English lad he was; but their attitude towards him resembled that of the great Dr. Johnson with regard to the pig. They were not greatly concerned with the excellence of his swinish caligraphy, all their admiration being claimed by the marvel that a pig should write at all. They rather enjoyed showing Saleh off to their friends, but they never dreamed of looking upon him as a human being susceptible to all the emotions of humanity. His racial inferiority for them was something so completely beyond the range of dispute that it passed into their acceptance as an axiom. It was so patent a fact that it called for no demonstration. It was a point upon which they were unshakably convinced. If Alice had been accused of flirting with Saleh, she would have resented the charge as a degrading insult, and her brother and sister would have felt themselves to be no less outraged through her; but the bare possibility of such an interpretation being put upon her kindness to the lad never so much as crossed the girl's mind. It would have seemed to her too grotesque, too absurd. Her whole conception of their relative positions would have had to be revolutionized before such a suspicion could even find an entry into her mind, for her very graciousness to Saleh was but an expression of the pity with which his inferiority inspired her.

Also, I think, Saleh's hairless, boyish face, which made him look to unaccustomed English eyes so much younger than his years, did him here a sorry service, for to Alice he seemed little more than a child, and it was as a child rendered piteous by irremediable deformity that she petted and flattered him. Yet Saleh, for all his apparent youth and his bare nineteen years of age, was a man full-grown. In his own country he would have entered upon the estate of the husband and the father before he was fifteen, and though the climate of England had done something towards checking his precocious development, he was now far more mature than are the majority of European lads six years his senior. Also the blood running in his veins was hot from a race which since the beginning of things has paired and mated almost in childhood, a race which holds with the primitive Adam that "it is not good for man to live alone." Circumstances, so far, had saved him from the divine obsession of love; but now in the daily companionship of Alice Fairfax the passion which his people name "the madness" came upon him in all its grandeur and its might. And the pity of it was that this was no mere calf-love, such as an English lad might have felt, nor yet the crude animal craving of man for woman which passes for love with the men of Saleh's blood and is called among them by too holy a name. For here the curse of his five years' training among English folk fell heavily. The spiritual side of the lad's nature had been developed by insensible degrees, giving him a higher range of aspirations, a greater acuteness and delicacy of feeling, and far more power of appreciation and delight than were his by right of inheritance; but endowing him also with a capacity for suffering infinitely enhanced.

Primitive men are denied many joys which may be tasted only by their highly civilized and cultured brethren. Their desires are few, and of a kind easy to satisfy. They are never thrilled and exalted by the dreams of a lofty ambition; but the most bitter of disappointed hopes means for them nothing much more difficult of endurance than a hunger-pang—a memory which the next full meal will triumphantly efface. Inasmuch as they are nearer to the beasts, in so much are they spared the deeper agonies of man; for just as the little mermaid in the German story could put on the likeness of a woman only at the cost of feeling the knife-blades eat into the feet with

which she trod the earth, so each painful step which
humanity has taken upon its upward path has made
it more and more vulnerable through its increased
sensitiveness, its finer perceptions. And Saleh, born
and bred a primitive, but lifted through the caprice of
the white men out of his native conditions, found himself, now on the threshold of manhood, possessed of
a refinement of taste and a yearning after higher
things such as his teachers had been at no small pains
to instil. They had given him all they might, but one
thing they could not give—the equal chance with
others to satisfy the aspiration they had inspired.

Left to himself, he would have loved many brown
girls, after the fashion of his people, with a rough
passion that made no demand upon his intellect and
asked no contribution from the stunted soul of him;
but transplanted as he had been from his natural environment, and forced to a development foreign to his
circumstances, he loved Alice Fairfax with all the fire
of his Malayan temperament, but also with the reverence, the purity, the idealism of a European lover.
And here again his utter denationalization smote him
shrewdly; for since the devout lover must ever think
meanly of himself when he raises his eyes to the
object of his adoration, Saleh presently began to torture himself with doubts and questions.

For some flawless days he had lived in a fool's
paradise, knowing only that he was happy, and dreaming not as yet that it was love which of a sudden had
made the world so good a place in which to live. Then
a chance word of Harry Fairfax had forced upon him
a realization of the truth. "When you girls are
married and settled down," Harry had said with casual
brotherly indifference, speaking of some plan of his

own, and immediately Saleh had understood that the
bare notion of Alice becoming the wife of any man
was a thing he could not endure to contemplate. He
asked for nothing for himself. He would be content
just to watch and love and serve her; but she must be
Alice Fairfax, not the wife of some other man. In a
moment it flashed upon him how bitter it would be "to
look at happiness through another man's eyes," and to
that thought succeeded a kind of cold despair, for the
humility of a reverent lover at last brought into focus
the elusive vision of himself as a being innately inferior, giving instantly a new meaning to the hints
and suspicions which of late had been haunting him.

Yet still he struggled manfully with his conviction.
He was eager to admit the supreme beauty and worth
of his deity, he was content to prostrate himself in
spirit before her, confessing that no man in all the
world could be deserving of her love. This, he
thought, must be the creed of any man who dared to
love her; but he fought with himself desperately to
prevent the truth from forcing him farther than that
admission implied. He tried to shut his eyes to the
gulf that divides the white men from the brown, strove
strenuously to persuade himself that though all men
were unworthy of her, he was not the most unworthy
of all, and then the insolent words of the little
Princess came back to him, mocking his grief. "You
black boy," she had called him, and the memory of the
words set him wincing anew. He was not *black,* he
told himself—not black like a Habshi. (He still preserved sufficient of his Malayan prejudices to feel the
deepest contempt for an African negro.) He was
dark, of course, but hardly more swarthy than were
many of the people he had seen at Naples on his

voyage to England; yet he knew now that it was this very matter of his color which had been troubling him ever since he first came to stay at Richmond. For a day or two after he had made the discovery that he loved Alice, the emotions that rent him affected him so deeply that his friends feared that he was ill, and Alice, more pitiful of him than ever, was doubly kind and gracious. Then the facile optimism of the ease-loving Malay came to his aid, and, seeing how good the girl was to him, he speedily persuaded himself that he had been frightened by shadows. Something of his former self-content returned to him; an echo of the belief, held so firmly by the natural Malay, that his race represents humanity in its highest expression, came to him, bringing him some measure of comfort in spite of its want of logic; he comported himself with his old proud independence, and though now and again reaction plunged him in despair, at other times his hopes ran high, and even the impossible seemed easy of achievement.

Chapter   *Eleven*

IT was in this spirit of intense exaltation that Saleh
went with the young Fairfaxes to the ball at Aston
Manor-House.   Harry undertook to chaperon his
sisters, but was far too busy to look after anyone save
himself and certain young ladies who claimed his
attention.   Alice and Sibyl, therefore, were left completely to their own devices, and the former chose, in
obedience to some momentary whim, to give a large
share of her dances to Saleh, an act which bore him
aloft on the wings of delight.   I have said that he
danced beautifully, and upon this evening the haunting suspicion of inferiority was forgotten.   The
music, the bright lights, the sheen of soft silks, the
rustle of women's skirts, the glitter and movement,
elated and excited him.   The open preference for himself which he thought to detect in Alice's favors intoxicated him.   Reason had ceased to whisper its
somber warnings in his ears.   A divine certainty of
success was his.   A tag of verse, committed to memory
laboriously at Mr. Le Mesurier's bidding, sorely
against the grain, came to his mind:

> "He either fears his fate too much,
>   Or his deserts are small,
> That dares not put it to the touch
>   To gain or lose it all."

He would test his fate to-night!

But, for all his new-born confidence, the courage
was for the moment lacking.   Perhaps he feared to
jeopardize such joy as was already his; perhaps,
almost unknown to him, the conviction that the risk

of failure was great still lingered; perhaps Alice's complete unconsciousness of the feelings with which she had inspired him had a certain repressive effect of which he was unaware. Whatever the reason, however, he danced the first four dances that she had given him without suffering a word to escape him that could prepare her for what was to come, and this though his mind was made up and his determination to tempt Providence unshaken. Reluctantly he yielded her up to another partner, and saw her float lightly away in his arms. Then he stood with his back against a door-post watching her animated face and graceful figure, and dreaming of the hopes that centered in her.

A hand laid suddenly upon his arm caused him to return to the things of the gross earth with a shock, and looking round he saw the little Princess standing by him. She was in evening dress, with a bodice of crimson satin cut low and trimmed with black chiffon; and with a kind of inward shrinking Saleh noted how dark the skin of her neck looked by gaslight and how swarthy were the arms now bared to the shoulder. She had a string of marvelous pearls round her neck, great gold bracelets on her wrists, and a second string of pearls twisted in and out among the black masses of her hair. Her great eyes were looking at him with a sort of elfish amusement.

"How do you do?" she said. "You are not dancing now?"

"No," said Saleh, "but I am engaged to dance presently."

"With Alice Fairfax, I suppose," she said, mischievously; "but as she is dancing with some one else now, you had better come and sit out with me."

"Thank you," said Saleh, with very little of gratitude in his voice; "but won't you dance instead?"

"No, thank you. I don't want to dance with you. These horrid people would laugh if they saw us dancing together. Besides, it wouldn't be proper, and I want to talk to you."

She led the way into one of the sitting-out rooms, and Saleh reluctantly followed. She had not seemed to notice the arm which he tentatively offered, and inconsequently enough Saleh felt hurt by the fact, though he lacked the perception to understand that this little Oriental shrank instinctively from allowing a fellow-Asiatic of the opposite sex to touch her, as any white man might have done without offense.

She threw herself down in the corner of a vast Chesterfield, arranging her skirts with a sort of cozy feline movement vaguely suggestive of her Eastern origin. Saleh seated himself beside her, pulling up the knees of his well-cut evening trousers and crossing his neat little feet in their pumps and silk socks.

"I was rude and unkind the other day," she began, "but you angered me. Now I am going to be rude again, but it is because I want to be kind. You think that you are in love with Alice Fairfax."

"How do you know?" asked Saleh, unconscious of the admission he was making.

The little Princess laughed.

"I know because I am not blind," she said. "Do you remember that I told you you were like one of my hounds? Well, if you could have seen yourself as you stood looking at her from that doorway, you would have needed no telling. Your eyes were following her about slavishly—just like a dog's. Now"—

as Saleh would have interrupted—"don't be angry. I do not mean to be rude. After all, she is so nice that you would not mind being *her* dog, would you?"

"No," said Saleh. Though his dislike of the little Princess was no whit diminished, to talk even to her about Alice was in itself pleasurable.

"I know," she resumed, "and that is why I am sorry for you and why I am talking to you now. Listen. You love her so much that you would ask her to marry you—isn't that so?"

"Yes," answered Saleh. "I mean to ask her."

"And I say that you shall do nothing of the kind!" cried the little Princess, with all the fire that she had shown at their first interview. "You do not know these English as I know them. They despise us: they call us 'niggers.' Oh, I know what you would say—that they treat us civilly, that you and I are guests here to-night, are received by them on equal terms. But that is nothing. Up to a point they can make believe to regard us as human beings, but only up to a certain point. They will talk with us, laugh with us, flirt with us, perhaps, but they will not wed with us! I know."

"But your brother, Prince Alexander, he has married an English girl. I have heard people talk of it," objected Saleh.

"And how have you heard them talk of it?—with disgust, with horror—as a degradation, a disgrace!"

The conversation at the Fairfax lunch-table recurred to Saleh's memory, fraught suddenly with a new meaning.

"I had not thought of it in that way," he said, haltingly.

"And the girl my brother married was not like Alice

Fairfax. She fell in love with his good looks, and when once a woman has got over something that is repellent to her, her passion is stronger than any ordinary feeling—while it lasts. It is morbid, and all morbid things are more violent than nature, because they have beaten nature before they have prevailed. I am sorry for my brother now."

"Why?"

"Because morbid passions are short lived. But Alice is not like that. She is just an ordinary, commonplace English girl—not in the least like the angel you fancy her, but even more unlike the neurotic morbid creature who is my brother's wife. She would never do what my sister-in-law did, and, though I hate her for it, I know that the reason is that she is more normal, more healthy, and could not sin against her nature, even if she would."

"If you are going to abuse Alice I won't listen to you," said Saleh, sullenly, drawing away from her.

"I am not abusing her. Can't you understand that I am praising her—as she would account praise? She would say that my brother's wife was a degraded, horrid woman."

"She did," said Saleh, musingly, blurting out the truth unthinkingly, more to himself that to his hearer.

The little Princess sprang into a more upright attitude, her cheeks darkened by the rush of blood under her skin, her eyes flashing with fury.

"She said that," she exclaimed. "The hateful, proud wretch! But I knew it, I knew it, and . . . and she was right! Nature did not mean brown folk and white to mate together; it is contrary to her law. In the East we Orientals feel the same repulsion; it is only those of us who are morbid, depraved, debased, who can overcome the repugnance inspired by the pale faces, which are like nothing so much as animated corpses, since death bleaches the color out of our cheeks; but people like you and me who have been brought up here in England have been robbed even of our nature. To us that which should be horrible has become natural, even attractive, it may be. The English who have taken so much from us, have taken that too. We cannot even keep our taste, our judgment."

"But they give us something in exchange," said Saleh. "I could never have felt about a girl as . . . as I feel about Alice—not if I had remained in the East, not if I had never come to England."

"And is that anything to be thankful for?" cried the little Princess, in bitter derision. "Can you be glad because you have been taught to feel as you ought not to feel, because you have learned to want what you cannot have?"

"But . . . you may be wrong. You hate the English, and you misjudge them." Saleh longed to convince himself, but the miserable doubts which of late had taken root in his mind had sprung up now into sudden maturity with the speed of Jack's beanstalk, and were flourishing luxuriantly, bearing a heavy crop of bitter fruit.

"I do not misjudge them in this. I *know*—I have good reason to know," the girl replied, her voice vibrating with passion. "Listen. If I had lived all my life in India—if the English had not robbed us, depriving us even of the surroundings which should have been ours by right of nature and inheritance—I should have scorned to think of a European with love. I should have felt about white people as . . . as they now feel about *us*. But I grew up here. I have never been to India. I have been made to associate with English people all my life, and so . . . so . . . when love came to me, it was . . . through an Englishman." Her voice was subdued to a whisper—a whisper that vibrated with intense passion. Saleh followed her words with an eager and painful excitement.

"Are you speaking of a man called Fred Castle?" he asked.

The girl gave a little inarticulate cry of pain, such as might have escaped from a tortured animal.

"Who told you?" She seemed to scream the words, though her voice was still hushed.

"I heard the Fairfaxes talking about it," replied Saleh, "but I did not understand. I mean that I did not know that it meant so much."

The little Princess wrung her hands, and then, clasping them together, let them fall into her lap. Saleh noticed that the knuckles stood out white and prominent, the skin strained over them by the violence with which the fingers were pressed into the palms. For a moment or two there was silence between them. Then the girl spoke again.

"I might have known," she said, and in her tone there was a sort of desperate rage and impotence. "I might have known that people talked of it and . . . laughed. I was not spared even that humiliation. To them it is something 'funny'—a jest, a good story!

"Yes, it was Fred Castle. I was fool enough to love him, and he—he loved me." She spoke the words softly, as though even in her pain the memory brought to her some measure of comfort. "But . . . he could not do it. He was too weak and public opinion was too strong. He went away to India—and people said,

I suppose, that 'he was well out of it,' and laughed at *me!*" Again she wrung her hands in that odd un-English fashion. Again she restrained her gestures with obvious effort, and clasped her writhing fingers in her lap.

"Why could not the English have left us alone!" she almost wailed. "I could have been so happy if I had been left alone!"

"You don't know what the life of women in the East is," said Saleh, bent on consoling her, for his sympathies were awakened suddenly by the sight of her pain. "If you had been born and bred in India, you would have been shut up behind the curtain all your life. You would not have been able to go about as you do in Richmond Park. You could not have gone to balls, or have played hockey, or . . . or anything."

The little Princess laughed a discordant laugh.

"How appalling!" she exclaimed, with bitter sarcasm. "No walks, no balls, no hockey! What immense privileges to have lost! And what sorry things I should have had in their place! Only love, and marriage, and . . . motherhood, perhaps! Only everything!"

Again the silence fell, and in the distance came the soft strains of a valse tune and the faint sound of dancing feet. Saleh felt that he had nothing of comfort to offer to her, and that he himself was all on edge from listening to her words. Yet even now he hoped against hope that her case might be unique, that it might have no special application to his own circumstances. An uneasy feeling impelled him to ask a question.

"Why do you tell me all this?"

"Because you ought to know. Because I do not want these English to have something else to laugh about. You do not belong to India, but you are a 'nigger,' too, just as I am." She laid a stress that was fierce upon the word, and Saleh winced.

"If you speak of love and marriage to Alice Fairfax, she will laugh at you. It will be one more humiliation for us all. I don't mean that to happen, if I can do anything to prevent it."

"She wouldn't laugh," said Saleh, indignantly. "You do not know. She likes me, I am sure. She is so sweet, so kind. She couldn't be cruel if she tried."

The dance had ended and the couples were beginning to overflow into the sitting-out rooms. The little Princess rose suddenly. "Take me over there," she said, indicating two vacant seats the backs of which rested against a tall screen. She led the way, and Saleh again followed her obediently. Somehow her talk, though it made him uneasy, miserable, fascinated him, much as a snake fascinates a bird. They seated themselves in the places she had selected, and the little Princess spoke again, sinking her voice to the lowest of whispers.

"You say that she is kind to you—you fancy that she is fond of you. I know what that is worth. She is much kinder to you than to any Englishman with whom you have seen her. Isn't that so?"

"I think she is," said Saleh, with something of triumph in his voice.

"Kinder, for instance, than she is to Major Dalton?" pursued the little Princess.

"Yes—much," said Saleh, joyfully. "She certainly likes me better than Major Dalton."

"That does not follow," said the little Princess,

blightingly. Her sex gave her the intuition which poor Saleh lacked. "She is nicer to you than to anybody. Do you know why? It is because you *matter less*. Because, being only a 'nigger,' you do not seem to her to stand on the same footing as other men. She thinks she can be kind to you without danger of seeming too kind. She can't imagine a mere 'nigger' even daring to fall in love with her!"

She spoke brutally, tauntingly, as though she took pleasure in the pain she was inflicting; and Saleh interrupted her with an angry exclamation that broke in upon her tense sibilant whisper.

"It is a lie!" he said. "I won't believe it. She isn't like that. You don't know her."

"Hush!" said the little Princess. "Hush!"

Saleh obeyed her mechanically, and in the silence that followed he became conscious for the first time of voices on the other side of the screen. He had been so wrapped up in his own affairs, his own painful emotions, that hitherto he had been totally unaware of all that was going on around him. A man's voice was speaking.

"I suppose you wanted to hurt me," it said. "You have given him four dances already."

"And why shouldn't I?" came the reply, in the low murmur of musical feminine speech. "He is our guest, you know."

The man's voice grumbled something that Saleh could not catch.

"You mustn't say that about him," the girl's voice objected.

"But it's true," said the man. "I should hate it if you flirted with anyone—but to flirt with a thing like that!"

"How can you say such a thing—such a hateful thing?" cried the girl, with real indignation in her voice. "I have never flirted in my life. But to flirt with a poor little creature like that! Why, the idea's horrible! How can you think such a thing of me? How can you?"

"It's all very well; but if you don't call it flirting to dance four dances with the same man out of the first half-dozen, I'm at a loss for a definition."

"But he's different. Nobody could flirt with him. Oh, it's dreadful that you should think such a thing possible!"

"Of course I have no right to object," said the man's voice, sulkily. "But the little beast is head over ears in love with you. You can't pretend to be blind to that obvious fact."

"He is nothing of the sort. He wouldn't dream of such a thing. It would be an insult. He wouldn't dare to feel like that."

"And I suppose you are going to give him some more dances presently?" hazarded the man, still sulkily.

"I was going to give him one," replied the girl, hesitatingly. "But . . . but . . ."

"Don't," pleaded the man. "Don't, Alice; I can't bear it. You must know. I care so much—so terribly."

There was the sound of a little happy sigh. Then very softly:

"Do you?" said the girl's voice.

"Yes—you know I do. And, dear, I don't want only this; I want—just everything. Do you care a little?"

The inaudible answer was accompanied again by that sigh of happiness, and then there was a silence through which Saleh sat rigid like one turned to stone.

"But you really were mistaken about him," the girl's

voice said, presently, in eager explanation. "He didn't
look at things in that way at all, any more than I did.
Don't you see that such a thing was impossible—quite
impossible?"

"Well, we won't bother about him; but you mustn't
give him that dance, Alice," said the man, masterfully,
with a ring of joy in his voice. "You see the little
beggar is a man for all he is a nigger, and I can't allow
my queen to become the idol of even a savage's
worship."

"I am Your High Mightiness's very humble servant,"
said the girl with a gay laugh, "so of course I must do
the bidding of my lord and master. You shall have
the dance yourself. You see I am beginning to honor
and obey already!"

"But I want you to love me too. Do you? Just a
little?"

The opening bars of a new valse drowned her soft
reply, and Saleh, suddenly conscious of what he had
been doing, sprang to his feet and turned a face, gray
under its brown skin, upon the little Princess.

"You brought me here on purpose!" he said in a
voice of concentrated passion. "You have made me
behave like a cad!"

The little Princess rose too, and laid a hand upon
his coat sleeve.

"Yes. I brought you here on purpose, though of
course I did not know what you would have to listen
to. It was Alice Fairfax and Major Dalton. I am
very sorry for you—sorry for your pain. I—I have
been through it all myself. There is nothing to be
said, but at any rate you are convinced; at any rate
you will be spared the humiliation which was in store
for you; at any rate you will not make an exhibition

of yourself—as I did! There is nothing for anyone
to laugh and mock at now. Let that comfort you.
We brown people have 'given ourselves away' enough,
and often enough, without you adding to the list. But
I am sorry, dreadfully sorry, and now you will understand how much you owe to the English. Oh, why
can't they let us alone!"

"It is not the English," cried Saleh, in a choking
voice. "It is not the English! It is we ourselves who
are all wrong! Oh, why was I ever born, why was I
ever born! *Allah-hu! Allah-hu!*" Unconsciously, in
his grief he made use of the cry of his own people.
At that moment he felt himself to have reverted suddenly to the condition of the Malay, to be utterly
an alien.

The little Princess watched him critically, noting
how in the extremity of his pain the veneer which the
white folk had superadded was stripped from him,
and from her heart she was glad because the brown
humanity they shared in common had not been exposed in his person to wanton insult. His individual
agony signified little in her estimation. That was
his affair, and he must make with it the best terms
he might. What really mattered was that he had,
through her agency, been spared the humiliation of
an inevitable rebuff, which, as being, in a sense, a
triumph gained by the white race at the expense of
the suffering Oriental, would have mortified her also
by proxy.

"Don't let them see. Whatever you do, don't let
them know," she pleaded now, earnestly, eagerly, half-
entreating, half-commanding. "Don't let this English
girl understand that she has hurt you, that she has had
the power to wound you. Don't let the English have

that satisfaction, too! Learn to hate them and to make others hate them, as I do!"

"I don't hate them!" cried Saleh. "I hate myself because I can't be one of them, because I am all wrong, made all wrong from the beginning; and I hate you because you are hateful, and cruel, and wicked, and . . ."

He broke off, stuttering and gesticulating. His hand flew to his belt and grabbed at vacancy just above his left hip. The movement was due to a slumbering instinct suddenly awakened, and had the *kris* he sought been in its place it would in that instant have gone hard with the little Princess, and Saleh, thrown back with a jerk upon his Malayan nature, might have run *âmok* through that English ballroom, his *sorak* clanging discordantly through the voluptuous dance music, his weapon stabbing indiscriminately the staid white shirt-fronts of men and the dainty frocks of screaming women.

The little Princess watched him with a kind of interested contempt. The traditions of her people had taught her to look for stoicism in a man, and a sneer curled her lips as she noted his working features and his frantic gesticulations.

"Even if you are a 'nigger,' don't let them . . ." she began, but she got no further. Saleh's hand came away empty from his hip, then was lifted above his head and an instant later was dashed into her face, wiping from it as by magic the half-pitying, half-jeering smile with which she was regarding him.

He had acted on the impulse of the moment, acted in direct defiance of all that he had learned since his arrival in England, but in obedience to the inherited instinct that held the brown woman as a chattel, and bade him chastise her when insolent. It was the stirring within him of the Malayan soul that had so long been lulled in anæsthesia; a stirring made more violent by the truth so abruptly, so mercilessly revealed, that his transformation into a white man—a transformation he had fondly believed to be triumphantly complete—was only a mockery, a sham. The bitter realization of his racial inferiority was upon him now in all its fullness, and while it inspired him with self-loathing, causing him to feel that, as he had phrased it, he was "made all wrong," it aroused in him a certain savage lust to give free play to his lower impulses. If he could not rise to the level after which he had yearned, he would put no further restraint upon himself. He did not argue, he felt; and so his hand fell and the blow brought him an instant's relief. If he could not kill, at least he could inflict pain! Then he turned away and passed through an open French window out into the night.

The little Princess was left alone in the deserted room, with one hand pressed to her smarting cheek. She felt dizzy, and physically sick with anger and indignation; yet in her, too, the blow had struck a chord of inherited memory, and though she would gladly have seen Saleh torn to pieces in punishment for that which he had done, he excited in her, for the first time in their intercourse, something of respect and even of admiration.

Chapter   *Twelve*

SALEH, bareheaded and in his evening clothes, passed out of the garden on to the road, and was presently climbing the hill upon which the Star and Garter stands. Once more the instinct of the forest-dweller had borne him in the direction of the Park, but the gates were closed, so, turning to the left, he skirted the high wall, following it mechanically, wholly unconscious of whither his steps were carrying him. His only desire was to get away—somewhere very far away from the men and women who knew him—so that he might do battle with his pain alone and unobserved. His was the dull misery—the sense that the world has come to an end—which any English lad might endure who has heard the love of the girl he had dreamed of making his own plighted to another man; but it was also much more than this. The tremendous reaction following upon the confidence, the triumphant hope almost amounting to certainty, which had been his during the early hours of the evening, caused the blank despair by which he was now overshadowed to assume a proportionately somber tint; but here, too, he was suffering no more than any Englishman might have suffered in the like circumstances. What differentiated his agony from that of the common run of men was the fact that, incidentally, his entire outlook upon life had been knocked out of focus. His was not merely the grief—poignant enough for the moment, but by no means necessarily eternal—of the lover who has learned that one bewitching maid is not for him. In the glare of dreadful

[85]

light that had been poured upon his circumstances he
saw at last that it was not only Alice Fairfax who was
denied to him by Fate, but that he was doomed to life-
long separation from all desirable members of her sex
and race. The morbid, the debased, the degraded—he
now understood that the little Princess had been right
when she had declared that these were the only
Englishwomen who would stoop to mate with him—
with him who had been taught to love beauty and truth
and womanliness and honor! Thus his trouble was irremediable; time could not alter or soften it. It had
its root in the fixed scheme of things—the sorry
scheme that nothing could amend.

And as it was irremediable, so also it owed no atom
of its force to any fault, any misdeed, any failing of
his own. He had been born a Malay—a "nigger," as
he now bitterly called it—and he had had no choice in
the matter, yet the accident of his birth was enough to
rob him of all the joy of life. He was not to blame,
yet on him alone fell the heavy, heavy punishment.
The immense injustice of it appalled, amazed him;
his utter impotence in the face of this unalterable,
this tremendous fact set him tearing at his heart, as
men in dreams struggle desperately with invisible
powers. Even now he could not understand the *why*
of it—why a man whose training had been that of
other English lads, whose views and opinions were
the same as theirs, who cherished their ideals, tried
his best to live up to their standards, should be banned
for all his days because his skin was swarthy. The
reason was hidden from him, though of the cruel, ugly
truth he no longer entertained a doubt; and then, in a
flash, he recalled how he had smitten the little Princess
in the face. No Englishman, no matter what the prov-

ocation, would have done that, he thought; and with unwonted clearness of introspection it dawned upon him that it was not only in the color of his skin that he differed from the men around him. In that moment of mad pain, and misery, and anger, his real self had come to the surface, beneath which it had lain hidden for years, and Saleh stood astounded at what it had revealed.

It seemed to him that he had been moving through a world of dreams, of smiling unrealities and had mistaken these mocking, delicious illusions for the truths of life. Now, in an incredibly brief space, enlightenment had been forced upon him, and for the first time he perceived something of the proportions of the facts that made his circumstances. A thousand half-forgotten memories crowded his recollection, piecing themselves together into a connected coherent whole, and the discovery was driven into his intelligence that his transformation into an Englishman had never been sufficiently complete to delude anyone but himself. He had been "taken in" by it, but he had been alone a victim of the deception He knew this now, knew that he had always been an alien, an outcast, an inferior, even to those who had been kindest to him, even to the Le Mesuriers, who had adopted him, loved him after a fashion. His affection for the Le Mesurier girls was that of a brother for his sisters; but he felt it in his bones now, that had that sentiment ripened into something more passionate, it would have awakened the same incredulous, almost horrified, dismay which the idea, when barely suggested to her, had aroused in Alice Fairfax.

Therefore, as Saleh plodded blindly through the

growing twilight of the early morning, he was bowed down by a burden of humiliation and self-abasement till little of fight was left in him. He had not the heart, the spirit, now to dispute the facts, to arraign their justice. Only he was utterly wretched, filled with a loathing for his body because it was not like the bodies of the white folk to whom he would fain have belonged; with a hatred of the soul within him, because it too had shown itself that night to be unlike that which he had learned to think that the soul of a man should be. As he still expressed it, shackled by the limits of his vocabulary, he felt himself to be "made all wrong" within and without, and the perception that this was not his fault that he could do naught to prevent it, only added to the bitterness of his rage and misery. Fiercely he longed for death, longed to be blotted out, to cease to be. His very existence had become to him a thing repulsive since this thorough comprehension of his inferiority had penetrated his understanding, and the feeling brought with it a mad fury against humanity at large. Suicide never presented itself to his imagination as a possibility; his Malayan instinct did him so much service. But he was possessed by a craving to hurt others, to make them feel pain, to force them to share in some kind the agony that preyed upon his heart. The impulse of the *âmok*-runner was gripping him, and though he barely realized what it was with which he was contending, he strove with it, summoning to his aid all the mastery of self which his five years spent in an English household had instilled into him. And all the while, underlying, interwoven with his other tempestuous thoughts, the memory of Alice Fairfax

haunted him—the memory of his love for her, of her
sweetness and kindness to him, of the soft, happy
sigh which he had overheard, of her joy in the love of
another man; and then he would fall to smiting himself cruelly upon the breast, as though he sought to
stun by blows the passionate demons of envy and
grief that were gnawing at his vitals.

The summer sun was shining brightly as he came at
last along Roehampton Lane, and so out upon the
Portsmouth Road, which leads across Putney Heath.
The road was empty save for half a dozen bicyclists,
in flannels and sweaters, with bath towels round their
necks, pedaling gayly riverward for an early morning
dip. These wayfarers looked at Saleh with amused
surprise, and he glared back at them in hatred, through
heavy, bloodshot eyes. Why should they sneer at his
misery? Many of them plainly were not even gentle-
men, he thought, and he—he was the son of a king!
Yes, but they were *white,* and in so much they towered
above him in unapproachable superiority. There were
white women of their own class, women who doubtless
represented to them the height of their desires, who
would love them, cherish them, and see nothing degrading, no covert insult, in the devotion which these
men could offer. "Women of their own class!" Yes,
that was it. There did not exist in all the world any
women of *his* class, Saleh felt. He had learned that
night that he was not, could never he, a white man;
but he knew no less surely that only an educated
Englishwoman could satisfy his ideals, could give
him the companionship, the kind of love for which he
hungered. With a wonderful distinctness the life
lived in his father's Court was suddenly pictured for

him by memory. He recalled the crowds of empty, vapid, giggling women among whom his early years had been spent—women whose very conception of love was only as a debased and debasing passion; women who had no minds, no ideas, no ambitions even, save the gratification of their cupidity and their vanity; women whose only conversation was a sort of reckless banter, whose only joys were the satisfaction of coarse appetites; women who sank uncomplainingly into mere slovenly drudges when their short-lived youth and beauty were ended. The thought of them set him shuddering, as in merciless contrast there floated before his mind's eyes those other women of whom Alice Fairfax was for him the type.

Presently he found himself at the bottom of Putney Hill, with the wood pavements of London beneath his feet. The passers-by were staring at his bare head, his disordered evening dress, his dark face. A knot of gutter children jeered him and he turned upon them a face so savage that they fled in terror. Then suddenly realizing the strangeness of his position, of the appearance which he must be presenting, he hailed a four-wheeler from the stand near the bridge and bade the driver take him to Jack Norris's address in York Street, St. James's. He knew few people in London; he could not bring himself to go back to the Le Mesuriers in his present circumstances and in a condition of such woeful disarray. Jack, he knew, would give him shelter, and also, it seemed to him, this white man, who knew and loved the Malayan land, would understand better than his fellows. Therefore he drove to York Street through the slowly waking town, hiding himself from curious eyes as best he might in the depths of the four-wheeler, and feeling jarred by the incongruity of this prosaic vehicle and by the self-absorbed indifference of London to the tremendous tragedy of which he knew himself to be the victim.

Chapter   *Thirteen*

JACK NORRIS, colonial civil servant, carried with him when on leave many of the barbarous habits bred by long exile, wherewith to outrage the eternal fitness of the civilization encompassing him. Thus he was an incurably early riser, a persistent devourer of "early morning breakast," a thrall of the insidious, poisonous, depraved, and wholly delightful early-morning cigarette. It was his custom to enjoy these luxuries lounging in a huge chair, with his legs thrown over one of the arms, with all that he required set within easy reach of his hand, and a book resting on his knee, its page partly obscured by the clouds of tobacco smoke. Also, during this hour of peace and quiet, ere the strenuous whirlpool of the day had sucked him into its vortex, he was accustomed to let the Oriental half of him—the half that had been absorbed little by little from his Malayan environment —assert itself. He thrust his bare feet into sandals, hampered his body by no garments save a loose silk jacket open at the neck, and a wide native waist-skirt knotted about his middle and falling to his ankles, like a plaid petticoat of innumerable colors. It was a relief to be free for a little space from the grip of the high collar and starched shirt—the rigid strait-waist-coat of civilization—and with his body thus released from conventional restraints it was easy for his mind to take on something of the peaceful indolence of the Oriental. By nature alive with energy, quick with force and with vitality, he was able, while the day was yet young and quiet, to look out upon life with the lazy philosophy of the brown man; to regard for

the moment toil and effort of any kind as a blame-
worthy and inexplicable madness; to dream dreams;
to dwell upon the past, upon things gone, without
troubling himself about plans for the future, difficulties that still waited to be overcome, and all "the
demned horrid grind" of active life.

He was sitting thus, smoking, sipping his tea,
dreaming, and making pretense to read, when Saleh
suddenly threw open the door and entered the room.
The boy was draggled and woebegone. His dress-
shirt was soiled and crumpled; his tie was out of place;
his clothes were powdered with the dust of the roads;
his pumps were trodden down at heel. His face, too,
was drawn and gaunt, robbed for the time of its air
of excessive youthfulness; his cheeks were hollow;
and the color of his skin had that gray tinge that
belongs to the faces of brown men who are the prey
of violent emotion. His eyes, deeply sunken by
fatigue and want of sleep, were bloodshot. They
glared with a sort of savage pain, and the dark bruise-
like smudges below them gave to them an unnatural
brightness. His hair was disordered; his forehead
knit into hard lines; his gums, drawn back a little,
disclosed the even rows of his set teeth. Jack noticed,
too, that the hands hanging by his sides were tightly
clenched.

Saleh stood within the closed door, swaying a little
from side to side, looking at Jack in silence; and for
an instant the white man gazed at him in astonishment. Then he leaped to his feet.

"What hath befallen thee?" he asked, speaking in
the vernacular.

The question was asked mechanically; but no answer
came to it beyond a sort of choking cry, such as might

have escaped from an animal in pain, and Norris, taking Saleh by the hand, half led him, half pushed him into a chair. He poured out a cup of tea and made the lad drink it. Then he seated himself on the arm of the chair and patted his visitor on the shoulder, soothingly, without saying a word, as a man might caress a frightened child.

Saleh remained silent, as though sunken deep in a dreary torpor, shivering a little now and again as with an ague, his quivering body held with a certain rigidity, his heavy eyes fixed upon vacancy. The silence of the room was broken only by Saleh's labored breathing and by the ticking of a clock upon the mantelpiece. Had his visitor been a European, curiosity might have impelled Jack to cross-question him, to try to discover the lie of the land, that he might the better be able to comfort him; but Saleh was a Malay, wherefore his white friend said no word, and waited with the exhaustless patience born of long habit. He felt the youngster's shoulder thrilling under his touch; with the corner of his eye he noted the twitching features, the clenched hands, the taut muscles; and the memory came back to him of a night long ago in the capital of Pĕlĕsu, when he had spent some anxious hours at the elbow of a Malay friend, with difficulty combating the devil which impelled him to run *âmok* since grief for a father's death was overpowering him. He remembered the hushed, breathless whisper with which the Malay had said to him:

"Don't speak to me! . . . Don't let any one speak to me! . . . I . . . I . . . I shall . . . I shall . . . I shall . . . I shall do them an injury! . . . Keep close, Tûan, keep close! . . . Let me feel thy hand gripping me! . . . Let me know that thou wilt not let go! . . . Keep very close!"

It had been an anxious time, a nightmare whose reality was horrible, for the credit of the British Agency had depended upon Jack's ability to subdue the possessing demon; and when the dawn had come and the Malay had sunk at last into a restless moaning sleep, Norris had risen up feeling aged and shattered and knowing that he, if ever a man had done so, had wrestled that night with devils.

It seemed to him that Saleh was now the victim of a similar nervous obsession; that he too was on the brink, tottering on the brink of that gulf into which from time to time a Malay, driven beyond the bounds of human endurance, plunges, seeking death amid the slaughter of his fellows. The incongruity of the idea struck him as wonderful—the incongruity of this savage instinct and the little English-nurtured boy whom he had known, the incongruity of such elemental passions and the staid, ponderous life, the orderliness of London! Yet for all that, he saw no reason to question the accuracy of his diagnosis: the shoulder that quivered under his hand, that nervous working face, spoke to him more forcibly than words; only there was a certain bathos in the situation here in this weaponless land, amid the organized systems that impose so crushing a restraint upon individual action. In the capital of Pĕlĕsu the thing had been very real, thoroughly in its place in the picture, inevitable, a natural circumstance. In the little sitting-room in York Street he felt it to be grotesque, farcical, a piece of pure burlesque. Yet to Saleh, of course, let the cause of his emotions be what they might, the thing was real, Jack was sure, and the lad differed

from that other Malay only because he was making a
more gallant effort to restrain himself. But for him
too, the presence of the white man who *understood,*
who needed no word of explanation, was a very tower
of strength. Jack's proximity, the sense of calm force
and determination exhaling from him, were tonics
that helped the sufferer to fight the rending struggle
that was going on within him; wherefore Saleh re-
laxed the rigidity of his limbs, and his stare lost something of its fixed intensity.

Jack was quick to note the change; and as soon as
he had satisfied himself that it was safe to quit Saleh's
side for an instant, he went into his bedroom, and
presently returned with a dose of bromide in a
tumbler. This, not without difficulty, he forced Saleh
to swallow, and in a little while the soothing proper-
ties of the drug began to take effect upon his exhausted frame. He sank back into the cushions of
the chair, his limbs hanging limp and loosened, the
fire dying out of his hollow eyes.

"I have spent the night among the fires of the
Terrible Place!" he said, drowsily, dropping into the
vernacular, which had so long been unfamiliar to his
tongue; and with that explanation Jack Norris had
to content himself, for nothing more fell from his
guest before sleep came upon him, and he lay, moaning a little, tucked into Jack's bed.

Chapter Fourteen

" 'THE evil that men do lives after them,' " quoted
Jack Norris. " 'The good is oft interred with
their bones.' We white folk have done a wonderful
lot of good in Pĕlĕsu, beyond a doubt, but it will take
a world of it to wipe out the memory of the harm we
have done to poor Saleh. From first to last we have
made a pretty bad break with him."

"I really cannot agree with you," said Mr. Le
Mesurier, earnestly. "He is suffering now, poor boy,
suffering cruelly; but against that you must place the
benefits he has derived from his education in
England."

"I don't fancy that his very slender book-knowledge
is going to help him much," said Jack, grimly.

"I was not referring to his books," said Mr. Le
Mesurier. "He has never distinguished himself as a
scholar—he lacks the mental energy and stamina for
that kind of thing. No; I was thinking of the improved moral standard which association with English
people has given him."

"I don't think you or anyone who has not watched
him daily, as we have done, can know how really
good the boy is," said Mrs. Le Mesurier, softly bend-
ing the gaze of her kind eyes upon Jack's honest, ugly
face. "He has learned to be quite punctiliously upright and honorable, and he has lived a life as pure
and manly as I could wish that of my own son to be."

They were seated in Jack's small sitting-room after
dinner, the men smoking, Mrs. Le Mesurier reclining
with tired grace in the one big armchair. Jack had
wired for his guests earlier in the day, and they had

come hurriedly in answer to his telegram. Saleh was lying in the next room, tossing in a high fever, and all his three friends had had an anxious and a busy day arranging for his nursing. Now they were resting from their labors, and were talking of the topic which for the moment filled their minds to the exclusion of aught, else.

"I dare say he is all that," said Jack; "but don't you see? It is because he is so malleable, so plastic, that you have been able to influence him as you have done. You have given him the training of an English boy, and he has taken to it like a duck to water. The only difference is that he has learned consciously what we all learned without knowing it. You have utterly changed him. You have given him improved standards of morality, I dare say, improved standards of everything, including taste; you have set an ideal before him of which he had never dreamed before, and you have led him for years to fight his way up to it. An English boy does not need to be taught to be an Englishman. It comes natural to him. But you had to make Saleh see, to begin with, that it is a fine thing to be an Englishman, and that once accomplished, you have done your best to help him to attain to the unattainable."

"But, as you must see for yourself, it has not been the unattainable in his case. The boy is English now in all his instincts," interposed Mr. Le Mesurier.

"Not all of them, I think," said Jack; "but that doesn't matter. The point is that you have taught him, between you, that the one thing for him to do is to become an Englishman—not a Christian, mind you, but just an Englishman. He has believed you, and now he is as near an approximation to a decent white man as a Malay can be."

"Ah, you admit that," said Mrs. Le Mesurier. "Is not that something to have accomplished?"

She spoke with a sort of passionate enthusiasm which Jack thought very tender and beautiful—tender and beautiful as only the dreams of good women can be.

"You have such faith in sheer goodness that I despair of ever making you understand," he said. "Virtue ought to be everything, oughtn't it?"

"I think it is everything—everything that matters," said Mrs. Le Mesurier, softly.

"I wish it were!" cried Jack. "Of course it ought to be, only—well, it isn't, you know. You have given Saleh an ideal—not purely secular, not a religious ideal; you have helped him to work up to it; you have helped him so well that it seemed to him that he had attained it; and then the events of last night happened and he found that he had mistaken the lowest valley for the crest of the unachievable mountain. You see there was a flaw in the theory from the beginning. A Malay hasn't got the rudiments of the Englishman in him; there aren't the materials there with which to effect the transformation; all you can do is to make of him an imitation, a sorry imitation, a sham, a fraud. Don't imagine that I question his good faith for an instant," Jack added, hurriedly. "The pliability of the poor little beggar, the very love of the approval of his fellows which is bred in the bones of a Malay, helped him to deceive himself—and you. He has been so busy aping Englishmen for so long, consciously at first, less consciously later, but *aping* always, that the thing had become a habit. You believed you had made an Englishman of him: he hoped that you were right —believed that you were right, very likely; and now suddenly, without a word of warning, he has brought up sheer against the Truth—the eternal adamantine Truth that swerves for no man. If you could have changed the color of his skin, the deception might have lasted a trifle longer than it has done; but that was a miracle that even your love and kindness and constant influence could not accomplish, that even his imitative genius could not fake; and the change inside him is no more complete, only you haven't eyes to penetrate into those depths."

Jack stopped, breathless, and Mr. Le Mesurier looked at his wife. They both shook their heads.

"I can't think you know him as we do," Mr. Le Mesurier said, gravely. "I refuse to believe that the change in him is only skin-deep, as you seem to think it."

"I don't *think*, I *know*," said Jack. "He told me things himself this morning after he woke up, before you came—things I can't repeat because you wouldn't understand. Don't mistake me, Mrs. Le Mesurier," he said, hastily, as Saleh's adopted mother turned anxious eyes upon him. "I am not referring to any sins against his acquired code of morality. I don't mean that he has been knowingly deceiving you. Nothing of the kind. Only, well, he told me enough to convince me that the Malay soul is alive and kicking, and very much its old unregenerate self. You see it woke up suddenly last night, and shook itself in a way that surprised even its owner."

"And you think that it is all wasted—all this love and care, all the hopes we have had for him?" said Mrs. Le Mesurier, leaning forward in her chair, her hands clasped on her knee, her eyes looking almost beseechingly into Jack's grim face. "You don't know how I have yearned over him, how I have prayed . . ."

"It can't be wasted—no kind action can ever be wasted. That much at least *must* be sure. But . . . oh, I feel a brute for saying it . . . the whole thing is just a gigantic mistake, the sort of mistake that white men make, with the most glorious intentions, and without an atom of foresight, in the name of Progress."

"I still think that you are wrong," persisted Mr. Le Mesurier. "The happiness of the individual, much as we may desire it, is not everything. Saleh will not spend all his days among English people. I only this morning received a letter telling me to arrange for his return. His training here will fit him for the government of his people. It will enable him to exert over them a beneficial, an elevating influence. His principles are acquired, I admit, but they are solid."

Jack groaned aloud.

"You don't understand, you can't understand," he said, hopelessly. "If you knew the Malays as I know them; if you had lived their life as I have done; if you had gone for a year at a time without seeing a white face or speaking a word of your own language, so that the strangeness of you had had time to wear off, and the natives grew to look upon you as one of themselves and let you get a real sight of their characters, not decked out for your inspection, but living, so to speak, in their shirt sleeves, you would see matters as I see them. You can form no conception of the inert bulk of that people, the sheer dead-weight of their inertia. They are incapable of feeling even the 'divine discontent' which is the beginning of new things, the

very groundwork upon which reform can be built up.
To you it is self-evident that they need elevating, that
they occupy an inferior position; but they wouldn't
agree with you. They are quite satisfied with themselves as they stand; they are altogether unambitious
of improvement; unconscious that, in so far as they
are concerned, improvement is either possible or necessary. You have taught Saleh to accept your point of
view, have put him utterly out of conceit with himself, with his lot, wholly out of touch and sympathy
with his own people."

"But now that he has learned to look at all things
from a higher standpoint, he will make a wiser ruler
than his father before him," said Mr. Le Mesurier.

"I am afraid that even that does not follow," replied
Jack. "You see, the British Government looks after
the administration of the country, and takes precious
good care nowadays that the Sultan doesn't oppress
his subjects, so the personality of the ruler—the nominal ruler—does not signify much. On the other hand,
the Sultan is the recognized mouthpiece of the native
population. His position is secure; he stands to lose
nothing by any concessions that the Government may
be led to make to his subjects; and since he is by birth,
by training, and by instinct a Malay of the Malays, he
is in close sympathy with the natives, knows what
they want, why they want it, what will happen if they
get it, and has no motive to conceal his knowledge.
But put Saleh in the same position. We have made
a sort of Englishman of him, taught him to see things
exclusively from our point of view, have estranged his
sympathies from his own people, have blunted his
understanding of their character and needs. They
will spot the change in him quick enough—trust them

for that—and the springs of their confidence will be dried up at the source. Far from making him a more useful instrument for the government of his people, the training we have given him will spoil him for the very work he could have done most efficiently."

"If you are right," said Mr. Le Mesurier, sadly, "this is a very miserable business. I confess that the matter has not appealed to me in this way before. I am beginning to wish that I had never had a hand in it."

"I would give worlds to believe that I was mistaken," said Jack, no less sadly; "but I know, I *know*. To sacrifice the happiness of the individual for the happiness of the majority is sound, no doubt. A heroic policy, perhaps, but utilitarian and just. I haven't a word to say against it. But in this case, it seems to me, the cause of the greater number has not been served and the hapless individual has been delivered up a whole burnt-offering—has been plunged into the fires of the Terrible Place, as he said himself, poor little fellow!"

"And what do you think is to be the end of it all?" asked Mrs. Le Mesurier, drearily. Neither she nor her husband seemed able longer to contend against Jack's merciless logic, backed as it was by such deep, sure knowledge.

"Heaven knows!" he answered. "You see, he has found out that he isn't and can never be the Englishman he had thought himself—that, in a word, everything for which he has been striving is unattainable. A reaction of some sort is inevitable in the face of this paralyzing discovery. For the moment, as far as I can make out, he is in desperate pain; but his strongest feeling is humiliation, disgust of himself because

of his limitations, physical and moral. That is bad,
but in a way it is healthy, too. If he sticks to that he
will suffer, but it won't do him much harm."

"Then what do you fear?" asked Mrs. Le Mesurier,
anxiously.

"All sorts of things. I fear that he may get to see,
as I do, the shocking injustice of the folly of which he
has been the victim. If that happens, it will embitter
him terribly. If he ever asks himself why he was
given false hopes, taught to cherish false ideals that
of their very nature were far beyond his reach, why
he was led on and on with fair promises to the brink
of the discovery that he could be an Englishman only
minus an Englishman's happiness and privileges, that
he has been robbed, too, of the power to appreciate the
lower, grosser life to which he was born, then, I am
afraid, it may play the very devil with him—I beg
your pardon, Mrs. Le Mesurier—I mean it may be
very bad for him indeed."

"His is a very sweet nature," said Mrs. Le Mesurier,
hopefully. "I can hardly imagine him becoming
soured. Besides, I don't think you allow enough for
the amount of principle he has."

"Don't you think that the principles might go by
the board when he saw what misery the whole system
of which they form a part had entailed upon him? I
do. Remember they have no root in religious
conviction."

"Oh, I hope not, I hope not," cried Mrs. Le
Mesurier, earnestly.

"Yet if he escapes the bitterness, if his love be not
turned to hate, his only chance of happiness is to
forget," said Jack, musingly, his eyes fixed with a
far-away gaze upon the empty grate, his chin propped

upon his hand. "The East is a wonderful place. It weaves its own spells—spells whose magic even a white man can feel. Perhaps it will take back its own. Perhaps when he returns to Pĕlĕsu the East will open its arms and draw him close to its tattered, gorgeous breast. Maybe the sun-glare on the wilderness of hot damp forest, the heavy air moving lazily through the sleepy land, the great rivers lumbering seaward, the utter quiet and calm and melancholy of it all, will lull him to a sort of peace. 'After a storm there cometh a great calm'; you know what old Thomas à Kempis says? Perhaps the East will be for him the Land of Cockagne, and in the voluptuous folds of it, drugged by the beauty of it, loving even the sickly sweet smells of it, he will sink down, down, down from the height to which you have raised him, till a certain animal joy be his in oblivion of the unattainable."

"I cannot hope that," said Mrs. Le Mesurier. "That would be the worst of all."

"I don't know," said Jack, gloomily. "In some ways, perhaps it would be the best that could befall him—perhaps it is all there is left to hope for."

A PRINCE OF MALAYA

Part Two

Chapter   One

IT was a graver, older, less exuberant Saleh that rose
up presently from his bed of sickness and began to
make languid preparations for his return to the Malay
Peninsula. Formerly he had not had a care in the world
—neither a care nor a grief—and introspection had
been to him an unknown occupation. He had been
wont to speak the thought which was in his mind
with all the frankness and some of the simplicity of a
child. Now he was silent, reserved, moody, watchful.
Even after his return to Winchester and in his old
place in the Le Mesurier family—"at home," as for so
many years he had been accustomed to call it—he was
no longer boyish and spontaneous, no longer completely at his ease. He had developed a new sensitiveness—the sensitiveness of the alien, who, amid foreign
surroundings, is morbidly suspicious, forever on the
watch for fancied slights—he who of old had identified himself so absolutely with the people of his
adoption.

The Le Mesuriers all noted the change in him, and
in their conversation even the young people went, so
to speak, on tiptoe, where formerly they would have
passed with reckless, unthinking tread. It made the
new relations which now subsisted between him and
his friends somewhat strained and uncomfortable.
The barrier of color, which Saleh himself and every
member of the family had learned totally to ignore,
was reared up suddenly in the midst of the family
group, destroying its homogeneity, and for this poor
Saleh, all unconsciously, was to blame. He had been
driven by circumstances to look upon himself in a new

light, and he forgot that that was not the light in which he was by this family regarded. To them he was just "Sally," the Sally who had lived with them for so many years, albeit they divined that he had undergone some subtle transformation; but to him they were no longer merely his old friends. They were white folk, and he was "a nigger." He suspected them of feeling this, as he felt it, and began to detest even their friendship as a kind of sullying condescension. They were uneasy weeks that Saleh spent at Winchester, and they went far to spoil the impression created by the years that had preceded them. I think that everybody concerned was glad when at last they drew to their close.

Yet for Saleh the separation from all those whom he had learned to love in England held many a heartbreak. It was a sudden violent severance of the ties which had bound him to a life that was, in some sort, the only life that he had even known. Dim memories of his Malayan past recurred infrequently, but they had long ceased to possess for him any attraction. Unconsciously, as he had absorbed so many ideas, he had acquired a certain contempt for his beginnings— for the mat-strewn floor of his father's hall of audience, for the loafing courtiers who squatted there unwearyingly to gossip and gamble, for the half-naked monarch, his father, blustering and fuming in their midst, with his mouth crammed full of betel-nut through which his words came thickly. All these things, as they rose up in his recollection, moved him to something resembling shame. He weighed them against the seemly orderliness of the Le Mesurier household, and found them appalling, no less. There was sheer panic in his heart at times when he recalled that it was to surroundings such as these that he was about to return. And yet, and yet. . . . It was there, not here, that he belonged. The white folk had rejected him; let the Le Mesuriers in their torturing kindness veil the truth never so deftly, that irresistible fact remained. And the brown men to whom he was returning? It was in his heart in his turn to reject them. He saw himself a waif of all the world— *of* the white men's world, but not *in* it; *in* the Malayan world, but not *of* it—an outcast of the nations! And all the while his heart was brimming over, for his love lay wholly in the quarter of the earth which he was now called upon to quit. A shackling inarticulateness, which made it impossible for him to frame his thoughts in speech, completed the measure of his miseries.

On the afternoon of the day which was the eve of his departure he crept away from his companions, like some wounded animal, and sought solitude in the little garden-house where once before he had found a refuge in the midst of his childish griefs, and here again his former instructress, Mabel Le Mesurier, now grown into a charming girl of some eighteen summers, chanced to light upon him.

He sat, as he had sat that day five years earlier, with his arms thrown out across the rustic table and his face buried in them; now, as then, his shoulders heaved and the faint sound of hard sobs came from him.

Mabel stood for an instant peeping at him, her trim, light figure poised on tiptoe, the sunlight struggling through branches overhead dappling her blue frock with little splashes of brightness and shadow.

And old garden hat was on her head, curls strayed over her smooth brow. Her face was filled with a grave concern, her blue eyes were soft with sympathy. She was not moved now, as of old, to chant, "Baby, baby bunting!" to him in derision of his unmanly grief; the years had developed in her, as they develop in most of her sex, a secret fellowship with the sorrow that finds expression in tears. Suddenly the memory of many days of childhood, in each of which Sally had his place, surged irresistibly upon her, coupled with the thought that Sally, their Sally, was about to be taken forever out of all their lives. A moment, and her eyes too were dewy.

She stepped softly to his side and laid a kind little hand upon his shoulder.

"Sally, dear Sally," she said. "We are all so dreadfully sorry that you are going away. You don't know how much we shall miss you."

He had acquired, together with other English notions, the idea that tears were shameful in a man. Therefore he continued to burrow with his face into the sleeves of his coat and his efforts to control himself caused the sobs to shake him convulsively.

"We are all so sorry, Sally dear," she continued, and now there were tears in her voice as well as on her eyelashes.

"Home won't be like itself without you."

She could feel the sobs throbbing through him under her touch, and suddenly a new, strange pity and tenderness overwhelmed her. She could know nothing of what the approaching banishment held for him; she had no inkling of all that awaited him at the end of that weary journey half across the world; but she

knew instinctively that she was here in close contact
with tragedy, the full measure of which it was not
given to her to understand. She was impelled at once
to comfort and to console; it was all that she could
do, all that there was to be done, since the fates were
inexorable and it was decreed that on the morrow Sally
must depart out of their lives.

Presently she was seated on the rustic bench at
Saleh's side, and a kind little arm began to creep
round his bowed neck. She had known him ever
since childhood, almost all her life, it seemed, and
there subsisted between them much the same sort of
relationship as that which ordinarily prevails between
brothers and sisters, with one single exception.
Never before had anything like a caress been given or
taken on either side. But here was "Sally" suffering
badly, in dire distress, heart-broken at leaving them,
and what could she do but comfort him just as she
would have comforted one of "the boys," her real
brothers?

But Saleh was the son of a race in whom the instinct
of sex is strong—so strong, indeed, that it may be
questioned whether it is by any Malayan ever wholly
forgotten. Mabel felt him thrill under her touch; a
moment more and he sat erect, looking at her with his
tear-stained face. Very gently he withdrew her arm
from about his neck.

"You . . . you mustn't," he said. And then with
bitterness, "Remember that I'm a *nigger*."

"Oh, Sally, how can you?" cried the girl, pained
and shocked by his tone. "You know we don't think
of you like that. You are Sally, our Sally, who has
been with us always, and who is going away. It is

like losing one of the boys!" And the catch in her voice matched the tears in her eyes.

"Do you . . . do you *really* feel like that about me . . . all of you?" he asked, eagerly. "Really and truly? You aren't just saying it to comfort me? You really feel it?"

"Of course! How can you doubt it?" cried the girl again. "What can people have been saying to you to make you ask such things? You are just one of us, and you know it, and we can't bear you having to leave us. I want to comfort you, Sally dear, but I don't know how. I'm not clever like mother. I shall go and send her to you."

She rose from the seat, and stood for a moment towering above him and looking down upon his sorrow-stricken face. Those great soft eyes of his, in which at all times there lurked such a veiled expression of brooding melancholy, were full of pain and fear like those of a dumb animal in torment. The brightness of high spirits which had been wont to animate his features so short a while before had quite departed. Once more, as she gazed, an overwhelming flood of pity for him surged up in the girl's mind, coupled with an intense longing to comfort him by some overt act of sympathy. Almost before she was aware what she had done she had stooped above him and kissed him on the forehead; then she was gone like a leaf blown by the wind.

Saleh gasped. For an instant or two he was stunned by this unexpected experience, and his surprise was mingled with tenderness and with gratitude toward the girl. Then the new-born bitterness in his heart reasserted its supremacy.

"She would never have done that if I had been a white man!" he thought.

When, ten minutes later, Mrs. Le Mesurier came to seek him, at her daughter's bidding, the garden-house was empty.

NEXT day Saleh got through his "good-bys" at Winchester ungraciously enough, I fear, although, or because, his heart was near to breaking, and traveled alone to Waterloo. Here Jack Norris met him and drove him to Liverpool Street, whence the special train for the outward-bound P. & O. bore them to the Albert Docks. The big steamer, with the blue peter at the fore, lay out in midstream, and the tender, packed with passengers and their friends, the former taking stealthy stock of one another, crept presently alongside.

On board there was the usual bustle which attends settling in a crowd of newly arrived passengers—stewards running and driving, lugging trunks hither and thither, pursued by anxious owners, the rattling of donkey-engines, the whine of steel hawsers, the clatter of hurrying feet upon wooden decks, the babel of many voices.

Jack, who knew the ropes with the thoroughness which comes of frequent voyages, led Saleh straight to his cabin; saw his things arranged there; sought out the chief steward, tipped him, and extracted from him a promise that Saleh should be well looked after and should have a good seat at table; and then introduced his charge to the captain and the purser, the two beings who were to play the part of Providence to the ship's little world during the next five weeks.

"It is finished!" he said to Saleh in the vernacular, when these duties had been performed. "Now, in a little space, I must go ashore. Remember the saying of the men of ancient days: 'Though it rain gold in a

stranger's land, though hailstones fall in our own, yet
our own country is ever the better!'"

"That is true," asserted Saleh in the same tongue.
"But behold this is *my* land," and he pointed an incongruous brown finger at the unsightly dock buildings with the smoke-haze lowering above them.

"Say it not, Ungku," Norris made answer. "Wait
for a while. Presently the smell of it will greet thee
—the smell of the *dûrian* and of much greenstuff."
As he spoke he expanded his nostrils and sniffed lovingly. "The smell will greet thee, and then. . . .
Thou knowest the ancient saying, 'The eel returning
to its mud, the *sîrih*-leaf to its vine, the betel-nut to
its twig!' Thus also wilt thou be."

"But my mud, my vine, my twig are *here*," groaned
Saleh. "Here, here! It is from home that I am driven
forth this day. It is as though the very life were
being drawn from out of me."

"Keep your pecker up, Ungku," said Norris, revert-
ing to English and laying a kind hand upon the
youngster's shoulder. "It's a wonderful place, the
East. I'm hungry for it myself already, though this is
my country indeed and in fact. You'll find that you
like it, in spite of all you may think; every man who is
born of woman loves it—can't help loving it. So buck
up, and may good luck go with you. I must get on
board the tender, unless I am to make the voyage with
you. Good-by!"

They clasped hands and stood for a moment looking
into each other's eyes—the sturdy, firm-featured
Englishman whose love of the East was a veritable
obsession, and the delicately formed, clean-cut young
Malay with the sensitive, mobile face, to whom return
to his native land spelled banishment. The sun-glare

of the tropics had parched the color out of the white
man's skin, leaving it yellow and taut save where the
hard puckers about the eyes told of much gazing
through a blazing-hot atmosphere. The East that he
loved had marked and marred him ere his time, and
yet he worshiped her. Saleh, on the other hand,
showed a glow of health under his evenly tinted, clear
olive skin. Even the illness and the harrowing experiences of the past few weeks had not availed to trace
one line upon his boyish face. The temperate climate
to which he had early become inured, and the clean life
which had hoarded his manhood, as never yet was
the manhood of an Oriental princelet hoarded in the
prodigal East, had combined to turn him out at the
end of his six years' sojourn in England as comely
and as promising a youngster as the Malayan race
ever yet produced. The white man, by reason of the
long years that he had spent among Malays, and the
deep sympathy with them and the profound understanding of their character which those years had
brought to him, had absorbed unconsciously more
than a little of the Oriental, much as Marco Polo and
his relatives, after their two decades of Cathay, are
described by a contemporary Venetian chronicler as
having had about them "an indescribable smack of the
Tartar." Yet though the temptation may at times
have been felt by him, never had he become denationalized, never had his robust faith in the ideals of his
race in Asia faltered or failed, He was an Englishman whom the East had tested, trained, and tempered,
but he would always be distinctively English. And
Saleh—poor Saleh? Until a little agone he had firmly
believed himself to be an Englishman in all save the
accident of birth; now he knew himself for one whom

an inexplicable stupidity had robbed alike of country, kith, and kin—a waif of the world. Yet his heart clung insistently to the land from whose people he knew himself to be in a manner outcast; shuddered at the thought of a return to the Malayan country, where dwelt a race with which he believed himself to have now naught in common.

The last that Norris saw of him, as the tender sheered off and began to puff shoreward, was a hand-kerchief waved spasmodically, a pitiful face uplifted for a moment and then buried in the arms that rested on the bulwarks, and, last of all, two heaving shoulders.

This was the fashion in which Râja Muhammad Saleh of Pĕlĕsu set out upon the journey that was to carry him—home!

THE Channel and the Bay took their toll of Saleh, and it was not until Gibraltar was sighted that he crept at last on deck. Quite forgetful of the fact that he had no share or part in the heritage of the British race, he felt a glow of pride warming him at the sight of the ancient fortress which the dash and enterprise of the island people won for their country, and which their stubborn courage has since held against all efforts to dislodge them. As the ship tramped along the coast of northern Africa, Saleh began to make acquaintances among his fellow-passengers; but the kindness of the older men—seasoned Anglo-Asiatics every one of them—was mingled with a certain reserve, which his sensitiveness at once perceived, while he lacked the high spirits which were needed to urge him to take a part in the games played on board by the Griffins and younger members of the little community.

Port Said, where the vessel lay many hours awaiting the mails from Brindisi, appealed to him curiously in a manner in which pain and pleasure were subtly interwoven. He experienced something of the sensation which comes to a man when old, dim things, deeply hidden in the recesses of memory, are stirred anew by a chance whiff of some more than half-forgotten scent. The air of licentious rascaldom in the place disgusted him, and yet at the back of it all there lurked something else which was at once attractive and familiar. He could not give to it a name until at sunset he saw the quay lined by turbaned Arabs, each one of them kneeling, squatting, or prostrating himself upon a cloth or praying-mat, with face turned gravely Mecca-ward. Then suddenly, after long years, Saleh recalled that he too was a Muhammadan, a member of one of the greatest, and by far the proudest, of human confraternities. Next, as he watched the worshipers, out of the mists of memory trooped words, rolling, sonorous words, the meaning of which was blank to him, and he found himself repeating them to himself under his breath. The Five Hours of Prayer! Their names, as they are pronounced by the Malays—*Suboh, Lohor, Asar, Maghrib, Isa*—flashed across his mind. Next afternoon, when the ship had made her way through the Ditch and was steaming down the Gulf of Suez, Saleh locked himself into his cabin, spread a bath towel on the floor, and stumbled painfully through the Maghrib prayers. The words came unwillingly; his prostrations were clumsy; he still was imbued by the Englishman's fear of ridicule and horror of being detected in the performance of any act of piety; yet the infection of Muhammadan enthusiasm was inexplicably upon him—upon him who for years had not thought upon the religion to which his folk belonged—and he was irresistibly drawn to the ritual of the Faithful.

The Red Sea was frankly abominable, as it usually is. The old and experienced Anglo-Asiatics on board "sat tight," avoided all exertion, even speech, shunned the bathrooms with their clammy, sunheated water, and waited with stolid patience for their release from this torture-chamber of nature. The greenhorns fumed and raved, adding the heat of impotent indignation to that of the breathless sea, and the apoplexy of resentment to the suffocation of the heavy atmosphere; and Saleh, who had forgotten what real heat is, thought that his head would explode like a bomb,

or that he would go mad. He was goaded by an un-
conquerable restlessness, and at the back of his mind
was a haunting fear—was not Malaya like this, too,
like this *always,* and was he condemned to endure heat
such as this for the remainder of his days? When at
last the ship made her way through the well-named
Portals of Affliction and Saleh found himself bathing
once more in sea water which was cool, he felt like a
man newly released from some odious durance, and
his volatile spirits rose triumphantly.

Aden, "like a barrack stove what's not been lit for
years and years," made to him no such appeal as had
been whispered in his ears by Port Said. Here, as
in Egypt, Muhammadanism dominated the minds of
men, but Saleh could not bring himself to recognize
any kinship between himself and the squalid black
Somalis with their greasy locks, sun-bleached or dyed
with yellow ocher, nor yet with the shining Seedy-
boys, whose faces had high-lights on them like those
on newly blacked boots. From his earliest childhood
he had always been taught to despise a "Habshi," and
his English training had not helped in the least to
eradicate the prejudice. It never occurred to him that
this feeling was merely another expression of the race
instinct of which in England he had so recently found
himself to be an innocent victim.

The Bombay passengers quitted the ship at Aden,
and the remainder—Anglo-Indians bound for Calcutta, a family or two for Ceylon, for Malaya, and for
China, and a number of homeward-bound Australians,
returning, most of them with open reluctance, to the
land of their birth—had by this time settled down into
a community whereof the members had developed a
surprising intimacy and knowledge of one another.

As the ship sped across the Indian Ocean on an even keel, the peace of the ship's life was broken during three unspeakable days by athletic sports of a primitive and violent character, followed each evening by a dance. Saleh, boy at heart that he still was, entered into the games with delight—reading, the only possible occupation of his enforced leisure, always had the ill-luck to bore him—and his activity won for him many prizes. The applause which greeted his success was very sweet to him: he loved to excel, and in these facile triumphs the haunting thoughts which of late had pursued him were thrust for the moment into the back of his mind. The Australians of both sexes treated him with frank good-fellowship, and by accident more than by design, seeking as it were instinctively the line of least resistance, Saleh found himself associating almost exclusively with them.

It was the last dance evening of all, held the night before the day which would see the arrival at Colombo, that the one untoward incident of the voyage occurred. The dancing had been preceded by the usual prize-giving and mock speech-making, and Saleh, the winner of numerous events, had been called up again and again through the applauding avenue of passengers to receive the trifling tokens of his victories. He was flushed with pleasurable excitement, and all racial prejudices and problems were for the moment far from his mind. He felt himself to be, in some sort, the hero of the voyage, and therefore, for the first time, he mustered sufficient courage to ask Stella Bambridge, one of the Calcutta passengers, to dance a valse with him. The girl was young and pretty, and he had worshiped her in a fashion from afar, because there was something about her that

reminded him of Alice Fairfax, the love for whom had
brought so much of sorrow and of disillusionment
into his life. She was traveling out to India for the
first time, in the company of her father, an old civil
servant of long standing and of income and importance to match, and hitherto Saleh had not dared to
approach her, save in such casual way as the association in deck sports had made necessary. He had regarded her with something of awe because she resembled Alice, and had been chilled, too, though of
this he was hardly conscious, by the cold though
courteous reserve of her father, and by the girl's own
uneasy avoidance of him.

Now he walked boldly up to her as she sat fanning
herself near the stern and asked her for a dance. He
saw a look of distress come into her eyes as they
wandered hither and thither over his shoulders, as
though in search of help; he saw her blush painfully;
he noted that she stumbled over the words which came
from her so indistinctly that he could not catch their
meaning; but he had danced repeatedly with all the
Australian girls on board, and, uplifted as he was by
the successes of the evening, he failed to put their
true interpretation upon these signs of confusion. He
repeated his request, and the girl, suffering evidently
from a painful embarrassment which her inexperience
did not enable her to conceal, rose reluctantly to her
feet, still casting about her those helpless glances of
appeal. Still Saleh was blind. He had danced with
hundreds of English girls, and he knew that he
danced, as the saying is, divinely. How should he
dream that any girl, or the relations of any girl, would
object to him, as a mere ballroom acquaintance, be-

cause Asia, not Europe, chanced to be the continent of his origin?

Stella was too new to life and its ways to find an exit easily out of a situation of such delicacy and difficulty as this. Presently her left hand lay unresisting in his clasp, his right arm was about her waist, in another moment she would be whirled away into the throng of the dancers—and "Whatever will papa say?" thought Stella in awful trepidation. But at this juncture the two young people were aware of a tall, gaunt, sun-dried figure standing in front of them, with grave, displeased eyes gazing at them out of a parchment-tinted face.

"Stella," said Sir Thomas Bambridge, "I think you have danced enough. It is time for you to go to bed. Come with me to Mrs. Dewhurst, who is just going below."

Terrified out of his wits by the stern face and the calm, domineering manner of the old civilian, and feeling inexplicably like a very naughty little boy caught red-handed in the commission of some unpardonable crime, Saleh released the girl and stood aside. She passed him with a little awkward, jerky bow; he noted that she was very red in the face and cruelly embarrassed. As he watched their backs retreating from him down the deck, the girl's face seen in profile, uplifted in voluble explanation, Saleh felt as though he had been dealt an unprovoked blow with a clenched fist. In all his experience in England nothing like unto this had ever befallen him. He had always been received with kindness and with courtesy, nay had often been petted and made much of by men and women alike; it was only when he had sought something dearer and more precious than mere friendship that he had met with a rebuff. But now . . . now? Was he, who had been brought up among English-women of culture and refinement, who had been taught to respect them as Englishmen respect their women-kind, and to regard their society as a necessity of his existence, to be cut off from all familiar intercourse and association with them now that Asia had been reached and Europe had been left behind? The notion, the thought of the banishment which such a decree would entail, smote him with a shock of which the violence was appalling. He could hardly believe the evidence of his own senses. If this thing were true, then was he indeed a waif and outcast of the nations, and the cruelty of the unwisdom which had weaned him from the life to which he had been born, which had painfully implanted in him all manner of artificially inspired cravings while denying to him the ability to gratify even the least of them, which had spoiled his original form of existence for him, had given him a glimpse of a better, and then had shut him out from it by a barrier that he might not scale, took to itself a new and still more sinister meaning.

Saleh, too, danced no more that evening; but for many and bitter hours he lay wide-eyed upon his bunk, listening to the throb of the screw, and seeking vainly, as many a better man than he has done before and since, some key to the great enigma, some explanation of the unmerited injustice of the Universe.

MORNING, with its cool, wan lights and its calm sanity, brought some measure of comfort to Saleh. The incident of the previous evening still caused him to wince when he recalled it to mind, but now in the daytime the mountains which the night and its broodings had reared about him began to shrink and dwindle into molehills. Sir Thomas Bambridge was obviously a dry old chip with a rebellious liver. His action, mortifying though it had been at the moment, was surely no criterion by which that of the bulk of Anglo-Asiatics could be gauged. Saleh brought all his experiences, not only in England, but with the Australians with whom he had associated on board, to fortify his opinion that Sir Thomas's prejudice was something peculiar to himself: and then came Colombo to distract his thoughts from mere personal matters.

Jack Norris had foretold that Saleh would find the Oriental soul within him kindle at the first scent of the East, and this was borne to him on the soft, wooing breezes blowing offshore as the vessel approached Ceylon. He leaned over the bulwarks and snuffed it lovingly, and it seemed to him that something stirred within him that had long been dead or sleeping. Old memories crowded upon him, memories of half-forgotten faces, of scenes once familiar, of a life whose indolently unmoral simplicity admitted the intrusion of no torturing problems, and now of a sudden all these things awoke in him a feeling of kinship and

affection. A tingling excitement began to take possession of him, an eagerness of curiosity and anticipation. He was in a fever to get ashore.

The broad, white-hot streets lined by glaring buildings, the moving pageant of the Oriental crowd, the
deep fringe of restless palm-fronds skirting the shore,
the clamor of strange tongues, the bright color of
costumes, the yoked oxen in the clumsy carts, the
crowding vegetation, and the warm, moist smells, as
of mountains of hidden fruit—each one of these things
made to him its separate and insistent appeal. It was
not Malaya yet, but it was Malaya's twin sister, and
Malaya was beginning to call across the seas to her
wandering son, bidding him welcome home. Saleh
said no word to his Australian friends—he had landed
with a party of fellow-passengers—of these tumultu-
ous sensations, but his eyes were bright, his nostrils
expanded, he was conscious of a vivid delight which
he cherished in his innermost being, but of which
the English half of him was more than a little
ashamed. So short a while ago he had believed himself to be entirely, invincibly British, and now—?
But it was good, good, *good* to drink in with all five
senses these revived impressions of the East.

The stay in Colombo was short, and then a smaller
vessel, China-bound, bore Saleh and a much diminished
band of fellow-passengers upon their way. The ship
which had brought them out pursued her long journey
to Australia.

The week that followed was to Saleh the longest
part of the whole voyage. He was wildly restless,
eager now with quite a hungry eagerness to reach his
journey's end. Colombo had whetted his appetite for

the East; the few hours spent at Penang put a new
edge on it; and then at last came Singapore, and at the
docks a knot of men, whose gnarled brown faces were
strangely familiar, greeted him with smiles and tears
and extravagant demonstrations of joy, and told him
that the Resident's yacht was lying, with steam up,
in the roads, waiting to carry him home. The Englishman in Saleh experienced some moments of acute embarrassment while his mother's retainers, old men who
had known him in infancy, squatted about his feet,
embraced his knees with tears and laughter, and bade
him welcome in their kindly and unself-conscious
fashion in the presence of his amused fellow-passengers, but the heart of him was touched by the
obvious sincerity of their greeting. Of a sudden it
was revealed to him that he was, in truth, returning
home—that this distant land held men and women
upon whom, in his self-absorption, he had hardly
expended a thought for years, yet who loved him with
a depth and a fidelity wholly different from the kindly
affection which he had won for himself even in the
warm-hearted Le Mesurier family. There, too, he had
been at best just "one of the boys," here he was a
prince and the son of a king! The incense of that
curious blending of familiar personal affection with
an inherited tradition of loyalty—whereof the Malayan people in a special measure have the precious
secret—was very sweet to him. Jack Norris had been
right when he had spoken of the East and prophesied
that Saleh would like it. The old proverb of the
Malays, which at parting he had quoted, recurred to
the lad's memory, "The eel returning to its mud, the
sîrih-leaf to its vine, the betel-nut to its twig!"

Where on earth is there joy like unto that of the home-coming?

After all, had Saleh been right, he wondered, when he replied that his mud, his vine, his twig were England?

Chapter   *Five*

THE arrival at the mouth of the Pĕlĕsu River and
the ten miles' journey upstream to his father's
capital caused a mighty vibration of the chords of
memory. The villages under the shady cocoanut
palms, the deep fringe of restless casuarina trees with
each delicate spine atwitter in the breeze, the long
yellow sand-spits, the thick-set wooden lighthouse
painted black and white and squatting squarely on its
four sturdy legs, the irregular, creamy line of the bar
where the waters of the river contended eternally with
the tides—every one of these things cried its separate
welcome to Saleh. Then came the noisy transfer from
the yacht to the native boat with its crowd of gayly-
clad Malays saluting him with lifted paddles and
curious, interested faces, and a somewhat ignominious
crawl into the wooden, palm-roofed shelter at the
stern.

Saleh seated himself on the carpet which covered
the deck of this cabin, and noted with interest the
spears slung from thongs from the roof. With a
shock of wonder he found himself recollecting not
only each spear, but the individual nickname that it
bore, and something even of its fabled record! The
very existence of these famous weapons, he was certain, had not been so much as remembered by him for
years. Where, then, he asked himself, had all this
lore, that now recurred to him so readily, been hidden
that long while? And yonder, upstream near the
bend, lay an island—a tiny piece of earth supporting
a dozen cocoanut palms and a hut—Pulau Kapas—
Cotton Island—though there was not a cotton tree

within a mile of it. How was it that the name, so long
unthought upon, leaped now unbidden to his lips?
And it was the same with everything—people, places,
things—he remembered each one of them vividly,
though the faces were older, the dimensions of inanimate objects had shrunk curiously, and with them
came rags and tags of story which he could never
even remember to have heard. Each one of the four
grave and aged headmen who squatted about the
cabin door in silence, their attitudes submissive, their
hands clasped in their laps, their backs to the straining men at the paddles, was known to him with an
intimacy that was startling, since no thought of them
had so much as crossed his mind for years.

There was to Saleh something vaguely disquieting,
even terrifying, about this sudden sharp assertion of
the powers of an unsuspected memory. It seemed to
him as though he were the possessor of a dual personality, and that one of the egos within him had been
long lapped in slumber and now was abruptly awakened. It was playing queer and uncanny tricks upon
him already. It was strange to him; he did not know
where to have it, what to expect from it. It made
him conscious of an extraordinary feeling of uncertainty, of insecurity about himself.

With the awkwardness bred of long desuetude and
emphasized by the fact that he still was clad in
European fashion, Saleh sat cross-legged on the carpet
just within the doorway of the tiny cabin, watching
the familiar landmarks come up one by one, each in
its turn to drop behind as the boat leaped forward to the
ordered thump and splash and rhythm of the paddles.
Above him hung the historic spears; before him sat
the grave courtiers, dressed in correct Malay costume,

kris stuck in their girdles, twisted handkerchiefs on their heads, their faces immovable as though carved out of mahogany. Over their shoulders Saleh could see the bright silks of forty paddlers in kaleidoscopic movement, as the shining paddle blades, dripping gems of the sunlit water, rose and fell. Beyond them again the long reach of the river, flanked by villages, set with islands, busy with the traffic of small craft, was visible in swiftly changing glimpses. The steersman, perched in the *mâgun* on the roof of the cabin, lifted up his voice and began to keen a boat song, an elusive, plaintive melody pitched in a minor key, instinct with the unresisting, patient melancholy of his race, and as the men at the paddles took up the refrain, Saleh felt as though the very heart-strings of his soul were being made the instrument of that music. A little puff of scent-laden wind wandered down the river and blew upon his cheek. It was to him as though the land that gave him birth was greeting him with a kiss. Yes, yes, yes, it was here, here that he belonged!

At the landing-stage which ran out into the water near the center of the Kampong Râja—the King's Compound—a long string of ramshackle buildings, each in its own ill-kept grounds, the whole surrounded by a high fence of split bamboos—a big crowd of natives had congregated to witness the arrival of their Sultan's son. As Saleh stepped ashore every soul present squatted suddenly, and as he stood still in momentary surprise, those who were following him immediately imitated their example. Saleh found himself in an instant awfully alone—the only erect figure in that wide multitude, every eye in which was fixed upon him. He felt himself flush painfully under his dark skin. He was conscious of a sensation of acute embarrassment. His European clothes, which for years he had worn quite naturally without giving to them a thought, seemed to him of a sudden to be incongruous, conspicuous, in a manner even grotesque. And the thought flashed across his mind, were they not the outward and visible signs of certain transformations within himself which would make him, too, as hopelessly out of place at the Court of Pĕlĕsu as was, he felt, the aspect of his trim Western figure alone in the heart of that squatting, gayly-dressed multitude? Yes, indubitably he was *of* this world, but not *in* it.

He was directed to one of the compounds, and the crowd surged after him, each individual rising to his feet and falling in behind, the moment Saleh had passed him. He picked his way along a narrow footpath, between wastes of rank grass strewn with a miscellaneous assortment of rubbish, to the door of a big building consisting of three large thatched houses, connected each with each by narrow covered ways. He clambered up a stair-ladder which led into a wide, mat-strewn room, and all the while he was subtly conscious that bright eyes were peeping at him from behind lattices and door curtains. He even fancied that he could catch the sound of the feminine giggles and light whispers of their owners. He felt at once embarrassed and outraged.

"*Tûan-ku bĕr-âdu!* His majesty sleepeth!" They were almost the first words that had been spoken since his landing, and how vividly they recalled to him the memories of childhood. They were a euphemism, as he, who had been free of the inner precincts of the palace, knew well, and they meant in plain language

that the king did not mean to allow himself to be
bothered. "His Majesty sleepeth" was what they had
always been wont to say when the Resident wished to
consult the king upon any affair of state, or to bring
him to book for one or another of his unspeakable
naughtinesses—when, in fact, the presence of the
monarch was requested for any purpose that was cal-
culated to bore him. Of old it had been a matter of
course; now it struck a chill into Saleh's heart. After
all these years of absence his father would not put himself out even for a moment to the extent of according
to his newly arrived son an immediate interview.

As many people as could contrive to find sitting
space had crowded after him into the low-ceilinged,
walled-in room. Saleh himself was seated near the far
end, opposite to the entrance, and a space of a few feet
square was left vacant immediately in front of him,
but very soon the atmosphere was insupportable. No
one spoke. All eyes were fixed upon him and he
dared not move his cramped limbs. He was abomin-
ably uncomfortable, body and mind.

"And Tŭngku Ampûan?" he asked. Suddenly it
occurred to him with a shock that he did not know
even his mother's name—only her title.

"*Gring*," came the monosyllabic answer from one of
the senior men present. "*Gring*"—a word which is
used only in speaking of a person of royal blood—
means "sick," and Saleh was to learn ere long that this,
too, was a euphemism. What it cloaked he also had
yet to learn.

Again the silence fell.

Saleh, his nerves sawed to excruciation by that host
of staring eyes, calm, emotionless faces, and silent
immovable figures, felt as though in a little space he

would be driven to scream aloud. Again and again
he tried to break the paralyzing monotony and embarrassment of the situation by asking a question or
attempting to start some subject of conversation, but
it was like tossing a ball to one who allows it each
time to drop to the ground through limp, indolent
fingers. Very soon he abandoned the vain endeavor
and suffered the pall of silence to cover all within the
room in its dense, stifling folds, but the Englishman
within him hated the inactivity of mind and body,
fumed inwardly, and protested vehemently.

There recurred to his memory the scenes that used
to be enacted in the Le Mesurier family when he or
one of the boys returned to it after a few weeks'
absence—how all rushed to greet him, how the
house was clamorous with welcome, how questions were fired at the newcomer with an eager interest that barely waited for any answers, and how the
joy of being "home again" was multiplied exceedingly
by the open rejoicings that celebrated the return.
What a contrast, he thought, were those hours of
exuberant welcome to this funereal and apathetic
reception; and even more than the lack of frankly
expressed interest and pleasure, the which wounded
his feelings more deeply than he cared at present to
recognize, the lack of energy and vitality in the assemblage hurt his acquired opinions of what human
beings ought to be.

HALF an hour, each one of the thirty minutes containing sixty æon-long seconds, fraught with its separate torture of sepulchral silence, embarrassment and *ennui,* crept by, and still the packed room was filled by the solemn, grave-eyed crowd, all staring placidly at Saleh, and still the lad himself sat there, not knowing how or whither to make his escape.

At last there came a diversion. A child of about six years of age, dressed in a gaudy silk *sârong,* or waist-cloth, and an immense velvet cap many sizes too large for him, swaggered up the footpath leading to the building. An aged courtier walked behind him, holding over his head a silk sunshade with a six-foot-long haft to it, and a rabble of small urchins, in various stages of impartial nudity, followed at his heels. He climbed up the stair-ladder, and the crowd made a way for him in their midst. He walked to the small open space in front of Saleh and squatted there comfortably. The bearer of the sunshade had closed it at the doorway, and he and the rabble of boys now squatted at their little master's back, each, as he took his seat, saluting Saleh with hands folded as in prayer, held with the thumbs against the nose.

"Tûngku Anjang," said a voice, "the son of Che' Jĕbah." And Saleh realized that he was looking upon one of his half-brothers—a son of his father by some favorite concubine. It occurred to him with a shock that there had probably been many such additions to the family during his absence, and that he did not know even of the existence of many of his brothers and sisters.

"This, then, is my brother," said the child in a clear, high-pitched treble. "Ya Allah! I should have said that he was a Nasareen!"

A "Sĕrani," or a Nasareen, means a half-caste, and a half-caste, as Saleh knew, is, in the estimation of the Malays, a social outcast of both races.

The bearer of the sunshade leaned forward and whispered a reproving protest to his charge in a hoarse, throaty whisper.

"But he is just like a Nasareen," replied the boy. "He dresses like a white man, but his face is black like ours, and his eyes, too, are black, not white eyes. Also, behold how he sits cross-legged. Ya Allah! He is very certainly a Nasareen!"

The faintest conceivable ripple of amusement ruffled the impassivity of the listening throng. Evidently the thought which the child had put into words found an echo in many minds. Saleh's embarrassment increased. He felt that the child was acting, in some sort, as the interpreter of the multitude.

"Come hither," he said, holding out his hands to the child. "I have come from afar. Come to me, little brother."

"Go," whispered the bearer of the sunshade; but the child held back.

"I won't," he said, shrugging off the hand which his follower had placed upon his shoulder. "I won't. Behold his feet! He weareth boots in the audience-hall! What is the name of manners and customs such as that? He is no brother of mine, but a Nasareen. I want to go back to Inche'. Take me back to Inche'. I shall tell His Majesty to send this Nasareen away. It is true what Inche' said, that his coming would do me injury. If you loved me, you accursed ones, you would drive him away."

The little fellow was on his feet by now, stamping and raving, lashing out with hands and feet at his embarrassed henchman, nor was he pacified until he had been lifted on to the latter's hip and borne storming out of the compound. Saleh could hear the little voice raised in angry abuse and threats long after the child had disappeared from sight, and a keen sense of mortification and distress was upon him.

This was the first greeting that he had received from one of his own blood upon his return to the land of his forbears.

Chapter   *Seven*

T HE coming of little Tŭngku Anjang and his
    stormy departure broke up the silent sitting in
the outer chamber, which otherwise, so far as Saleh
could see, might have endured for all eternity. A
voice speaking from the doorway at his back said that
his gear had been brought up from the boats, and suggested an inspection of the room assigned to him.
Saleh scrambled up into an erect position as nimbly
as his cramped limbs permitted, and passed through
the curtained doorway into the interior of the house.
It was a sort of rabbit warren of a place, with narrow,
crooked passages, the floors of yielding bamboo laths,
the walls of plaited wattle, and it was so dark that it
was with difficulty that Saleh could see his way. He
came at last, however, to a big room, the center of
which was filled by a great square platform raised
about two feet above the level of the floor. Upon this
was spread a flock sleeping-mat, covered with crimson
silk, with a huge stack of square impossible-looking
pillows piled at its head, and with ample curtains of
glaring Manchester chintz looped up into untidy,
twisted knots. For the rest, there were no traces of
other furniture, save a vast brass vessel which memory
told him was intended for a spittoon; and the contents
of his dressing-case and a number of his clothes were
ranged, the former in neat rows, the latter in incongruous heaps, by the side of the brilliant sleeping-mat.
The whole thing had a curiously hybrid aspect, illustrative, so it seemed to Saleh, of the uneasy blending
of the civilizations of Asia and the West.

    Saleh took off his European clothes, put on a *sârong*

and a short silk blouse which he was told had been
sent to him by his mother from the women's apart-
ments, and as the delicate scent of sandalwood filled
his nostrils it seemed to him that with his English
garments he was putting off many other things, and
that, with the loose, soft, fragrant Malayan silks he
was resuming some part of his strayed Oriental self.
There was a measure of consolation in this. Never,
during all the years that he lived among white men,
had he felt more completely isolated, estranged, and
outcast than he had in the room yonder while his
little brother looked at him with childish, disapprov-
ing eyes that received from the silent assemblage an
indorsement of their adverse verdict.

And now the real welcome to his home began. Chill
formalities were for a moment at an end, though
Saleh's rank, which in England he had almost forgotten, still hedged him about with much ceremony.
Through the doorway there filtered a trickle of dim
figures—old men and women who crept toward him
one by one, caressed him with soft hands, and kissed
his knees with broken words and tears. They cooed
over him, praising, petting, belauding, flattering him,
sounding notes of admiration at the manly growth to
which he had attained, at his likeness to his mother in
her youth; hinting (and this set Saleh's cheeks flam-
ing again) at the love which the sight of one so comely
would breed in many hearts. They were a little bewildering, a little embarrassing, a little fulsome even,
but Saleh was hungry for the warm family affection
which had always animated the Le Mesurier household, and it was pleasant to find at last some people, at
any rate, who seemed to be genuinely glad to see him.

He remembered them all, though they had aged considerably, and also, so it seemed to him, were more shabby than of old. They were retainers of his mother's household, and he was touched by their obvious delight at his return. He did not know that in the eyes of each one of them he was the incarnation of a last hope; that for months all his mother's people had been building airy castles which had his return for their foundation; that they looked to his advent to wean the Sultan, his father, in some degree from his grasping concubine, Che' Jĕbah, and cherished expectations that the light of the royal countenance (which carried with it a full share of the royal wealth) would be led, through him, to shine once again upon the derelict queen and her establishment. A Malayan court is ever a hotbed of intrigue and counter-intrigue, the main prize of which is the fickle favor of the king, and Saleh, disarmed in advance by his British ignorance and innocence of such things, was already a piece in the game round which revolved a thousand plannings and schemings. But for the moment he knew naught of this, wherefore the coming of these "old faces of his infancy," whose gladness at his return had every appearance of being inspired by the purest personal affection, brought to his sore heart not a little of satisfaction.

He ate his evening meal of cunningly concocted curry and rice sitting upon his sleeping-mat, with a score of these family retainers grouped around him, chatting to one another easily, and ministering to his wants. There was present no one of a rank that warranted him in sharing a dish with Saleh, so the meal was eaten at once in solitude and in public, the discomfort being increased by the fact that it had to be eaten native fashion, with unaccustomed fingers,

under a host of critical eyes. It requires a sturdy
appetite to eat much in circumstances such as these,
and as soon as the meal had been dispatched, Saleh
inquired once more for his mother. There followed
much passing to and fro between his room and the back
of the ramshackle buildings, and a great buzz of
mysterious whisperings, but at last he was informed
that Tŭngku Ampûan was well enough to receive him.

He was led along a narrow, tumble-down passage to
a room at the rear of the building, passed through a
frowsy curtain obscuring a doorway, and entered his
mother's apartment. It closely resembled the place
which had been allotted to his own use, save that it
was smaller and that the chintz curtains shrouding the
central platform were not looped up. Dim figures
darted into the corners, like scuttling rabbits, at his
approach, to the sound of much feminine giggling.
The only light was cast by a lamp which stood on the
floor of the central platform behind the curtains, upon
which grotesque shadows danced mockingly.

Obeying the whispered suggestion of the old woman
who had brought him hither, Saleh lifted up the hem
of the curtain, crept under it, and seated himself upon
the platform. The kerosene lamp which he had seen
from without flared and stank at his elbow; the ceiling cloth overhead sagged low in great stained
patches; the platform was covered by a thick flock
mattress; the whole place was reminiscent of the interior of a very foul four-poster bed.

There were two figures in the place—an aged woman
lying upon her side with her back toward him, both of
whose hands clutched what looked like a short thick
piece of polished bamboo, one end of which was held
between her lips, and a young and very pretty girl

who squatted upon her heels and leaned with indolent grace above a tiny lamp with a glass shade open at the top. As Saleh watched, this girl fished some choco-late-colored substance out of a little jade pot with a thing like a knitting-needle, held it above the flame of the lamp till it bubbled into big swelling blisters, and then, at the psychological moment, thrust it with the skill born of long practice into a tiny hole bored in the centre of the terra cotta pipe-bowl in which the thick bamboo terminated. The place was stiflingly hot and reeked with the stale fumes of opium.

The woman who lay upon her side puffed in the smoke luxuriously three or four times, inhaling deeply, then suffered the pipe to fall upon the mat-tress, and presently blew out great, quick clouds through her mouth and nose. She gave, when this was done, a sort of guttural grunt of satisfaction. The girl, peeping slyly at Saleh, bent above her and whispered something in her ear.

"Who? Where?" said the woman, vaguely.

"Here, on the right," said the girl with a little laugh which to Saleh sounded full of insolence.

The older woman pulled herself together, rolled on to her back, and then sat up, gathering her legs under her. For an instant she peered at Saleh as though she saw him with difficulty, then she gave vent to a sudden, inarticulate cry, threw out her arms, seized him round the back of his head, and buried his face in her bosom. It was done so quickly, so unexpectedly, that Saleh was near being thrown off his balance, and with his nose and mouth forced into the folds of a frowsy bed-gown that seemed to have been soaked in a mixture of sandalwood and opium, he found it difficult to recipro-cate the embraces to which he was being subjected.

Also, do what he would, the thought of Mrs. Le
Mesurier and her dainty sweetness and refinement,
and of the cruel contrast which his adopted presented
to his real mother, would obtrude itself. The revelation which the past few minutes had brought to him
was horrifying, no less—his acquired European prejudices were responsible for that; but what shocked him
in an almost equal degree was the discovery that no
filial instinct within him responded to the endear-
ments of this poor, broken-down, opium-sodden old
hag! This, too, warred against his European concep-
tions of the eternal fitnesses, for with many of the
white man's prejudices he had acquired much of the
white man's sense of moral obligations, and he belonged, moreover, to a race among whom the love of
the mother that bore him is to the average man the
strongest love of his life. It was dreadful to him that
he should see this woman, after many years of separation from her, not with the tolerant eyes of a son
whose grateful memory refuses to recognize uglinesses which are patent to others, but with the cold,
critical, appraising judgment such as any white man
might have used. Ah, indeed, those who by educating
him in England had given him so little save an added
capacity for pain, had taken from him ruthlessly much
that was very precious, much that it passed the wit of
man ever to replace.

These thoughts crowded through his mind, jostling
and hustling one another, not distinct and clean cut as
they are here set down, but in a host of dim, half-
formed, but scalding impressions, the sum total of
which was a horror of the mother that bore him, in
whose frowsy embraces he lay suffocating—horror of
himself because he could not feel toward her as a son

should feel, horror at the thought of something taken from him that could never be made good, and a keen self-pity. Soon he, too, was shaken with sobs, and to the woman that wept and crooned and mumbled over him, the convulsive clutching of his hands seemed the natural expression of a heart brimming over with emotion.

At last he was released, and his mother, turning abruptly toward the girl who sat at her side, struck at her savagely.

"Begone!" she cried, and the girl forthwith vanished, casting as she went a languishing glance at Saleh. She saw in the newly recovered son of the household a rising power with whom it would be at once pleasant and profitable to be on terms of intimacy. Besides, young Saleh was very good to look upon.

Tŭngku Ampûan drew Saleh toward her, so that he occupied a seat by her side with his back against the stack of pillows, and, taking his right hand between both her own, she held it in her lap, caressing it.

"*Al-hamdu-l-Illah!* Thanks be to Allah!" she mumbled, repeatedly. "It is to me as though the moon had fallen this night into my lap! Oh, my child, my child! How my heart hath longed for thee all these years, and now at last thou art come! But thou art no longer my little sweetheart. Thou hast grown into a man, and comely. All the girls of the palace will be mad for thee, my son! But step cautiously, Chik!" (How the long-forgotten pet name recalled to Saleh the memories of his childhood!) "Be wary in thy love-affairs, lest thou chance to anger thy father."

"I shall have no love-affairs," said Saleh, with conviction. To him, after his long intercourse with refined Englishwomen and association with clean-minded men, his mother's light and complacent reference to low intrigues as a thing of course jarred upon and shocked him.

Tŭngku Ampûan laughed.

"Ya Allah, little son of mine!" she cried, playfully. "No love-affairs indeed! The cat and the roast, the tinder and a spark, a boy and a girl! All be ill to keep asunder! No love-affairs forsooth! But the palace hussies will have a care of that, comely as thou art! But step with caution, for Underneath-the-Foot is as jealous as of old, and that slut Che' Jĕbah is to him eyes and ears and nose for the detection of intrigues. Also it is for thee to help me, thy mother."

This was to Saleh's thinking a better channel in which to let the conversation flow.

"Willingly," he said. "How can I help thee, O my mother?"

Tŭngku Ampûan threw a suspicious glance over her shoulder to assure herself that there were no eavesdroppers. Also she sidled nearer to Saleh, thrusting her chin almost into his face. For the life of him he could not prevent himself from noting that her skin was dry and parched, as is the way with confirmed opium-smokers, that it was covered with grimy wrinkles, that her hair was frowsy and unkempt, that her habit had evidently developed in her the inevitable distaste for cold water and contempt of cleanliness which are among the penalties it inflicts upon its victims.

"Thy father," whispered Tŭngku Ampûan, hurriedly, still casting apprehensive glances about her. "His conduct toward me hath not been fitting. Here be many months—more than I have the wit to count— that he hath not entered my dwelling, the which is a sin against the law of Allah and his Prophet, so those learned in the Scriptures tell me. For me, I neither read nor write, but those who are well versed say that it is a sin, for I am his *istri*—a wife of rank equal to his own—no mere *gûndek,* mere concubine, like that slut Jĕbah, who of old was one of mine own tire-women. That I could endure, for my body now is no longer young, but of all the money which the *kompani* (government) giveth to him every month he spareth me no portion! It is true that the *kompani* maketh provision for me also—a monthly pittance, a mere nothing, barely enough to pay for my betel quids—but it is fitting that I, the queen, the principal wife, one upon whom the title of Tŭngku Ampûan hath been conferred, should share in the wealth of the king."

"Surely," said Saleh, not knowing what else to say.

"Therefore, Chik, I trust that thou wilt insert certain advice into thy father's heart, showing him how evil is his conduct, and urging him to give me money, more money. Also, thou who canst speak the white man's tongue, I trust that thou wilt take order to bring to the knowledge of the Tûan Resident the full measure of my calamities and the so evil behavior and carriage of the king, thy father."

To Saleh, filled with prejudices imported from England anent the privacy of family affairs, there was something grossly indecent in the idea of celebrating his return to Pĕlĕsu by a grand washing of the domestic linen of his mother's establishment in view of every white man in the country; but he felt that it would be vain to attempt to explain this feeling to the old woman at his side who alternately pleaded and stormed for money, more money.

She was storming now.

"It is all the fault of that slut Si-Jĕbah!" she cried. "To think that the minx was once a girl in mine own house! To think that it was mine at pleasure to pinch and slap her, to bend back her fingers till they cracked and the screams came, to suspend her by her thumbs that she might know the torture of the live embers! To think that I might have done that and more, that I might have had my will of her in any fashion that I chose, and that there was no man to hinder, since such things come but rarely to the ears of the Tûan Resident! But she was cunning, the accursed one— cunning and meek and willing and soft-spoken in those days. She wheedled *me* then, as she wheedleth thy father to-day, and I never saw, blind eyes that were mine! how she was scheming. Wherefore she never received aught of punishment from me while she dwelt within my household. *Ya Allah! Ya Allah! Ya Allah!*"

Tŭngku Ampûan was rocking herself to and fro, to and fro, in a paroxysm of grief at the thought of these precious opportunities which she, lacking a prophetic vision, had so shamefully neglected. To Saleh, robbed through no fault of his own of the filial affection which might have helped him to pardon that which he could not approve, this exhibition of savage vindictiveness was something to turn one sick with horror and disgust. The abominable, opium-laden, stifling atmosphere of the place was making him physically giddy. The whole experience held for him something of the torturing unreality of a nightmare, yet throughout he knew that this was happening in fact, not in the fictitious agony of a dream.

Fortunately, perhaps, his mother was too drug-sodden and self-centered to be able to take much heed of the impression which was being created in her son's mind, and for nearly an hour she continued to pour forth her complaints and her rage. For months, almost for years, she had not stirred beyond the narrow limits of the half-bed, half-room in which she sat, and her ideas, her loves, and her hates had been whittled down to dimensions almost equally restricted —anger against her husband, hatred for Che' Jĕbah, and an impotent craving to torture her, a fierce desire for money, more money, which in its turn would help to feed her only love—her opium pipe! She went through and through the whole gamut of these emotions, not once, but with endless, aimless repetitions, for Saleh's benefit, and when at last he succeeded in making his- escape he felt shocked and outraged, as though he had been called upon to witness some hideous indecency, or as though he had been forced (as indeed he had) to become the unwilling recipient of disgraceful secrets.

Shortly after his return to his own quarters he received a visit from two aged crones, tire-women of his mother's establishment, who with much mysterious paraphrase informed him that they had been sent by Tŭngku Ampûan to borrow from him the sum of one hundred dollars. They had much to say, and they said it with elaboration, and many details to give, and they spared Saleh no fraction of their squalor, bearing on the subject of the sordid poverty of the house; and the poor young fellow, with a feeling of intense repulsion at his heart, gave the money demanded of him in a frantic desire to be rid of the hags. As she reached the doorway, one of them stealthily returned and whispered hoarsely and with much mystery into his ear, that Mûnah (which, it appeared, was the name of the girl whom he had seen filling his mother's opium pipe) was fallen deep in love with him and sent him greeting. The old witch added slyly that Mûnah awaited his commands, weeping and beating her breasts in her distraction, and that she, the old witch aforesaid, was sorely in need of a five-dollar note.

It was then that the strain which the experiences of the day had put upon Saleh proved to be too much for his self-control. He broke out into angry, petulant, half-tearful rage, and the old woman fled from him in dismay to impart her firm conviction to the other members of the household that their mistress's son had returned to them, after many days, possessed by the incomprehensible devils which notoriously inhabit the bodies of white men.

NEARLY a week had elapsed after his arrival at the court of Pĕlĕsu before Saleh was permitted to see his father. If the king was really "asleep" on one occasion out of every ten when this was reported of him, he was certainly the most somnolent person alive; and when he was not "asleep" he was either "eating" or "bathing"—at least so the members of his household stated in reply to all Saleh's messengers. With the recollection of his mother still very fresh in his mind, it seemed to Saleh to be at least a satisfactory feature in his father's character that he should be so much addicted to the bath; but as the days passed, and the duties of his bedchamber, his meals, and his toilet still held the king a close prisoner, the youngster began to wonder which disgusted him the more, the lack of paternal, nay of human, interest in him which caused his father thus to postpone their meeting, or the poverty of invention among the royal retainers which was responsible for such flimsy explanations of his action.

But though the light of the kingly countenance was so steadfastly denied to him, Saleh saw during these days a great deal of some of his other relatives. His interview with his mother was repeated with frequency, and always resolved itself sooner or later into a long-drawn-out complaint about her wrongs, her poverty, and the unspeakable wickedness of Che' Jĕbah, his father's favorite concubine. Tŭngku Ampûan would keep him by her side in the loathsome atmosphere of her bedroom for an hour at a time while she delivered herself of these unvarying mono-

logues, lying on her side and sucking at her opium
pipe, or squatting with her back to the pile of pillows,
chewing betel-nut as a cow chews the cud. Little by
little Saleh began to perceive that she was not, as he
had thought at first, an old woman, that in all likeli-
hood she had not yet turned her fortieth year; but
that she was wrecked prematurely by too early marriage, unhealthy living, and addiction to the opium
habit. For the rest she was, to all intents and purposes, a monomaniac. He learned to dread his interviews with her quite indescribably.

He made the acquaintance, too, of his three sisters,
one of whom was older, while two were younger, than
himself; but he found them hardly more satisfactory.
He was never permitted to see them alone, and in their
eyes he was primarily a *man,* and a man, too, about
whom clung something reminiscent of the European.
They would sit side by side, first in a decorous silence
and an immobile modesty that baffled Saleh utterly,
and later, when they became more accustomed to him,
they would huddle together, as though for protection,
and would exchange little foolish personal remarks
about him one with another to an accompaniment of
much childish giggling. Had he been suffered to
grow up in daily association with them, poor Saleh
thought he might perhaps have learned to know his
sisters, for surely they must each have some sort of
individuality concealed beneath the cloak of these
stifling futilities; but as it was, he was to them a
stranger—a strange *man*—and the barrier of sex made
a wall between them which he could not scale.
Against his will the memory *would* recur of the frank
brother-and-sister relations which had subsisted between Mabel Le Mesurier and *her* brothers, between

the two Fairfax girls and Harry, nay, even between Mabel Le Mesurier and himself. The contrast was merciless, and he, who during the last few weeks of his stay in England had fancied himself to be terribly alone, found that he was here, under his mother's roof, discovering the meaning of real loneliness.

The only relative for whom he found it easy to feel some real affection was Râja Pahlâwan Indut, a cousin fifty times removed, whom Saleh remembered from the days of his childhood as a figure at once awful and heroic. There clustered about him a whole world of legend and romance, wild stories of love and war, in each of which he had played the leading part. Men said, Saleh recalled with a smile, that Ungku Pahlâwan, as he was usually called, was invulnerable; that he had the power of assuming invisibility at will; that his magic was only equaled by his valor, and the latter had been proved time and again, as even the white men acknowledged, on many a hard-fought field. Saleh, with these facts still crowding the nooks of his memory, was astonished to find the Ungku a singularly quiet, thick-set, little man, with quick, humorous eyes, square, capable hands, a mustache like a cat's whiskers, and a particularly gentle voice and manner.

That was the first impression which he created, but, as Saleh learned to know him better, Ungku Pahlâwan developed certain qualities which differentiated him from his fellows. To begin with, he was not in the least bit afraid of the king, and laughed openly at the rail-sitting courtiers who, he averred, did not dare to pay their respects to Saleh until they had had an opportunity of judging for themselves in what fashion his father was likely to receive him. Also, he went in no awe of the Resident and of the white men, and he held and frankly expressed very strong opinions concerning the precise effect which the coming of these people had had upon Pĕlĕsu.

"They have robbed the land of manhood," he would say. "Our youth grow up knowing naught of arms nor of the lore that maketh the warrior. If to-day there chanceth a quarrel between two young cockerels, it is not fought to a finish with the 'steel spurs,' as quarrels between men should be fought, but straightway both fly headlong to the police station, there to make complaint after the fashion of weeping women. Of old, Ya Allah Muhammad Al-Rasul!—of old there were deeds to be done that it were fitting for a man to do. Now ... In the days which the white folk have filched from us, for a man who was a man supplies lay ever at the tip of his dagger! I never lacked for aught in those so glorious times! Now ... "

And the spittoon would be called into request as the only sufficient means of expressing his deep disgust.

He would tell Saleh tales by the hour together of the adventurous past in which he had been so prominent a figure, always comparing that eventful, lawless time with the ordered, dull monotony of to-day, and Saleh, boy that he was, would find himself kindling with enthusiasm for the romance of Malaya the untamed. He did not stay to think of the misery and the oppression from which the coming of the white men had relieved the bulk of the common people. He only knew that his own life had seemingly been spoiled by the Englishmen's determination to force a blending of the East with the West, the which, so Ungku Pahlâwan declared, when applied to

the whole of Pelesu, was rendering the country one
unfitted for the habitation of a man who was a man.
He was utterly out of love with the present; that of
itself set him longing for the past. He knew that his
English education and training had put him completely out of tune with surroundings which by right
should have been congenial, and for the rest had
given him, so he thought, little save an increased
capacity for suffering. Where the English had been
guilty of so hideous an error in the case of a single
individual, was it not only reasonable to suspect that
they had made blunders even more deplorable when
dealing with a country and its entire population?
It had been shown to him with merciless clearness
that he could never be an Englishman; it followed,
therefore, that he must be a Malay, but not a Malay
of the present time, of which Ungku Pahlâwan spoke
so scornfully—a Malay with all the romance, all the
adventure, all the thrilling interest of the unfettered
past taken from him,—but a Malay of the bygone days
whereof the stories warmed him with so strange an
excitement.

Râja Pahlâwan Indut began to perceive that he had
not only a sympathetic listener, but promising material lent to him for his hand to mould, by the kindness
of Allah, the Merciful and Compassionate God. He
summoned another distant relative to his aid, Râja
Haji Abdullah, a little wizened sage dressed always
in an immense green turban and flowing *jubah* of the
same color, who had much to say on the subject of
the Muhammadan religion and the indignity offered
thereto by the fact that in Pelesu infidels took it upon
themselves to rule the children of the Prophet.
Saleh had felt the contagious enthusiasm of the

Muhammadan stirring in him unbidden when he first came into contact with it at Port Said. He was, at this period of his life, sorely out of countenance with things as he found them in this best of all possible worlds, and he longed to find something connected with himself of which he might feel that he had a right to be proud. Râja Haji Abdullah's teaching supplied this need. Saleh thrilled to remember that he was part of the greatest brotherhood upon earth; that he belonged to a faith which was the religion, not of love, but of hate, which regarded all infidels as food for slaughter and for the fires of Jehannam, and that in the eyes of millions he was the unquestioned superior of the white men, who had outcast him, because he was a Muhammadan. These lessons were taught gradually, cautiously, and spread out, as we shall see presently, over a period of many months; but it was during the first few days of his stay at the court of Pĕlĕsu, when he stood most sorely in need of consolation to his wounded spirit, that there were implanted in his soul the seeds of an active discontent with the ways and works of the white men, and the beginnings of the fierce, devouring fanaticism of the Muhammadan.

The two men whose words had upon him so strong an effect were perfectly well aware what it was that they were doing. Like the hungry retainers of his mother's household, they, too, had their plans and their schemes, and to them also Saleh was an important piece in the game they hoped to play.

THE interview with his father, when at last it did take place, was a very frosty business. The king sat cross-legged on a mat at the far end of his hall of audience, a great oblong building, open to the air on three sides, its veranda raised some eight feet from the ground, and fringing two tiers of platform. The princes and nobles of the court, sitting on one or another of the tiers, according to their rank, squatted immovable, with elbows on knees, hands clasped in their laps, backs bowed, and their eyes glued to the face of the king. They formed a sort of horseshoe, and the Sultan had his place between and a little beyond the two horns.

The monarch was older and fatter than when last Saleh had seen him, and was dressed in an absurd assortment of brilliant colors, while a yellow cap, much too small for him, perched crazily upon his shaven scalp. His face, with its small eyes and the loose rolls and creases of flesh, resembled that of a fat but rather fierce hog. He breathed heavily, and his upper lip bulged over an immense wad of shredded tobacco, red with areca-nut juice.

Saleh, who had been carefully drilled in his part by the anxious inmates of his mother's house, and had been forced, sorely against his will, to don for the occasion full native costume, clambered clumsily up to the top platform and squatted cross-legged opposite to his father, the whole length of the hall dividing them. The king did not so much as spare him a glance. Saleh felt as though he were dressed for a fancy ball and was going through a set of laboriously acquired tricks, like a performing dog. His hands shook as he laid them palm to palm in his lap and raised them so that the thumbs rested against his forehead. Then he shuffled up the carpet a few yards and repeated the operation. He was uneasily conscious that his progress was a sadly awkward affair and that the courtiers were watching him critically with the tails of their eyes. Again he shuffled forward, sweating with embarrassment and agitation, and again he raised his hands in the salute. He was quite close to his father by this time, but neither by word nor by sign did the old man give any token that he was aware of his son's approach. There were real tears of mortification in Saleh's eyes as he bent at last to kiss the king's knee. Still no notice of any kind was taken of him, and he shuffled, still maintaining his sitting posture, to a point at the end of the right-hand tip of the horseshoe of courtiers.

The king rolled slowly, as though turning upon his axis, and addressed a gayly dressed man who occupied a seat upon the side opposite to Saleh.

"Your servant desireth to go upstream to-morrow to snare doves," he said. The man he spoke to was of royal rank, and the "servant" to whom he referred was the celebrated Che' Jĕbah. Since she was not a woman of the blood-royal, she was nominally "the servant" of every râja in the land, though practically most men and women in Pĕlĕsu that day were her slaves.

"Majesty," said the man addressed, and forthwith a slow trickle of talk began to flow on the subject of decoy doves, their points and their records. Saleh felt chilled to the core. What a welcome, what a home-coming to his father's house was this!

At last, when the subject of decoy doves began to

show signs of running dry, the king turned abruptly
to Saleh and fired a question at him, using the vocative,
and something of the manner which a Malay generally
employs when addressing a dog. Saleh was startled,
hurt, and offended, which was a pity, for if he had
been bred in Malaya instead of England he would have
known that he had no cause for indignation. Most
Malaya râjas pet, caress, and indulge their children in
a quite extravagant fashion so long as the days of
childhood last, but adopt a certain truculent brutality
of manner toward them so soon as the boys become
transformed into men. This, it is felt, is necessary, if
paternal authority is to be preserved, and it is often
salutary, since no one save the king himself dares treat
a cubbish young prince with the withering contempt
and blistering frankness which the health of the souls
of such gentry commonly demands. If the whole
trend of your education has taught you to gratify, not
to restrain, your passions, it follows that violent
methods are necessary if you are to be by anyone con-
trolled, and it is in this fact that the Malayan râja's
bearing toward his sons finds its justification; but
Saleh, poor fellow, had not been brought up in the
haphazard fashion that prevails at a Malayan court,
and to him his father's manner was sheer outrage.

"Heh, you there! You know nothing about doves, I
suppose?"

Saleh saluted hurriedly.

"Nothing, Majesty," he stammered.

"And very little about language and religion? [1] You
sit cross-legged in ungainly fashion, and your tongue
speaks with a bad accent. Yet you have been to the

[1] *Bhâsa ugâma*, literally "language and religion," conveys a far more
comprehensive meaning than the words themselves imply. The phrase
means manners, carriage, behavior, conversational style, etc.

white men's country, they tell me. What then did they teach you there if you know naught about such simple things as decoy doves?"

"I learned all manner of things out of books," faltered poor Saleh. "Also what is fitting and what is not fitting according to the codes of the white men."

"And yet," said the king, disapprovingly, "you salute clumsily. Did they not even teach you the manners that befit an inmate of a court over yonder in the land which lies above the wind?"

Saleh hung down his head. He despaired of being able to make his father understand the nature of the things of which a knowledge had been imparted to him during his sojourn in England.

"It is a long way off, is it not? Heh, you there! It is a long way off, is it not?"

"Yes, Majesty," said Saleh.

"Is it as far away as *Kâyang-an*—as fairyland?" asked the King.

Saleh smiled. He took this question to be a royal jest.

"What are you grimacing at, you there? Are your ears deaf? Is it as far away as *Kâyang-an?*"

Saleh looked around in bewilderment.

"There is no such place as *Kâyang-an*," he blurted out at last.

The wrath of the king was instantly tremendous and threatened forthwith to become apoplectic. His voice rose to a roar and broke discordantly upon a high note.

"What profits it to say such things?" he cried. "What meaneth it that you, you whose age is barely a year of maize, come hither and tell me—*me* that there is no such place as *Kâyang-an?* There always has been such a place, the books are full of brave tales concerning it, and you—you who say that you have learned much out of books—tell me that there is no such place! It seemeth to me that you are vainly striving to display cleverness! No *Kâyang-an*, forsooth! Heard ye ever the like?" He turned to the assembled courtiers. "Do ye hold with this young jackanapes that there is no such place?"

"No, Tûan-ku," the obsequious chorus made answer. "It is very certain that there is such a place, even as Thy Majesty sayeth."

"And how far is it from the white men's lands which lie above the wind?" asked the king.

The courtiers looked at one another inquiringly, and then one of them, a great authority on such matters, answered with the gravity which the royal question demanded.

"The white men's country," he said, "is distant a matter of a month and a half in a ship—about twice as far as Mecca. *Kâyang-an* must be at least as far away again, for the books say that it is 'more distant than the eye can see, farther than a horse can gallop, even farther than a bird can fly without falling exhausted.' *Kâyang-an*, Majesty, according to thy servant's reckoning, must be more than twice as distant as the white men's country. It would take approximately three to three and a half months to get there."

The king turned triumphantly to Saleh.

"See there!" he roared. "That be good talk! And you would have us believe that there is no such place! Ya Allah, Muhammad! Even in the matter of book knowledge it seemeth that you are sadly deficient."

Saleh saluted in silence. Self-satisfied ignorance

such as this was, he felt, something with which it were vain for him to attempt to compete.

"And in the white men's land the people are without manners, decency, or morals," continued the king, dogmatically. "You lived there many years, and your manners obviously have suffered thereby, but you noticed that things are as I have said—eh?"

"No, Majesty," faltered Saleh. "I noticed nothing of the kind."

The courtiers gazed at him with astonishment. There must be a fine blending of madness and audacity in one who made bold thus to differ with the king.

"What?" roared the monarch, rolling about grotesquely in the extremity of his wrath. "You have certainly learned to lie. It is not fitting to tell such things to me. Not noticed such things, forsooth! Do not the men wear trousers without any waist-cloth to cover them from thigh to belt? Do not the women wear garments that fit their bodies so closely that they might as well be nude? Do not these same women bare their necks and their breasts shamelessly in the evenings, and thereafter consort unblushingly with men—men who are not even bound to them by ties of kindred? Do not the white folk have orgies which they name 'dancing,' when the men, to the encouragement of music, embrace the women indiscriminately, this man with the other's wife, this youth with some neighbor's daughter? Do they not, when the 'dancing' is over, retire, two by two, to certain dark places prepared for the purpose, there to make love, while the husbands and the brothers of these shameless women lift no finger to prevent the scandal? And you have noticed none of these things! Perhaps you will tell me that they are like *Kâyang-an*—that they have no existence!"

"Such practices prevail, Majesty," faltered poor Saleh. "But indeed there is no harm—such as . . ."

The king cut him short with a roar.

"No harm, you say! No harm, forsooth! Ya Allah! Would you make my eyes blind? Are not these folk men and women? Then how can there be no harm? No, it is as I said. In the white men's land there are no manners, no decency, no morals. Is it not so?"

And again the courtiers spoke in chorus—

"It is very certainly so, O Majesty!"

Saleh had no word to say. Explanation, he felt, was hopeless. He was paralyzed by the patent impossibility of making his father regard these things from his, from the Englishman's, standpoint; and stated as the king had stated them, even the most innocent practices sounded like damning proofs of the truth of his assertions anent the depravity of white men. Yet he longed to defend his friends, to vindicate the honor of the race which numbered Alice Fairfax among its daughters, and it seemed to him that there was something grotesque in such a condemnation being pronounced upon it here, in the court of Pĕlĕsu, of whose happy-go-lucky lack of morals he had already obtained more than a passing glimpse.

"And you," continued the king, brutally—"you, I suppose, you have danced with these shameless women, eh?"

"I have danced with English ladies, and I am very fond of dancing," said Saleh, sulkily.

"I make no doubt of it," said the king, unpleasantly, and the chorus of courtiers echoed the royal laughter.

"But . . . but . . . really it is not as thou thinkest, Majesty; there is no evil in it."

The king spat out a coarse vernacular proverb that made Saleh's cheeks burn with indignation, and again the ready laughter of the courtiers greeted the witticism of their monarch.

His facile victory over his son had put the Sultan by now in an excellent humor with himself and with all the world, a fact which was proved by his proceeding to relate a number of anecdotes, every one of which was of a character more or less unpublishable, designed to illustrate the soundness of his contentions anent the frailty of human nature. Saleh, as he listened, was astonished to find that these appalling tales were robbed of the major portion of their offense by the fact that they were being told in the vernacular. He tried mentally to translate one of them into English words, and the result fairly took his breath away. Yet the story-teller was his own father, and it was his father who but a moment since had been pointing the finger of scorn at Saleh's English friends for what he held to be their notorious and shameless immorality! The tangle and topsy-turvydom, the crooked vision and the distorted travesty of the truth which result from looking at the West through the eyes of the East, and of judging the Oriental from the standpoint of the European, were impressing themselves upon Saleh's understanding in a bewildering fashion. It appealed to him as a hopeless task, no less, to attempt to unravel such a surprising confusion of cross-purposes.

Presently men trooped into the hall bearing great trays of sweetmeats, and Saleh was gruffly bidden by the king to share his dish with him. He partook of these delicacies with difficulty, for their luscious sweetness sickened him, but he felt that his startled assent was justified when the king, in a bullying voice, told him that such dainties could not be produced in England.

Very soon after these abominable refreshments had been disposed of, the king retired, and Saleh was conducted back to his own quarters. He went feeling like one who has just received a severe and public whipping, and he noticed that the more prudent of his father's courtiers gave him a wide berth. In his mother's household there were weeping and wailing that night, and Tŭngku Ampûan railed at and scolded him for an hour on end. It was held that Saleh, in his first interview with the king, had not acquitted himself well.

Chapter Ten

SO far Saleh had not had the fact forced upon his
perception that the white men, who had taken
it upon themselves to play the part of Providence
to the state of Pelesu, were in any wise concerning
themselves with his destinies; yet it was the British
Resident, not his parents, who had decreed that he
should spend the first unbroken month of his return at his father's court.

"He must begin by remaking the acquaintance of
his own people," the Resident had said, nor stayed
to think what that experience would hold for a lad
of Saleh's upbringing. "It is a thousand pities, to
my thinking, that he was ever taken out of his
proper environment. The Malay guided by white
influence is all right; the denationalized Malay is
the devil. Anyway, he must begin by fitting back
into his own groove before we try to work him on
European lines."

Baker, the district officer who had charge of the
two thousand square miles of country in which the
king's court was situated, had been absent on duty
at some distance from the capital at the time of
Saleh's return, and the only two remaining white
men in the station, the medical officer and the inspector of police, had been occupied with their own
business, and had not thought it necessary to in-
trude upon the new arrival.

Upon the evening of his disastrous interview
with his father, however, Saleh learned that Tûan
Baker had returned, and before he went to his rest
a note was put into his hands. It ran thus:

[167]

DEAR TŬNGKU MAT SALEH,—I am just back
from a long trip down the coast, and write this line
to welcome you to Pĕlĕsu. I hope that they are
giving you a good time on your side of the river
and that you will let me know if there is anything
that I can do for you. I had a letter from Mr. Norris
by last mail very full of interest in you and your
affairs. I have a lot of work awaiting me after my
absence, but I will come across and see you to-
morrow afternoon, unless you care to come and see
me some time earlier in the day.

Believe me sincerely yours.

ARTHUR BAKER.

"Ambûi, O Ma' Tŭngku! How clever thou art
to be able to decipher writing such as that!" cried
the retainers who were present when Saleh read
this note, and they crowded round him in undis-
guised admiration when Saleh, writing under considerable difficulties, scrawled an answer saying
that he would call upon the district officer on the
morrow.

The boat which had brought him up from the
mouth of the river carried him next morning across
the broad stream to a neat landing-stage, and Saleh
was at once struck by the trim orderliness of the
place, which was in such abrupt contrast to the ill-
kept grounds of the royal compounds. Here were
streets straight as a die, houses and shops of uniform pattern, well-built, airy bungalows for the
white men, a broad parade-ground, with police
barracks on one side of it, and a big jail building on
the other; lawn-tennis courts, golf greens, and a
large block of government offices. He had left

behind him on the far bank of the river a native
court untouched by the years—slovenly, dirty, un-
disciplined, immoral—a place where law and order
gained at best but a precarious foothold; only a mile
and a half of running water separated it from a station
where all things, from the carefully constructed roads
to the grim wall of the jail, told of organized administration, enforced cleanliness, and obedience to well-
understood rules. With the teachings of Râja
Pahlâwan Indut fresh in his mind, it seemed to Saleh
that the white men's coming had robbed the court of
Pĕlĕsu of all the romance and the unfettered, masterless freedom which of old had been its heritage, leaving in their stead only the dirt, the squalor, and the
unloveliness, and had availed nothing to mold it into
even a distant likeness to this station, this little piece
of the West thrust thus incongruously into the heart
of the disordered East. Pĕlĕsu, the ancient, the inviolate, the unreformed—the Pĕlĕsu of which Râja
Pahlâwan had such stirring tales to tell—stood out, in
Saleh's imagination, as the representative of one ideal
—the native; the trim little station on the left bank
of the river represented, to his thinking, another—the
ideal of the white men. The court of Pĕlĕsu, as he
had learned of late to know it, appeared to him to
approximate neither to the one nor to the other—to
be, in fact, a hybrid creation of two opposed and clashing civilizations, hateful at once to the European and
to the thoughtful Malay. In it Saleh winced to trace
in some sort a picture of his own soul.

There remained, then, to choose between the two
ideals—the Malayan and the European; of the unlovely
hybrid he would have nothing. His hopes must be
fixed either upon the future or the upon the past; the

present was unendurable. Must he strive with the
white men to reduce the land of his birth to the regu-
lated monotony which this trim station typified, or
must he dream with Râja Pahlâwan of a return to the
old order of things before the coming of the white
men, and with Râja Haji Abdullah of the temporal
supremacy of the Children of the Prophet? Already
this question was beginning to obtrude itself upon
Saleh's understanding as a problem to which, sooner
or later, he would be forced to supply a solution.

Arthur Baker was sitting in his office under a swinging *punkah,* with a huge pile of official papers cumber-
ing his writing-table. He was a lean, lantern-jawed
man of thirty, spare and muscular from hard exercise
and a low diet, sun-tanned to a dingy yellow tint, and
with light-blue eyes, which looked lighter than they
really were through contrast with his discolored skin.
He rose from his chair, shook hands with Saleh, and
bade him be seated.

"What's the news?" he said in the vernacular. Then
he added in English: "Look here, it is absurd for me
to talk to you in Malay. You speak English as well as
I do, I suppose."

"Yes, I speak English all ri'," said Saleh.

"Well, then," said Baker, throwing himself back in
his chair and lighting a cigarette, "how do you like
Pĕlĕsu?"

"Pretty well," said Saleh, feebly.

"A bit of a change after England, isn't it?"

"Yes," said Saleh.

"Where are you living?"

"In my mother's house—Tŭngku Ampûan's you
know."

Baker whistled shrilly, then caught himself up with haste.

"Oh yes, quite so—quite so," he said, hurriedly.

There followed an awkward pause.

"Seen the king yet?" asked Baker.

"Yes, I saw him yesterday," said Saleh.

"Was he nice to you?"

"No," said Saleh and his face flamed.

"I am sorry for that. I had hoped that you would be able to work the king. He's difficult, you know—most infernally difficult."

"How do you mean?" asked Saleh, rather stiffly.

"Well, he's most uncommonly inaccessible, for one thing. Can't get him to attend to business at any price. I have a host of things here"—and Baker thumped a pile of official papers—"that I must see him about, and Heaven only knows when I shall get hold of him. The worst of it is that if there is too much delay, the powers that be put it down to incompetence on my part and then I get my hair pulled."

"I see," said Saleh.

"I tell you what," continued Baker. "You might cast your eye over these papers and see if there are any about which you could say a word to the king if the chance offers. I wish you would, like a good fellow."

Saleh took the bundle of dockets, pleased to think that he might perhaps be of use, and began to read them. They were all petitions addressed to the Resident by people who claimed that they had been aggrieved by the king. Here was one from a man who said that his wife had been lured into the house of Che' Jĕbah and had there undergone treatment which may not be more particularly described; here was another complaining that while upriver snaring doves the king and his youths had stripped his fruit trees of their crop; and there were a half a dozen others, all containing charges ranging from petty theft to aggravated assault. They were not pretty tales to read about one's father, and the worst of it was that Saleh's instinct told him that they were true. He laid the papers back on Baker's table without finishing his perusal of them.

"Oh, have you read 'em?" asked Baker, glancing up from the writing which he had resumed.

"Some of them," said Saleh. "But . . . I do not think you understand. I cannot speak to the king about such things. You forget that he is my father."

"I beg your pardon," said Baker, looking very much embarrassed. "Upon my soul, it didn't strike me in that light. You see, you talk English so well, and all that. I was speaking to you as I might have spoken to a white man. I didn't connect you with the king— not in that way. I'm awfully sorry."

"And all these complaints, are they true?" asked Saleh.

"Oh, well, yes. I am afraid they are," said Baker, reluctantly.

"And what can you do?"

"Oh, I shall see the king and speak to him like a Dutch uncle. I really beg your pardon—I mean I shall have to put matters to him very straight, and of course he will have to pay compensation all round— and heavy compensation at that. It is the only thing we can do, and he hates having his allowance docked. I shall have a beast of an interview with him, and I loathe the job as cordially as he can do; but, you see, it is what I'm here for."

Again there came a pause.

"Is the king treating Tŭngku Ampûan any better now?" Baker asked, presently.

Saleh felt outraged. The question might have been asked without offense to a Malay and in the vernacular; but Saleh was only in part a native, and the language being used was English.

"I do not think that I can discuss the affairs of my family with a stranger," Saleh said, just as any Englishman might, in the circumstances, have replied.

Baker laughed a short, hard laugh.

"I'll tell you what it is, Râja Mat Saleh," he said; "I find it most infernally difficult to know where to have you. If I talk to you as I would to a white man, you pull me up short with the remark that the king is your father; and when I ask you a question which no Malay râja of my acquaintance would resent, you take offense because you look upon it from a white man's point of view. I tell you this kind of thing is a trifle too difficult for me. Let us discuss the weather."

They did not discuss the weather, but talked instead about England, a subject concerning which they at least were not beset by bewildering confusions, and presently Saleh took his leave. He felt that he disliked Baker and that his own indignation had throughout been justified. It was only natural that he should fail to perceive that he had been placed by circumstances in a position whose delicacy and difficulty rendered such conversational disasters almost inevitable. Unfortunately, also he belonged to a race whose susceptibilities are more easily wounded than those of any breed of men extant upon this earth.

THE conclusion of the month which had been allotted to Saleh for the purpose of "remaking the
acquaintance of his own people" found him utterly
confirmed in his opinions as to the worthlessness of
Malayan life in its latter-day developments. He was
little given to philosophizing, and he had scant skill
in putting into words the conclusions which formed
themselves in his mind, but he began dimly to perceive something of the causes that were at work. By
the coming of the white men to Pĕlĕsu a transformation had been wrought; but it was not the natural
growth of a gradual evolution, itself the result of pro-
pulsion from within. On the contrary, it was produced and maintained by wholly artificial means, in
bitter conflict with inherent instincts, inherited traditions, innate tendencies, characteristics, and genius,
whether racial or individual. These changes in a habit
of life infinitely old, it seemed to Saleh, had wrought
nothing, but had ruined much. Existence at the court
of Pĕlĕsu, he saw for himself, was as empty, as vapid,
as useless to God and man, as sordid and as licentious
as it had ever been; but to-day there had been taken
from it all that of old had lent to it worth and force
and glamour and enchantment. Men sinned as aforetime, but they sinned with caution, mindful of the
white man's law, in cowardly fashion, and upon a puny
scale; men were as immoral as of old, but no longer at
the peril of their heads; men loafed and sauntered
through their lives, but now they lacked the frequent
tonic of warfare, and there came to them no longer
any opportunity for individual deeds of valor, or

chances to display courage or loyalty wherewith to
break the dull monotony of their ill-doing. No, the
tawdry shell of the ancient court life remained, but
the soul within had atrophied; all its failures and
futilities were intact, but the daring, the reckless manhood, the headlong loyalty, the true Malayan fighting
spirit—all the few but precious virtues which it had
fostered—had been filched from it. In Saleh's eyes
there was justification in all this, ample justification,
for *laudator temporis acti*.

In spite of his secret contempt for life as he saw
it lived around him, Saleh found that he had no alternative but to conform to things as he found them. It
was useless to rise early, since there was nothing doing
until the afternoon brought with it a measure of coolness. Therefore he took to lying late abed, in itself a
demoralizing practice in a tropical climate. When at
last the sluggish stream of life began to flow once
more, he could only kill time, as his fellows killed it,
by joining in long, grave discussions about the points
of rival fighting-cocks or decoy doves, by witnessing
occasional matches arranged to test the prowess of
these birds, by listening for hours to the trivial gossip
of the court or to the tales, in number past all counting, of the brave days of old, each one of which served
to make more manifest to Saleh the ugliness and the
hollowness of the present. In this fashion the afternoon would be whiled away, and then would come the
evening meal, an event of importance. Once or twice
Saleh had crossed the river and had played a game or
two of lawn-tennis with the white men of the station,
but he had found himself somewhat *de trop*. Baker
and the medical officer were well matched, and had
formed the habit of playing singles daily. The in-

spector of police did not play, and a third man was a
nuisance. The tennis over, piquet was played till
dinner-time, but from this Saleh was rigidly excluded.
It was against the unwritten law of the white man in
the Peninsula to play with a Malay for money, and no
exception could be made in Saleh's favor. To these
Englishmen, who had lived so long among Malays, the
accident of Saleh's upbringing counted for little. In
their eyes he was primarily a native.

The lad was accordingly thrown back upon the
society of his own people for distraction, and his evenings would be passed for the most part in playing at
chĕki a very elaborate form of the card game called
Ma poule crie, with his father, Che' Jĕbah, and a select
coterie of men and women, in the favorite concubine's
house, or at Chinese dice in the audience-hall. This,
too, was demoralizing, for the gambler's instinct is
part of the psychical furniture of most Malays, and in
his own heart, Saleh presently found, it was warm and
quick.

Play would continue until the east was yellowing
for the dawn, and Saleh would go to his rest with a
wasted day behind him and a morrow of little profit
awaiting his waking.

In England Saleh had always been accounted
"slack," and indeed his energy, judged by European
standards, was by no means super-abundant; yet the
training which he had received sufficed to make the
deadly inertia into which the court of Pĕlĕsu had
fallen a thing utterly revolting. To him it was a degradation that he and his should thus saunter through
profitless lives, suffering the white men meanwhile to
usurp all those functions of government which it is
the sole *raison d'être* of a royal caste to exercise. The

Sultan was still nominally the ruler of the state, he was euphemistically said to govern "by the advice of the British Resident," all things were done by the white men in his name; yet Saleh saw very clearly that his father had no power, and very little even of influence, save among the inhabitants of his disorderly court. Again the tawdry shell, the valueless husk, had been left to the Malay by the Englishman; but the soul which it had once sheltered, the soul which had given to it meaning and force and value, had been reft from it.

Yet the Sultan, Saleh recognized with disgust, did not resent this very bitterly. In the old days, all affairs of state which did not directly or indirectly affect his own comfort, pleasure, or convenience, had been wont to bore the king to distraction. Such things had a knack of making demands upon his time and of disturbing his easeful self-indulgence. That the white men, in their folly, should be willing to concern themselves with such gross and sordid details was clearly, in the king's sight, cause for much thankfulness; it was only when the theories of the Englishmen clashed with some lawless whim of his own that the Sultan was inclined momentarily to resent the presence of the aliens in his country.

This, however, naturally enough, was a point of view which Saleh could not share, and for the rest he rejected the one thing in life which gave for all at the court of Pĕlĕsu a savor to existence. Men and women alike lived in this little hotbed of iniquity mainly for the prosecution of their inconstant *amours,* and this was yet another phase of Malayan life for which Saleh's British upbringing had unfitted him. To others increased leisure, additional opportunity,

diminished risk, all due to the presence of the white
man in the land, might enlarge the field for pleasure
and afford compensation for much; to Saleh these
things furnished one proof the more that Pĕlĕsu was
undergoing a process of rapid degeneration, the responsibility for which must be laid at the doors of the
English.

Yet, as a young celibate at a Malayan court, Saleh
was, and felt himself to be, an almost grotesque
anomaly. His mother was frankly ashamed that her
son should be such a milksop, and said so with a pungent emphasis which made poor Saleh wince. Mûnah
and half a dozen other girls who had ogled him persistently began presently to offer him a hundred little
covert insults, illustrative of the contempt they entertained for such a laggard in love; and Saleh was made
uncomfortably aware in half a thousand ways that his
conduct, far from inspiring respect, was making him a
public laughing-stock among his own people. Yet
during the whole of the month which he spent at the
court of Pĕlĕsu he clung feverishly to his acquired
notions of right and wrong. It was an uphill fight,
and he got small joy from it, but the memory of Mrs.
Le Mesurier and her daughter, and, more still, the
thought of Alice Fairfax, kept him true to his ideals.

And two others also helped him. Râja Pahlâwan
Indut fed the flame of enthusiasm for the Malaya of
the old days with calculating sedulousness, while
Râja Haji Abdullah expounded the faith of Muhammad to him with fanatical vigor. Râja Pahlâwan was
quite ludicrously distressed by Saleh's rigorous celibacy, and even Râja Abdullah, professional holy man
though he was, derived from it more surprise than
edification, but by common consent both avoided all

reference to the young man's peculiarities in their conversation with him. Among themselves they discussed the marvel freely.

"Unquestionably he hath become possessed by certain devils, such as the white men breed," Râja Pahlâwan would say. "But therewith he hath perforce acquired much knowledge concerning white men and their tortuous ways. When the great day dawneth, brother, that knowledge will be useful to the Cause. I, for one, would not have him other than he is. I behold in him a weapon tempered by the white men for their own destruction. *Allah Akhbar!*"

"Surely, brother, surely," Râja Abdullah would reply. "He is a true son of the Faith, notwithstanding such devils as the white men have implanted in his soul. Already he is afire with the enthusiasm which in the end will work destruction upon the infidel. As for those same devils of the white man, their coming upon him is plainly due to the unclean things which he hath been made to eat in the white man's land in defiance of the Prophet's law. Now hath he put away all such uncleanness, but the power bred of knowledge may not be put off. That, as thou sayest, brother, is a weapon ready to our hands."

"And our hope lieth ever with the young men," Râja Pahlâwan would cry, "with the young men who know only the romance of the past, not with the old men whose memories recall the days when they were as driven cattle before prince and chief; and he, he also, is young! He kindles to my stories of the past; he hateth the mean to-day, even as we hate it. Presently all the young malcontents will find in him a leader. Verily, brother, the white men in their folly have armed us for the Great Battle."

What time poor Saleh, holding firmly to his path in obedience to his acquired principles, and conscious of a growing contempt for the present, an increasing enthusiasm for the past, and a newly kindled, fiery pride in the faith of his fathers, would have scorned the notion that he was being influenced, bent to their will, steadily, gradually, carefully, and with calculation, by two ignorant Malays, who, the one for purely secular, the other for religious, motives, took delight in the dreaming of wild dreams.

THE month wore to an end at last, this month which had held for Saleh so many startling experiences; and presently word was sent to him by Baker that a steam-launch was in readiness to carry him upriver to the administrative headquarters of the state. Saleh, who had seen his father almost every night as long as it was a question of playing cards with him, found it curiously difficult to arrange a meeting for the purpose of formal leave-taking; but as soon as this had been accomplished and his farewells to his mother had been said, he started upon his journey. He did not go alone, for Râja Pahlâwan Indut and half a dozen other men, retainers of his mother's household, attached themselves to him after the frankly parasitic Malayan fashion. Râja Pahlâwan, by virtue of his rank and past prowess, drew a monthly stipend from state funds, but the rest of the party had determined, after due deliberation, but without consulting the person principally concerned, to live for the future with and *on* Saleh.

Kuâla Pĕkâra, the administrative capital aforesaid, lies some two hundred and fifty miles up the Pĕlĕsu River from its mouth, close to which the court of the king is situated. The river flows grandly from the interior through magnificent forest country, receiving on either bank the frequent tribute of other great streams, and its banks are now marvelous cliffs of jungle—tangles of giant tree, crowding underwood, clinging vine, and festooning parasite—rising sheer from the water's brink, now long clusters of villages deep in the shade of palm and fruit trees, now wide expanses of grass-grown meadow, where the grazing-grounds dip to the river, and the banks are cut into huge, trampled clefts by the passage of the kine trooping down to drink. Occasional wooded islands break the monotony of the river, or yellow sandspits and big wedges of granite run far out into its course; and over all by day smiled the joyous Malayan sunshine, while at night the tropical moon turned all this riverine world to the likeness of a fairyland.

Saleh, lying in a long rattan chair at the bow of the launch, drank in the scenes which succeeded one another in bewildering succession, and felt himself thrilled by an almost fierce appreciation of their beauty. This faculty of enjoyment he owed to his English training, for Malays set little store by the loveliness of inanimate nature, but the thoughts which crowded his mind were not sympathetic to the white men and their works. This miracle of beauty, he told himself again and again, was the country over which his family had ruled from time immemorial; it was his, his, *his*—his inalienable right and heritage! The folly of his father, who was content to barter so glorious a birthright for empty days wasted among his women, his decoy doves, and his trivial pleasures, appealed to Saleh now as sheer madness. The king, perhaps, was constitutionally unfitted for rule, but he, Saleh, was cast in a different mold. This country was his country, these people were his people: Allah, the Merciful, the Compassionate, had dowered him with high estate. Was it not iniquitous, shameful, that his authority and his responsibilities, both equally the gift of Allah, should be suffered by him unresistingly to be usurped by white men who were infidels?

If the English had "left him alone," he, too, would

have grown up in a Malayan court, content with such
paltry pleasures as such places can afford to a prince,
and inclined as little as was his father to take an active
part in the administration of his country. But the
English in their wisdom had decreed that Saleh should
not be left alone; wherefore, having robbed him of a
taste for such things as are wont commonly to keep
young Malayan râjas quiescent, they had inspired him
with cravings and ambitions which the whole practice
of their administrative system rendered it impossible
that he should ever adequately gratify. Saleh did
not fully understand this as yet, nor did the white
men; but the former, as he journeyed through the land
of his fathers, was torn by discontent and resentment
because the old order changing had given place to the
new, and because the reawakened Muhammadan within
him whispered that in this sorry transformation God
surely was *not* fulfilling Himself.

Here and there the riverine landscape was set with
a trim British station—a cluster of bungalows in well-
kept grounds, a police barracks, court-house, and
hospital, each putting the seal, as it were, upon the
administration of the country, Saleh's country, by the
white men. In each of these stations there were one
or more fine-run young Englishmen, lean from much
hard work, who were "in charge" of so many hundreds
of square miles of country, and responsible therefor,
not to Saleh or to his father the king, but to the Resident at Kuâla Pĕkâra. They came on board the
launch, greeted Saleh courteously, generally, he
noticed, in the vernacular, invited him up to their
bungalows while the launch took in firewood, and introduced him to hosts of grave-eyed chiefs, village
headmen, and elders. It was an added humiliation to

Saleh that he should have to be made known to these men—men who by birth and immemorial tradition were vassals of his house—by white men; but what hurt him far more shrewdly was the position which he found himself to occupy in regard to the chiefs, as compared with that held by the white district officers. From the great territorial chiefs, who of old had had power of life and death in their hands, to the meanest villager, every one treated him with the same marked and ceremonious respect, saluting him as a royalty with uplifted hands, declining to be seated in his presence otherwhere than on the floor, and styling themselves "thy slave" in conversation with him; but it was not to him, but to the young white men, Saleh noted, that these men turned instinctively for instructions or advice. Again the tawdry husk was his; all that it had once cloaked had passed into the keeping of the English.

Chapter   Thirteen

KUÂLA PĔKÂRA is one of the most beautiful places in the world. It is situated on a high, flat promontory at the point where the Pĕkâra River falls into the Pĕlĕsu, both streams being of about the same size and volume, and measuring at this point a matter of a hundred yards from bank to bank. The British Residency stands high upon the point, with great terraced gardens falling like a giant's staircase to the river's brink. Behind it is the European quarter, bungalows in big compounds, separated from the numerous government buildings by a wide savannah. Beyond that again, occupying an area of flat land some twelve square miles in extent, is the town, laid out with the regularity of a chess-board and filled with shops owned by Chinese, Tamil, and Bengali traders. The unsightly tin-mines, which make the wealth of the place, lie farther inland still, and are mercifully hidden from view by the masses of town buildings.

From the Residency lawn you look first down a noble reach of river, on the banks of which the forest has not been suffered to be touched and so over miles of seemingly primeval jungles to a blue amphitheater of hills. From the forest at night times come the plaintive musical notes of the tree-frogs, the hoot of little owls, and the occasional strident scream of the argus-pheasant. Turning upon your bed in the darkness, you are tempted to believe that you are far away in the heart of the untouched wilderness. Pass inland, however, and you find yourself first in a well-ordered British station of the East, with its clubs, its lawn-tennis courts, its stone bungalows, and its solid government buildings, all designed to endure the ravages of time, and so to the town, which, on a smaller scale, is a replica of the Chinese trading quarter of Singapore. The whole place, rightly judged, is a miracle, for Kuâla Pĕkâra had been conjured out of the wilderness by the energy and administrative ability of the white men, aided by the enterprise and commercial genius of the Chinese, in a matter of a couple of decades, yet for once the work of man has not been suffered quite to mar the magnificent handiwork of the Creator.

Kuâla Pĕkâra, coming upon him after days spent in steaming upriver through Malaya, the unchanging, the seemingly inviolate, fairly took Saleh's breath away with astonishment; yet his first impressions were uniformly painful. The British Residency was the first palace that he had seen in this land, of which his father was the reputed king! He could not know that the Sultan, obstinately conservative and a deep hater of new ways, had refused absolutely to allow a proper palace to be built at his court for his accommodation. His objection, if the truth were known, had really been based upon a fear lest an army of imported workmen should interfere with the monstrous regiment of palace women. This, however, was a detail; but what struck Saleh with a species of despair was the thought of the energy and of the genius for organization and government which had gone to the creation of such a place as Kuâla Pĕkâra. Beside these things, in contrast with them, the futility of life as he had seen it lived at the court of Pĕlĕsu was presénted to his imagination as something so paltry as to be at once vile and degrading. And men of his race and house (the persecuting thought *would* obtrude itself) had pos-

sessed this land, to have and to hold, to do with what
they would, from time immemorial! They had had the
same chance as the white men; they, too, might have
made of it what these strangers had made. They had
had their opportunity; they had had centuries to
devote to the work where the English had had only
as many years; yet they had accomplished nothing,
nothing, where these aliens had wrought miracles!
The old torturing doubt anent the inherent weakness
of himself and of his race, the which, perhaps, lurking
at the back of color prejudice, furnished its justification, rose up in Saleh's mind anew to daunt and harass
him. And there was nothing to show that Kuâla
Pĕkâra was a town of Malaya. The bungalows and
the great government buildings were designed by
Europeans; the trim grounds, everywhere in such
spick-and-span order, had been produced under the
direction of the race which, as Saleh knew, boasted
that it had mowed and rolled its own lawns in the
homeland these five hundred years; the shops were
Chinese or Indian; everywhere the Malay, the native
of the country, had been quietly eliminated, forced
out of existence by superior energy, superior ability
to compete successfully in the struggle for wealth and
power. Again the doubt assailed him, but now it was
hardly to be called a doubt: it was rapidly being transformed into a conviction.

And the very solidity of everything appalled and
paralyzed him. Of late he had dreamed dreams of
what might have been his lot as his father's heir in the
old days before the coming of the white men; and the
task of administration had seemed to him a simple
affair while he journeyed upriver through the sleepy
Malayan villages. But here was something with which

he could not cope, something too vast and complex for his powers; and the alien rulers, he felt, knew this, and were, withal, so firmly seated that nothing could ever dislodge them.   Let him strive as he might to convince them of his desire, his passionate desire, to rule this country, the throne of which must some day be his by right of inheritance, to rule it wisely, justly, moderately, as a country should be ruled, these strangers would greet his aspirations with a smile. The semblance of authority, and perhaps some measure of personal influence, might some day at the best be his, but the real power would remain in the hands of the Resident.   They would not tell him here that he was "a nigger," and the thought, stated in that crude fashion, would not even present itself to their minds; but the disparity between the white and the Malayan race was, he felt, an article of faith with the rulers of Pĕlĕsu—an article of faith fortified, as all things around him attested, by a thousand convincing proofs. These devotees of administrative efficiency, it was certain, would never permit a Malayan râja, even a man of Saleh's upbringing, to be his own British Resident, and when all was said and done, the British Resident for the time being, and no other man, was the only king of Pĕlĕsu.

Once again poor Saleh found himself confronted with the crushing, paralyzing, heart-breaking injustice of Fate.

HE was met at the private landing-stage at the bottom of the Residency grounds by a young Englishman, who introduced himself as the Resident's private secretary, and he was driven in a high mail-phaeton up the beautifully graded road which led to the summit of the hill. The Resident was waiting to receive him in the great cool hall, and, after shaking him warmly by the hand, threw himself into a big leather-covered armchair and bade Saleh seat himself in another opposite to him.

"Well," said the Resident, cordially, "I'm very glad to see you. I hope you had a pleasant time at the court and that Baker looked after you all right."

"Yes, thank you," said Saleh, shyly.

The Resident lit a cigar and examined Saleh curiously. He was a man of some seven or eight and forty years, sun-dried, and with a firm, hard nut of a face. His gray eyes were quick and piercing, his nose prominent and the tip was blistered by the sun, his chin was square and resolute, his clean-shaven lips thin and straight. He had the indefinable air of mastery which comes to a man who, during long years, has said, with the Centurion, to one "Go!" to another "Come!" to a third "Do this!" while he has stood a little aloof watching them work obedient to his will. His name was Ralph Craster, and he had some five-and-twenty years of Malayan experience at his back. He had succeeded Jack Norris as Resident of Pĕlĕsu, and had carried on the latter's work, with the same devotion to efficiency, but with something less of the deep sympathy with

[189]

Malays and knowledge of them and of their character, which his predecessor had possessed.

"Mr. Norris saw you off from London, he tells me," Craster said, presently. "He has written me a tremendous long screed about you. He's a good deal interested in your future. So am I."

"Thank you," said Saleh.

"My wife and I—I'll introduce you to her presently —want you to stop with us for a week, and after that I shall put you into harness. You'll have to begin at the bottom of the ladder, of course, like one of the cadets, but we shall be able to push you on more quickly than we can any of them. You see, your knowledge of the language will be a great pull. You have not forgotten your Malay, I suppose?"

"No," said Saleh. "I had forgotten it a good deal, but it came back to me wonderfully."

"Quite so. Well, now I'll show you to your room."

"There is one thing," said Saleh, faltering a little in embarrassment. He still had the Englishman's reluctance to make any display of religious scruples. "You are kind enough to say that I am to stay here for a week. About my food. . . . You see, I'm a Muhammadan. I cannot eat anything that is *hâram*—sinful."

"By Jove! yes, of course," said Craster. "Oh, we'll manage all that, I dare say. I'm glad you are particular about such things. A Malay râja should always remember that he is a Malay and a Muhammadan."

So Saleh spent a week at the Residency, as he had previously passed a month at the court of Pĕlĕsu, and the sudden return to a life modeled so closely upon that which he had known in England was to him, by turns, pleasant and distressing. Mrs. Craster was kind and motherly; the Resident, deeply immersed in work, was also kind whenever he could spare time to give the lad a thought; and the machine-like precision of a well-ordered English household was grateful to Saleh after the strange mingling of dirt and squalor and tawdry magnificence which had prevailed in his mother's establishment. The half-dozen parasitic followers who had attached themselves to Saleh when he left the court declined to abandon him and were the cause of some discomfort. They camped upon the veranda of his bedroom, and reduced it in no time, as Mrs. Craster told her husband in semi-humorous despair, to as near a likeness to a dirty Malay interior as circumstances rendered possible. They despised, too, and were in their turn despised by, the Chinese servants who moved so noiselessly about the Residency, and the feeling quickly developed into an open feud. They quarreled about the rations served out to them in a manner which shocked Saleh, who remembered that he and his party were guests in the house; they almost came to blows with the Chinese cook, whom they accused of attempting to put unclean things into the dishes served to them and at the Resident's table for their master's consumption. Once they even brought *dûri-ans* into the house, and stank the place out with that most delicious and malodorous of fruits, and this, it must be confessed, did cause more than a momentary commotion. When the week was over and Saleh moved into a bungalow set apart for his use, Mrs. Craster said that the veranda of his room was in worse case than Lady Macbeth's hands. All the perfumes of Araby, she laughingly averred, would not sweeten that little plague-spot!

Saleh's own bungalow was presently reduced by the parasites to a very similar condition. He fought against the growing disorder and uncleanliness, but he fought in vain. His followers had no eyes for such things, and it passes the wit of any single individual to keep a house neat and trim if he shares it with half a dozen men, no one of whom has the remotest inkling of what neatness and trimness are. Very soon Saleh abandoned the vain struggle, and his bungalow speedily became as untidy and disordered as the interior of any ordinary Malay house. Presently, too, he lost all sense of discomfort in such surroundings.

He was attached to the Secretariat, and was set to learn the office routine daily from ten o'clock to four. Routine of any kind is a weariness of the flesh, and to Saleh, who had always hated books, the sedentary life would in the best of circumstances have been highly distasteful. Now, however, he felt resentful because he was chained by the white man's will to the task of mastering such gross details. What cared he about the system by which official papers were indexed and registered, about the formalities of correspondence, about which heads of departments must be allowed to note certain decisions when they had been recorded, and about other similar trivialities? What had things such as these to do with the science of government? It was not for him to realize that work of all kind, if it is to be done to perfection, depends largely upon attention to, and acquaintance with, a multitude of tiresome details. He only knew that he was badly bored and that he resented the drudgery as a wrong. He was surprised that his fellow-cadets, young Englishmen of much higher educational attainments than his own, accepted the dull work allotted to them with complete contentment, took a keen interest in it, seemingly, simply because it chanced to be their work, and made no complaint of the drudgery imposed upon them. But then, he remembered, these men were not as he, the son of the king of the state. Yet any one of them might rise to be a British Resident and *de facto* ruler of the land, while he . . . !

For six months Saleh was kept in the Secretariat, and I fear that no very satisfactory reports of his work reached the Resident. Then for six more months he was mewed up in the offices of the audit department for the purpose of learning the details of the whole elaborate system of public accounts. The permanent staff were up to their eyes in work and could not waste time upon a would-be pupil. Other cadets, by applying themselves resolutely and learning with eagerness everything that could be learned by personal endeavor and occasional questions, obtained in some fashion or another an intimacy with the system which Saleh found perfectly dazzling; but the thing was altogether beyond him. It did not excite his interest and he could not apply himself to anything so wearisome.

Meanwhile the other cadets were racing one another in view of the periodical examinations in language and law. The language presented no difficulties to Saleh, of course, and his examinations in this branch of knowledge were purely formal, but law meant drudgery again, and here once more Saleh failed. It was all like going to school for a second time, and he always detested book learning; also he could not convince himself of the necessity, of the utility, of the knowledge which was being instilled into him. As a ruler, not by mere profession but by right divine, he resented the tyranny that bound him to such galley work.

For the rest, he lived during this year at Kuâla

Pĕkâra a sort of dual existence—one half native, the other half European—like the hybrid which the Fates and English blundering had made of him. His bungalow, as I have said, became rapidly transformed into an integral portion of the Malaya from which in the beginning it had been rescued. Native chiefs, on a visit to headquarters, camped on the veranda, as a matter of course, without permission sought or given. They and their followers contributed to the accumulations of dirt and made the already prevailing confusion worse and worse confounded. Loafers from all parts of the state straggled in, and were made welcome by the parasites. Everybody who could do so, as already said, lived with and *on* Saleh. Many of them borrowed money of him, which he found it impossible to refuse. All of them plundered him when the opportunity offered, and if detected smilingly quoted the Malayan proverb, "Where should the lice feed if not upon the head?" The white men might have robbed royalty in Pĕlĕsu of many things, but the inestimable privileges of keeping open house and supporting all and sundry at his sole charges were not to be counted among the duties of which a prince of the blood had been relieved. Saleh's allowance—he was paid from the civil list as a native chief—was more than double the salary of any of the English cadets, but his people spent it for him, as a Malayan râja's money should be spent—royally! Saleh found to his distress that it went a surprisingly short way, but the motto *noblesse oblige* forbade economy or retrenchment.

He frequented the club occasionally and played billiards there, what time the parasites, of whom he could never even momentarily be rid, squatted in a picturesque group round the door, making him, and

in some sort the race to which he belonged, ridiculous
in the eyes of the white men and ladies. The card-
room was practically closed to him, and, being a Muhammadan, he had no use for the bar; wherefore he
usually returned to his bungalow, the parasites string-
ing out at his heels, with the feeling that he was in the
white men's club something of a fish out of water.
His very horse and trap, he felt, speedily became unlike
those of his English companions. The parasites were
a hopeless set of loafers and inefficients; they would
admit no strangers to their company, so Saleh had
very soon to dismiss his Boyanese horse-keeper; and
the grooming of the horse and the washing of the
trap were thereafter home-made affairs, desperately
amateurish and slovenly.

Saleh dined at the Residency not infrequently, and
on such occasions he always took Mrs. Craster down
to dinner. He also attended such balls as were given,
but, though all treated him with kindness and courtesy, many even with distinction, he quickly learned
that the close intimacy which he had enjoyed with
Englishwomen in Europe was something to which in
Malaya he could not hope to be admitted. The men
of both races met on terms of friendship and much
equality, but the womenkind of each was something
which, by mutual consent, both tacitly agreed to
ignore.

Saleh, too, was gradually, almost insensibly, imbib-
ing many of the sentiments of his people. It is a mistake to suppose that color prejudice is a feeling confined to white men. Everyone who knows his Asia
is aware that the Oriental regards the familiar association of his own women with Europeans with a disgust as passionate as any that is excited in ourselves

when the position is reversed. Saleh, from time to time, had listened to much casual talk among his own people on this and kindred subjects, and as old instincts and sentiments revived within him, he learned to perceive that the barrier of difference—the question of inferiority or superiority does not enter into the matter—was held by the Malays to divide them from the white men with a wall which they regarded as a rampart of defense and which they would not for any consideration suffer to be laid low. The determination to keep the race unsullied by mixture with an infidel strain was as much present in the Malays as was the fixed resolve to keep their blood untainted a deeply rooted instinct of the white men. By both alike was the half-breed despised. Only—and here, Saleh felt, lay the whole difference—the Malays did not try to transform white men into Malays, while the white men had essayed in his case to work a miracle equally impossible, equally undesirable in its results.

And so, as the months rolled by, Saleh found himself more and more distinctively a Malay, less and less an approximation to a white man in point of view, in sentiment, in affections, in his ambitions and his aspirations. As Jack Norris long ago had foretold, the East was holding out her arms to her wandering child, was drawing him closer, ever closer, to her gorgeous, tattered bosom, and slowly, but very surely, was reclaiming her own.

Chapter Fifteen

AFTER Saleh had been some twelve months at Kuâla Pĕkâra, the Resident decreed that he should be transferred to Bandar Bharu, as the station situated on the right bank of the river opposite to the court of Pĕlĕsu was called. This decision was arrived at after the Resident had had a conversation with the Secretary to Government, Mr. Dennis Drage, under whose immediate eye Saleh had been acquiring his official education.

"The youngster is doing very little good where he is, sir," Drage had reported. "He's a nice little fellow, but he's a regular Malay. Work—real hard work—is hateful to him. I've tried to keep his nose to the grindstone, but it's no sort of use. He hasn't got it in him."

"Most boys are inclined to shirk grinding at dull routine," said the Resident. "Young Mat Saleh is not peculiar in that."

"In a way, no," assented Drage, thoughtfully. "All boys shirk at times, sir, as you say; but with Saleh there is a difference in kind rather than in degree. His indolence when he is not interested—and I am beginning to think that the sort of things which we can teach him in our offices can never interest him—gives one the impression that concentration is with him an impossibility."

The Resident now was thoughtful in his turn.

"That's curious, you know, isn't it?" he said. "That's clearly inherited. I've never known a Malayan râja of the old school who did not create precisely the same impression every time one had to discuss busi-

ness with him in which he did not chance to be per-
sonally interested—the impression not that he
wouldn't give his mind to it, but that he simply
couldn't. In spite of the English education and
training, this boy is, after all, a Malay râja. The fact
can be seen sticking out all over him, like the plums
out of a pudding. They tell me that his bungalow is
a disgrace, and no one who was not by birth a Malayan
chief could tolerate that 'tail' of scallawags who de-
vour his substance and trail about at his heels."

"Quite so, sir," said Drage. "And therefore I think
we must try him upon different lines."

"If he were an ordinary cadet, we should have to
set him back for failure to pass his law exams. and
for want of application to his other work; but this is
a cadet whom we cannot set back or get rid of."

"Precisely. My proposal is that we attach him to
Baker at Bandar Bharu. The work in the court district may, perhaps, interest him a bit, and it is just
possible that he may be useful. Anyhow, it seems to
me to be his best chance, and it can't do much harm."

"All right," said the Resident. "Attach him to
Baker. Send him to me before he goes, and I'll give
the young man a good talking to."

The "talking to" was duly administered, and Saleh
came away from it with a sore heart. He had been
made to understand very clearly that, so far, he had
failed; and yet he knew with an absolute certainty of
conviction that the kind of things which had been required of him demanded the possession of qualities
and abilities which he did not possess. As the Resident had said to Drage, his shortcomings were due,
not to a refusal to apply his mind to the mastery of
dull and uninteresting matters, but to an inability to

concentrate when his interest was not aroused. The transfer itself, however, presented prospects which elated him. At last, he thought, he would take his share in the work of practical administration, and that in a district inhabited, not by Chinese or other foreigners, but by men and women of his own blood. Baker was considerably less contented when he learned of the Resident's decision.

"I've been begging for a competent assistant for ages," he said to his friend, the medical officer, "and now the mountain, having been in labor, has brought forth *ridiculus mus!* They are sending me young Tŭngku Mat Saleh. From the wisdom of all Residents, good Lord, deliver me!"

Saleh, accompanied by the jubilant parasites, journeyed down the Pĕlĕsu River in a launch, the distance being covered this time in a couple of days, for the current now was in his favor; but again Malaya, the inviolate, cried her appeal in his ears. After a year spent at Kuâla Pĕkâra, a place from which the combined efforts of the white men and the Chinese had contrived to eliminate almost all traces of its Malayan origin, Saleh felt that he breathed more freely when he found himself once more among the sleepy, sun-steeped villages, the spreading rice-fields, yielding full crops in return for a minimum of expended energy, the broad grazing-grounds over which buffaloes and peasants wandered with much the same indolent content and the somber masses of forest, which from the beginning of things had remained unmarred by the disfiguring works of mankind. This, he felt even more strongly than he had a year ago, was his native land, his proper, his natural environment. He drank in the sights that crowded his vision, snuffed lovingly at the scents borne to him from wood fires, from spicy fruit groves, from village and from forest, and was conscious of an exquisite feeling of freedom, of release. Kuâla Pĕkâra and the miracles which human ingenuity had wrought in that portion of the state possessed for him no sort of attraction; rather they repelled him. In his mind they were connected now with the never-ending, monotonous, spiritless toil and grind of administrative routine. The reaction resulting from his year of servitude was strong upon him. Never before had he felt himself more completely, more passionately, more enthusiastically a Malay—a member of that race in whose eyes, be it remembered, the thing which we call "energy" is as naturally repulsive as is vulgarity to the refined European.

His first few days at Bandar Bharu, too, were to him sheer delight. The disorder to which the parasites had reduced his bungalow at Kuâla Pĕkâra had blunted his senses in many directions, and things which had offended his fastidiousness when he came to the court of Pĕlĕsu straight from an English home passed now almost unnoticed. Besides, had not the Malay in him been growing and gathering strength all these months, and was not this place the proper environment for a Malayan râja? Nightly he passed across the river to chat and gossip with old friends and acquaintances, at play at *chĕki* at Che' Jĕbah's house, or to gamble at dice in his father's audience hall. The parasites, gayly clad in silks purchased with his money or looted from his wardrobe, followed him everywhere; and Saleh, more in tune with his surroundings than ever before, enjoyed the distinction which was his by right, the deference shown to him, the flattery lavished upon him as the eldest son of the king. There was here no question, at any rate, of being tolerated, of being "a fish out of water," and his bruised self-conceit found balm in the knowledge that the interest which he excited, the loyal affection which he inspired, the ceremonious treatment which he received, were things personal to his Malayan self, in that no white man could ever occupy at the court of Pĕlĕsu a position in any degree similar. It was all so different from what it had been on the occasion of his first visit. Then he had been in a manner aloof, adrift, separated by impalpable barriers from his own people; now they recognized instinctively that he had identified himself, thrown in his lot, with them, and they welcomed him—home.

Chapter Sixteen

BUT at the end of the first ten days untoward events began to occur. Baker had silently determined to give his new assistant so much law—so much and no more. You cannot spend the hours of the night in high Malayan society on one bank of a river and next day attend office and do the work required of you satisfactorily upon the opposite bank; and Saleh, naturally enough, had devoted himself more successfully to play than to toil. On a certain day Baker called him into his office.

"Look here, Tŭngku," he said. "I want to speak to you. This place is a work-producing machine, and every one of us is a cog in the wheel. Each cog has got to take its share of the strain. At present you are sagging loose. That's not the game. Understand?"

Saleh did understand, but he was not pleased with either the matter or the style of Baker's address. During the past few days he had become more deeply impressed than ever before with the fact that he was the son of the king, the heir to the throne, and a person deserving of a full measure of consideration. All these things were true, and Baker, who was well used to dealing with Malayan royalty—the ordinary unadulterated brand—would have been the first to recognize their force, had not the whole issue been confused for him. When a sensitive Malay râja, of all but the very first rank, occupies the anomalous position of your junior assistant, and speaks to you in English almost as perfect as your own, you are perhaps hardly to be blamed if you regard him primarily as your junior assistant, and treat him as such small fry are treated in the cub-chastening civil services of the East.

"Yes, I understand," said Saleh, sulkily and resentfully.

"Therefore, my son," Baker continued, "I am going to put you on to a job that will give you something to do, mentally and physically—principally physically. I want you to go up the coast—it's a matter of fifty miles—to Kuâla Bûyong. You can annex a boat of sorts there, and make your way up the river. There are a lot of arrears of land rents to be recovered, the jungle produce collections to be taken over from the village headmen, and one or two complaints to be inquired into. The work will take about a fortnight or three weeks, and I haven't got the time to spare, myself. You had better start to-morrow."

Saleh had no alternative but to obey. It took him and the parasites nearly a week, however, to make their preparations, and during that time there was much talk in and out of Saleh's presence about the indignity which Tûan Baker had put upon him.

The journey was an abominable experience. Saleh and the mob of followers who had decided to attend him made their way up the coast, sometimes along endless stretches of burning sand against which the sea lapped with a sleepy monotonous whisper, sometimes along the narrow footpath which threaded a tortuous course between the gnarled trunks of the casuarina trees that fringed the shore; now floundering through evil-smelling mangrove swamps, again wading breast-deep through rivers, or tight-roping along logs felled across narrower streams. To Saleh it was all a labor of Hercules—the merciless sun, the plodding toil of monotonous exertion, the drenching sweat

that trickled into his eyes, the sand into which his feet
sank, the swamps which stained his clothing ink-black,
and at the back of all the memory that he, the heir
of the kingdom, was enduring these miseries at the
bidding of a white district officer in order to collect
coppers from a reluctant peasantry to help to fill the
overflowing Treasury.

"*Ta' pâtut!* It is not fitting!" said the parasites at
every turn, as wrung themselves by the unaccustomed
exertion, they witnessed with keen sympathy, and even
keener disapproval, the labors and the sufferings of
their prince; and the phrase found a ready echo in
poor Saleh's heart. It was not fitting, it was abominable, outrageous, that he, he, Iang Mŭlia Râja Muhammad Saleh, a scion of a royal house, should be
called upon in any circumstances to perform "coolie
work" such as this! The whole idea of the thing
was inexpressibly offensive.

Young English district officers, men like Baker
and his fellows, were wont to welcome the chance
of similar expeditions as a delightful release from
drudgery in office. The interests of the district and
its people usually became with them a species of
monomania, and they were never happier than when
traveling through it, giving a word of advice here,
a word of warning there, admonishing a village head-
man, sanctioning a remission of taxes where crops
had failed, listening patiently to long-tangled stories
told by men little skilled in the use of words, who yet
had some real grievance to disclose, helping in half
a hundred ways to advance the material, and in a
measure the moral, welfare of the countryside which
was their charge. Baker, Saleh learned, had done that
tramp from Kuâla Pĕlĕsu to Kuâla Bûyong, that fifty

miles of unspeakable sand and swamp, often and often in a couple of days—five-and-twenty miles to the march—and afterward had been a better and a sounder man in body and mind therefor. Yet Saleh and his people loitered over the same piece of country during a five days' journey, and every member of the party, far from deriving enjoyment from the experience, saw in each additional furlong, in each new obstacle, a fresh indignity to their prince.

The trip up the Bûyong River, though this was accomplished by boat, was hardly more inspiring. The place swarmed with mosquitoes, who greeted Saleh, not as a seasoned native, but as a newcomer from Europe, and feasted upon him with much satisfaction. The people were obsequious to their prince, and allowed his followers to pillage them at pleasure. The parasites, declining to regard the expedition as a visit paid to the district by a government officer, transformed it as nearly as possible into a royal progress, and clung closely to the tradition that such peregrinations should result in much loot. Unknown to Saleh, they rifled the hencoops, made open love to the wives and daughters of the villagers, and slaughtered goats at every halting-place. They also compelled the terror-stricken people to bring buffaloes and other gifts to Saleh, who had no notion that these were not voluntary offerings which could not be declined without offense. It seemed to the parasites and to the villagers that the "good old days" or the "bad old times" —the description depended upon the individual point of view—had returned once more.

As for the work which Saleh had been sent to perform, that he left to Krâni Uda, his principal follower, for he could not bring himself to squeeze arrears of taxes out of these indigent people; and Krâni Uda, secure in the ignorance of the peasants, took care that payment was made in full, with something over for the benefit of the tax-collector. Of all of which things Saleh remained in perfect innocence, for the natives, who would have approached a white man with their complaints with the utmost confidence, were held dumb by their inherited fear of a prince of the blood. Besides, royal progresses in the district, as every old man could tell them, had always been conducted upon similar lines.

When Saleh got back to Bandar Bharu—he had been absent for some seven weeks to the unspeakable disgust of Baker—he was speedily followed by a host of complaints from the inhabitants of the stricken valley, and Baker had to rush off to Bûyong on his own account to prosecute the necessary inquiries. On his return he had an interview with Saleh, from which that unhappy scion of royalty emerged livid, limp, and weeping. The conversation had this time been conducted in the vernacular, which lends itself to pungent and forcible expression, and Baker, on occasion, had a tongue to raise blisters. He brushed Saleh's tearful protestations of innocence and ignorance of his followers' actions aside with a curt "Then thou must be a person lacking full intelligence!" and the quotation of a rather coarse vernacular proverb anent pupils outdoing their masters. He concluded by saying that Saleh's allowance would be docked of an amount sufficient to pay ample compensation to those who had suffered, adding that, as a lesson to Saleh, he had computed the damage done on as liberal a scale as possible.

Saleh for the moment was cowed and crushed, but

later resentment was the sentiment to which the incident chiefly gave birth. Who, after all, was Baker? What earthly right had he to interfere between the people of Pĕlĕsu and the râjas to whom they owed hereditary loyalty and allegiance? What business had he, an alien, an interloper, a man who made his living out of a country upon which he had no possible claim, to use language such as he had held in his interview with one of that country's hereditary rulers? The expedition had been forced upon him, Saleh felt, not sought by him, and most of the offerings made to him, he was still convinced, had been voluntary tokens of fealty. From this time onward Saleh found himself more than ever *laudator temporis acti,* more than ever discontented with the present, daily in conflict more and more acute with the dominion of the white men in the land.

"And by all that's impossible, this is what the Resident sends me when I apply for an assistant!" stormed Baker to his friend the medical officer. "A pretty assistant, upon my soul! Of all the lunatic businesses that I have ever struck in this Bedlam of an East, this is the most insane! Still, here he is, and here, I suppose, the young man has got to bide; but I shan't send him on any more out-district work. I shall put him on to the accounts, and I can only pray that the devil won't move him to rob the till."

So, as one of the results of his fiasco, poor Saleh was presently condemned to the most uninteresting of all branches of government business, the management of a small Sub-Treasury; but the expedition bore other fruit. Saleh brought back with him from that mosquito-haunted river the seeds of malarial fever, not the mild, chronic malaria to which all Malays are more or less subject, a disease that for the most part works little harm, but the virulent, pernicious tertian, which is generally reserved exclusively for the entertainment of Europeans. Once more the English were to blame. The denationalization of Saleh they had attempted: the declimatization of him they had achieved. In the former case the success attained had been only very partial; in the latter it was far more complete; yet those responsible for the insensate experiment, it seems to me, were only less to be congratulated on their achievement than was their luckless victim.

Chapter Seventeen

MALIGNANT malaria of this particular type, it
is popularly supposed by the natives of the dis-
tracted heat-belt, is sent as a special dispensation—
by that Providence which notoriously tempers the
wind to the shorn lamb—for the chastening of the
otherwise insupportable energy of the white man.
Lacking some such salutary check as this imposes
upon the European's morbid appetite for toil—which
includes a desire to make all mankind partake, in
equal measure with himself, of a full share of work—
the tropics, it is thought, would speedily be rendered
unfit for habitation by the races whom Nature has
taught from the beginning to live by her aid, and,
so living, to idolize Ease. But malignant malaria is
one of Nature's watch-dogs, set to guard her shrine
and to punish intruders upon its peace. It seizes the
strongest in its jaws, shakes him till his teeth chat-
ter, and when it has had its will of him, casts him
aside, spent, shattered, feeble in mind and body, and
whimpering like a little child. Some—and their number is past all counting—are broken once and for all;
others gather themselves together after a space, and
carry on the struggle, albeit with a certain new so-
briety and caution; but let the victim be ever so ener-
getic, ever so full of vitality and force, he bears the
scars and the memory of that encounter with him to
his grave.

Saleh, in the natural course of things, ought not to
have been exposed to any such ordeal, and Nature,
in mistaking him for a white man, showed something
less than her usual perspicacity. The lad, in truth,

had no great store of superabundant energy and vitality of which to be purged. None the less, he suffered, not like a Malay, but like any other newly imported stranger. Nature, ruthless as is her wont, milked the manhood out of him with both her busy hands, racked him with aches and pains, shattered him with chills, scorched him with the fever fires, pursued him with despairing visions, and hag-rode him without mercy. All the men and women whom he had known in life, all the stories and legends that he had ever heard, all the sensations which he had experienced, all the facts which he had learned—but each one of these things contorted and distorted wonderfully—danced through his mind in a tangle of combinations, intricate, incongruous, inconsequent, monstrous, but informed throughout by a deadly but elusive logic. At times it would be Alice Fairfax, hideously transformed, her personality subtly interwoven with a complaint from a native chief, a severe pain in the head and back, a rudeness of Baker's and the *Pons asinorum,* proving with clarion din that the angles at the base of the color question are a pair of enormous boots in which two microscopic feet wander and lose their way. At other times the vision would change to some combination even more intricate, even more harassing—people, places, facts, inanimate objects, and even sensations welding together in ghastly, brain-stretching conglomerates, instinct with individuality and personality, strikingly human, yet torturingly inhuman and impossible. The barriers which divide the worlds of idea, sensation, and reality seemed to have been thrown down. The mind had become a wilderness overrun by hordes of unruly imaginings, masterless, panic-driven, maddened, and maddening;

but under all, trampled upon by all, spurned by all, tossed hither and thither restlessly, abided the agony of the fever-rent body, the travail of the fever-haunted soul. Also, through all the visions two arch-persecutors asserted their supremacy—the Horror of Effort and the Futility of Endeavor.

To the immense disgust of the medical officer, the parasites insisted upon carrying their master across the river, where they lodged him in his mother's house. A crowd of women filled the stuffy sickroom and rebreathed the exhausted air. They plastered Saleh's body with yellow turmeric and other messy concoctions. Prayers, charms, simples, and incantations were called into request, with a fine catholicity of faith, to aid the resources of the British pharmacopœia. There was also a general belief entertained at the court of Pĕlĕsu that Saleh's illness—the virulence of which demanded explanation—was due to the evil magic of a certain wizard of great repute who chanced to be among the number of the aggrieved peasants of the Bûyong Valley. Many and bitter, too, were the murmurings against the white men—for in the good old times, men recalled, the wizard would have suffered various and evil things until he had thereby been compelled to exorcise the familiar by whom, at his bidding, poor Saleh was manifestly possessed. This aspect of the case was discussed so frequently in the hearing of the patient that he got the idea interwoven with all the other inconsequences running riot in his fever-wearied brain, and more than once he called aloud upon the wizard by name, or in his ravings confused his own with the identity of the familiar. After this, what further proof was needed? The worst suspicions were confirmed, and Baker be-

gan to have much ado to keep the king, Tŭngku
Ampûan, and the courtiers quiet, and had to send word
to the police at Bûyong to guard the wizard closely,
since at this time his chances of dying a violent death
were extensive. Even chill-blooded Europeans are
apt to wax wrathful when the superstitions of others
frustrate the action of common sense; and to the
Malays of Pĕlĕsu the refusal of the white men to accept the proven fact of the guilt of the wizard appealed as the grossest and most mischievous piece of
superstition of which they had had any experience. If
Saleh had died, I think that the wizard would have
died too with surprising celerity, even though one or
more loyal people had to swing at a rope's end as the
price of their devotion to duty.

Saleh, however, did not die—and for this, perhaps,
the clean life which had been his for years may have
been partly responsible; but instead he crept back into
existence, still haunted by the twin demons which had
so possessed him while the fever held—the Horror of
Effort and the Futility of Endeavor.

Saleh had always been "slack" at the best of times,
but now all that there had ever been of energy in his
composition had been dredged out of him; and for
this, be it remembered, the race which puts energy
shoulder to shoulder with courage in the forefront of
the manly virtues, not Saleh, was responsible. It was
surely no fault of his, poor lad, that the white men,
in the course of the experiment of which he had been
the hapless victim, should have robbed him, among
other things, of his natural immunity to the climatic
influences of his native land.

Chapter Eighteen

I HAVE spoken of energy as a virtue, but reflection suggests a doubt as to how far that term can with accuracy be applied to it. A virtue, I take it, is a quality that can be brought into being in a man's soul in the course of that eternal conflict between the forces which Thomas à Kempis names *nature* and *grace*—a quality which, once generated, is thereafter capable of infinite development. If this definition be correct, it is clear that energy cannot be placed in the category of the virtues, since energy is merely a transmuted form of some existing force which, in one shape or another, has had its being since the Creation. In other words, virtue is a growth, energy an adaptation; the former is drawn from a limitless reservoir, the latter from a certain well-defined supply. The one may be produced in defiance of Nature; the other is a dole which Nature grants from her store of hoarded forces.

The point is interesting, because the possession of energy is the accident which will be seen principally to differentiate the people of the temperate zone from the people of the tropics; and the reason is not far to seek. In the temperate climates the ability of mankind to exist has depended upon the maintenance of an eternal, but on the whole successful, struggle with Nature. Nature has had to be pillaged to provide clothing, food, shelter; Nature has had to be overcome in a thousand ingenious ways to reduce her to servitude; Nature has been stern, inimical, waiting only for her opportunity to slay, and in the ages of man's earliest developments a constant watchfulness was necessary to ward off her blows and to frustrate her sinister designs. Farther north and farther south, in the arctic and antarctic regions, Nature has secured the victory and mankind has accepted defeat, has been eliminated, or has merely clung to life and to the frozen earth as lichen clings to a rock, an impotent parasite, powerless to mold or alter its unyielding habitat. In the tropics alone has Nature adopted the *rôle* of the great Mother, suckling her offspring tenderly, lavishing upon them her best in return for a minimum of languid effort, aiding them at every turn, and wooing them to idleness. In all their history, the peoples of the tropics have never been called upon to accept sustained exertion as the alternative of extinction. To the white man's thinking, sparing the rod, has gone far to spoil the child.

And there we have forthwith the whole key to the difference between the men of the temperate and the men of the tropical regions. The former, having found in the transmutation of natural forces into energy his only means of survival in his fight with Nature, has learned to make an idol of his preserver; the latter, having been taught to lean on Nature, to look to her for all his necessities, to claim her aid rather than to rely upon his own efforts, has learned to idolize ease. These widely divergent points of view have long ago become stereotyped, and are fused now into the innate characters of the peoples. The natives of the tropics and the natives of the temperate zones cherish ideals diametrically opposed one to the other: their sacrifices are burned in the shrines of rival and mutually inimical deities. Yet if the *summum bonum* sought by mankind from the beginning be the greatest happiness of the greatest number, then surely the apostles of ease, "on the hills like gods together," lying

> "beside their nectar, while
> the bolts are hurled
> Far below them in the valleys,"

are nearest to the achievement of the desired end. A divine discontent is undoubtedly the beginning of all progress, but who shall deny that it is for many the end of all happiness?

So think the Malays, typical children of the heat belt, and so also thought Saleh when he at last arose from his bed of sickness. He had sampled the work which the white men were doing in the land that was his by inalienable right, had sampled it in the office and in the field, and had found it little to his taste. Office work bored him, wearying his mind; field work tired him, putting upon his physical energy a strain greater than anything for which the history of his ancestors had made adequate preparation. He was not only a Malay, but a Malay *râja*—the breed which has been pampered by man, as the race has been pampered by Nature—and always he was conscious of the feeling that an indignity was put upon him when he was required to make an expenditure of energy, in obedience to the white men's will, for the better accomplishment of ends with which he increasingly felt himself to have but scant sympathy. "Why?" he asked himself

> "Why should we only toil, the
> roof and crown of things?"

Day by day his love for the Malaya which of old had existed before the white men came to break in upon

its æon-long sleep, grew and strengthened; but now
it was the peace, even more than the freedom from
foreign interference, which appealed to him. Even
white men, now and again, when the muscles of their
spirits have been worn slack by the long effort and
their souls are borne down with weariness, ask themselves the grim question, *Cui bono?* as they think upon
the unending toil in which in Asia they are engaged,
and find at such moments scant comfort in the answer.
Saleh asked it, too, and, unlike the white men whose
lives are devoted to the work they have in hand, had
no inducement to nail himself to a faith in the utility
of British endeavor. The twin demons which had
haunted his bed of sickness clung still to his skirts,
and Râja Pahlâwan Indut and Râja Haji Abdullah
fostered his discontent. Saleh could only see that
the white men had spoiled his life for him, that there
was no place for a Malayan râja, who desired to rule
as his fathers ruled aforetime, in the new scheme of
things which the English had evolved, and a keen
sense of injustice—keener far than it would have been
but for his training in England—fanned his hatred of
the present and his longings for a bygone time. He
was dropping back more and more into a Malay, and
into a Malay of royal birth and tradition. His sympathies were now wholly with the old order; and, surrounded by the monotonous peace which the white
men had imposed upon the land, it was not easy to re-
construct in imagination the evils, the horrors, and the
uglinesses of native rule from which that land had by
the same agency been freed.

Chapter *Nineteen*

EANWHILE Saleh accumulated some curious
experiences.

The girl Mûnah had helped to nurse him while he
lay sick in his mother's household, and after his recovery she renewed her former advances. Saleh had
learned to be pleased by her presence about him, and
was grateful to her for her kindness. When he
returned to his bungalow on the opposite bank of the
river, he missed her; and his parasites, who from the
first had felt something akin to shame on account of
their master's determined celibacy, urged him to take
the girl into his house. But Saleh, albeit many of
the impressions which he had received during his
sojourn in the Le Mesurier family were wearing thin,
had acquired certain prejudices (incomprehensible to
his *entourage*) of which he could by no means be rid.
The memory of Alice Fairfax, too, had stood hitherto
between him and every other woman's face, but now
the vision of Alice was fading. It is not in youth to
cherish a vain hope eternally. At the end of a few
weeks of indecision he made up his mind to marry the
girl—a step of no great moment in itself, since Muhammadan unions are dissolved without difficulty if
they prove to be unsatisfactory.

Accordingly, he sent for Râja Haji Abdullah and
asked him to celebrate the marriage. Râja Haji
hummed and hawed a great deal, showed symptons of
obvious uneasiness, and eventually referred Saleh to
his mother, to whose household Mûnah belonged and
in whose gift she was. But news of what was afoot
had already spread across the river, and when Saleh

entered his mother's room he found the place in great
disorder. Tŭngku Ampûan was screaming with rage.
Mûnah was in tears—very real tears, not only of mortification, but of pain; for Tŭngku Ampûan had been
practicing upon her some of the minor tortures which
it was the dream of that worthy woman to inflict upon
"that slut Jĕbah." Saleh himself was greeted with
virulent upbraidings.

"*Ya Allah! Ya Tûhan-ku!*" screamed Tŭngku Ampûan when the first spate of violence was expended.
"That a son of mine should so disgrace my house!
That he should thus smudge soot upon my face, soot
that may not be wiped away! That he should speak
of marriage with a wench such as this accursed
Mûnah! What have I done, what crime have I committed, that so great an infamy should befall me! *Ya
Allah! Ya Tûhan-ku! Ambûi! O ma!*"

Saleh was utterly bewildered.

"But what is it? What have I done?" he cried.

"It is not thee, my unhappy one, it is not thee!"
sobbed his mother. "It is this accursed girl who,
making use of magic and love potions, hath done us all
dishonor. She hath certainly taken advantage of the
opportunities conferred by thine illness, and thus it
is, beyond all doubt, that thou art this day devoured
by the 'madness'—madness of this hussy's making—
else surely thou hadst never dreamed of an act so
shameful as marriage with this Mûnah-thing, this
scrap left over from the dish whence many have
eaten!"

"But it was thee, mother, who in the beginning bade
me take this girl," protested Saleh. "In this court of
Pĕlĕsu, seemingly, a man may not live single and at
peace. The girl pleases me and I design to take her

to wife, if only to silence wanton tongues that weave
forever false stories about my name."

"*Ya Allah! Ya Tûhan-ku!*" cried Tŭngku Ampûan
in a species of despair. "Heard ye ever the like?
Take the girl if she pleases thee. Hang her on high,
sell her in a distant land, burn her with fire, souse her
with water, scorch her with the sunrays, do with her
what thou wilt—she and all her kind are thy property
from generation to generation! A thousand times
have I bidden thee take her; but *marry* her!!! *Ya
Allah Muhammad!*"

As of old, the baffling diversity of the point of view
which he owed to his English training and that of his
own people rose up as a barrier separating Saleh from
his kind. Too often, he realized, his right was their
wrong, his wrong their right. On this occasion, however, he was not prepared to compromise. Râja Haji
Abdullah had instructed him in the teachings of his
religion, and the lessons had not been taught in vain.
Saleh could see no sense in sinning when marriage
and divorce were such simple affairs and duly sanc-
tioned by the religious law. Therefore he held firmly
to his resolution, bribed a priest to perform the ceremony in his bungalow across the river and took
Mûnah to wife. His action caused a hideous scandal,
and the king and Tŭngku Ampûan alike were furious.
The latter even went the length of complaining to
Baker that Saleh had abducted one of her girls, and an
embarrassing explanation became necessary. Tŭngku
Ampûan was informed that the girl was a free agent
and that Saleh had married her legally. The latter
fact, it was piously supposed, would pour balm upon
her wounded feelings, whereas, of course, it was precisely this detail which was the occasion of her wrath.

Saleh suffered horribly during the whole transaction, and was conscious of a feeling of meanness, almost of treachery, because his action was upheld by the white men in defiance of native prejudice.

Mûnah, too, promptly took advantage of her new position to quarter hosts of indigent relatives upon Saleh, and the peace of the bungalow was broken. There was war to the knife between the new mistress and the parasites. A fresh set of vultures had fastened on to the carrion, and the "lice," as they frankly and expressively termed themselves, were nowhere. There was no holiday, however, for the victim.

The only remedy that could be found for the dishonor which Saleh's family had brought upon his house lay in his marriage to a wife of his own rank, and negotiations to this end were speedily set agoing. Now, in the vernacular, when some great domestic event is in progress in the royal household, the phrase used is "The king worketh," and considered as "work" it is in truth an extraordinary manifestation of energy. Languid pourparlers are protracted during weeks and weeks of indolent negotiation; still more languid preparations for the ceremonies are made during several ensuing months, the monotony being broken by periodical processions—the procession of water for the bathing of the bride and bridegroom, which is accompanied by much aquatic romping; the procession of the henna, for the staining of the toe and finger nails; the procession of rice, for the bridal banquet; and, finally, the procession of the bride and bridegroom themselves. The objects to be borne in procession are placed on enormous tinsel litters, under the weight of which fifty bearers stagger, and all the warriors of the court dance madly around and in advance of it with naked weapons brandished aloft, wild, excited faces, and shrill outcry. Later there is a banquet spread in the king's hall, and the whole population are fed at the royal charges, but the offerings which custom exacts render the business sufficiently profitable. Now, however, that loyalty finds no stimulus from fear, the expenditure is apt to exceed the receipts, greatly to the injury of the royal temper.

All these ceremonies took place duly, and every evening there was much gambling in the hall of state. The king was combining Saleh's marriage with the circumcision of little Tŭngku Anjang, his son by Che' Jĕbah, and the two half-brothers shared the honors of the occasion. Saleh threw himself into the enjoyment of the time with zest—it was all in a fashion a revival of the past, and there were moments when he found it possible to cheat himself into the illusion that Malaya was still as it of old had been. Even when he found himself decked out wonderfully in tinsel and gold ornaments, seated upon a vast litter surrounded by a dancing, whooping crowd of temporary maniacs, he was thrilled rather than embarrassed. Inherited memories seemed to stir in him and make the whole experience congenial. He had obtained three months' leave of absence for the purpose of celebrating his marriage, and the sight of Baker walking in the crowd and looking at his quondam assistant with amused eyes did not disturb him. To-day Baker was nobody in that throng, and he, Saleh, had come to his own for a space.

The girl selected to be his bride was a first cousin, a child of twelve, whom Saleh had never even seen. She was to him, and to most people apparently, the least important detail in the transaction. Saleh himself rather shirked the thought of her. He foresaw that she would bore him, and the memory of all that he had once dreamed that marriage might mean to him would arise to stab and torture him.

His marriage with Mûnah had not been a success. The palace-bred girl spoke to him quite openly, nay, boastfully, of her numerous amours, which she held to be so many proofs of her irresistible attractions, and Saleh would catch himself writhing with anger when he met any of the heroes of these love-affairs. There again the English half of him made unnecessary trouble, for Malays care nothing for the past of a woman. Their sole concern is with her present, and Mûnah, knowing this, made herself hateful in her husband's eyes when most bent upon exciting his admiration. She was extravagant, too, sought wit in pertness, was capricious, and had never acquired the habit of fidelity. Saleh knew—and the knowledge made him miserable—that he could not trust her for a moment, and that life in the palace had taught her to reduce deception to a fine art. The whole position was humiliating, and his knowledge of what purity in womanhood can be—such purity of thought and feeling as he had noted in Mrs. Le Mesurier and others of her kind—made it frankly intolerable.

Very soon Mûnah was divorced and replaced by another wife, married according to Muhammadan law, who presently was in her turn divorced. Once begun, the process was fatally easy to continue, and before the first twelvemonth of his stay at the court was ended, Saleh had been married and divorced four or five times, and was leading a life which, to a European, was indistinguishable from one of violent dissipation.

Marriage with his first royal wife, little Tŭngku

Mĕriam, wrought no change. The girl was a mere child, frightened out of her wits of Saleh, tongue-tied in his presence, without an idea seemingly in her little empty head. Though she was of his own class, and could "thee" and "thou" him publicly without offense, she was even less of a companion than the other women who passed in rapid succession through his household.

Saleh all this while, be it remembered, was obeying the letter of his creed. His sin, if sin there were, lay in the fact that he had allowed himself to be weaned from his ideal, the ideal which a marriage with such a girl as Alice Fairfax typified, yet it was not his fault that such a union had been denied to him by circumstances. The pathos of the whole position centered in the fact that he had been shown the light, had been taught to long for it unspeakably, and then had been shut out into the exterior darkness. Now, having seen the light, he knew that this indeed was darkness, and in it he found much weeping and gnashing of teeth.

Chapter   *Twenty*

FACILIS descensus Averni. At the end of five years, dating from the time of his return to Pĕlĕsu, there had been evolved a Saleh—the Saleh of the exterior darkness—very different to the sweet-tempered, light-hearted, careless youngster whom his friends in England had known and loved. The old Saleh had been full of health and boyish spirits, a bit lazy, it was true, but withal as "decent" a little fellow as one could wish to find in a long day's tramp. The new Saleh was prematurely aged by frequent attacks of fever and by an irregular life in a climate to whose eccentricities long years of absence had unaccustomed him. The easy good temper and the high spirits also had deserted him, for he felt himself to be the victim of a whole series of injustices, and the memory thereof made him sullen. He was beset, too, by cares and anxieties. His allowance, judged by British standards, was handsome, but those who fixed it had not taken into account the appetites of the parasites, male and female, who battened upon Saleh, the frequent calls upon his purse made by the borrowings of his mother and other relatives, the possibility of heavy gambling losses in Che' Jĕbah's house or the king's audience-hall, and the innate improvidence of a Malayan râja. He was up to his ears in debt, and was harassed and humiliated by the duns who, though they could not take civil action against him for the recovery of their money, made matters hot for him by petitions to the Resident, and subjected him to insults which, in the good old days, would have been punished by a violent death. Yet all the while the revenues of the state were enormous, and in Saleh's eyes these moneys were the property, not of the Government, but of his House. It was one injustice the more that, when the public treasuries were overflowing with wealth, he should be in daily difficulties about money matters.

The white men shook their heads over him. He was a hopeless young waster, they declared. He had been given every chance, had been trained and educated in England at great expense, had been set to learn in his own country the business of practical administration, had been afforded every opportunity of showing what capabilities he might possess, and in every direction he had signally and notoriously failed. There was not even a trace, they averred, that he repaid his teachers by exerting a salutary influence over his father or over any of his fellow-countrymen. After the manner of the English, they judged by results, making no very diligent search after causes, and did not attempt to look at things from Saleh's point of view, or to consider the enormous weight of the inherited tendencies and the shackling traditions wherewith the lad was handicapped. To them, given the initial fact of an English education, it was quite natural that young Saleh should be prepared to take up official life on the same low rung of the ladder as that which contented any other newly imported cadet. Also, the education aforesaid should, in their opinion, have fitted him for such work. They forgot that every one of the boys with whom he was expected to compete had generation upon generation of hard workers behind him to stiffen his character and steel his energies, while Saleh had for his forbears as many generations of indolent, pleasure-loving, self-indulgent, dissipated Malayan royalties. They forgot that the English youngsters had made a deliberate choice of the profession to which they were apprenticed, while Saleh's life had been ordered for him without any regard paid to his predilections or capabilities. They forgot, too, that while the last joined cadet could hope some day to become a British Resident, whose power and authority is well-nigh autocratic, Saleh could look forward only to filling the empty office of a Merovingian king. This was a closing of the gates upon ambition to one in whose veins ran the blood of hundreds of absolute rulers.

All these things the white men forgot, and so doing wrote Saleh down a "hopeless young waster"; but Saleh remembered, pondered them in his heart, brooded over them constantly, and, finding scant contentment in the present, fumed against the alien rule which had robbed the country of all that had made its history picturesque, his father of his sovereign power, and him of his birthright.

And all this while subtle influences were at work upon him. In Malayan lands we English have wrought some wonderful changes, have increased the wealth and well-being of the people enormously, have relieved them from evils and oppressions in number past all counting; but, given the character of the Malays, it were vain to hope that our rule will ever be universally popular. To begin with, it must be remembered that our hatred of injustice is largely a sentiment bred of training and hereditary transmission, that it is not shared in anything approaching equal measure by the Orientals whom we make it our business to relieve from grinding tyranny. A Malay will accept gross ill-treatment from his own chiefs with a philosophic calm quite baffling to the understanding of the average

European. In nine cases out of ten, far more indignation is excited in the white man who hears a tale of
cruel wrong than in the Malay who chances to be the
victim of such oppression. Similarly, the white man
attaches far more importance to the fact that our rule
has relieved a people of unbearable oppression than
is credited to it by the people themselves. Also, the
East is at once the land of very short and of very long
memories. The good that men have wrought does not
wait to be interred with their bones; it usually passes
into oblivion during their lifetime. Men who have
lived under the old *régime,* and under that which we
have established, speedily forget that life for them
was ever other in material security than it is to-day.
On the other hand, in a land where a discussion is
decided, not by the production of a new argument,
but by the quotation of an old wise saw, the Past ever
seems to overshadow the Present. Even those who
knew and suffered many evil things under native rule
dream fondly of the days that are gone, which after
all, were the brave days when they and all the world
were young. Tales of those lawless times are forever
on their lips, and the young men, shackled by the
monotony which the coming of the white men has imposed, chafe and fume because their world has been
marred for them, and fall to dreaming dreams that
the past may be made to live again. The old men forget and, looking backward, see all things through the
glamour that hovers about the youth of every one of
us: the young men, chafing at restraint, see through
the old men's eyes, and know naught of the misery of
those days when their forbears were helpless as driven
cattle before râja and chief.

But of late years there had been yet another in-

fluence at work, the which was already making itself
manifest throughout the littoral of northern Africa, in
Arabia and the Sudan—the influence of the Sanusi
Brotherhood. About the time of the Crimean War a
certain Saiyid—a descendant, that is, of the Prophet
Muhammad—retired, after many wanderings, to a
little oasis in the Sahara. During a long lifetime, he
had initiated a movement for the reform of Islâm upon
purer lines, and had preached as a first tenet that the
temporal subjugation of the followers of Muhammad
by the Infidel is an abomination in the sight of God
and man. Shortly afterward he died; but his sons and
their sons after them trod in his footsteps, and the
organization which he originated, for a space, flour-
ished exceedingly. Mecca, the annual resort of thousands upon thousands from every quarter of the Muhammadan world, was made the center of their propa-
ganda, and during the decades that followed millions
of pilgrims were initiated into the Brotherhood and
returned to their homes to spread its tenets broadcast
through their native lands. For a time it seemed that
the Muhammadan world was becoming honeycombed,
root and branch, by the Sanusi Brotherhood, and that
in its tenets had perhaps been found at last the cement
destined to weld the True Believers into a single,
cohesive and formidable whole. The leaders of the
organization, moreover, appeared to possess in unusual
measure the rare virtue of patience; to be prepared
to devote to the perfection of their plans the lifetime
of more than one generation; to be bent upon holding
their hands and biding their time until Islâm could
strike like one man with paralyzing effect. Their
disciples were not always equally prudent, and many
sporadic outbreaks of what Europeans term "fanatic-

ism" among Muhammadan peoples who submitted unwillingly to an alien yoke, were thought to be trace-
able to the influence of the Brotherhood. Nowhere,
save in northern Africa, did its doctrines make a
stronger appeal or take a firmer hold than among the
Muhammadans of the Malayan Archipelago whose
autonomy had been so completely reft from them by
the white intruders from the West.

In the fulness of time, the hopes centered by its adherents in the Sanusi Brotherhood were destined to
prove illusive. The extraordinary heterogeneity of
race, of nationality, and of material interests which
exists among Muhammadans has so far rendered any
really effective Pan-Islamic cohesion, such as that of
which the Saiyid and his adherents dreamed, impossible of realization; and though the ideal survives, its
translation into actuality seems to be as remote to-day
as it was in the time of Saleh and his counsellors.
Then, however, success was thought to be not only
possible, but imminent, and Râja Haji Abdullah and
Râja Pahlâwan Indut were forever at his elbow to
feed such dreams, to quicken his energies and his
resentment, to rowel his fanaticism, and to hound him
on to action. They were both men of a certain age,
and for them time was slipping by at a desperate pace.
Malay-like, they, having dreamed dreams, could see no
step between a magnificent conception and its immediate attainment. In a word, they lacked the prime
quality of the head of the As-Sanusi Brotherhood, the
quality which has made his organization what it is
and that makes the man himself so dangerous—the
restraint which knows how to wait. Moreover, they
and Saleh were convinced that all the youth of Pĕlĕsu
was at their backs.

Chapter Twenty-one

THE crisis came, as such things are apt to come,
very suddenly.

Saleh was at that time in charge of a district consisting of a big river which falls into the Pĕlĕsu on its
right bank at a distance of about a hundred and twenty
miles from its mouth. It formed an appanage to a
much larger district ruled by an Englishman named
Wilson, to whom Saleh was directly responsible.
Wilson himself bore the reputation of "a glutton for
work," and one of his preoccupations for many months
past had been an attempt to get a measure of steady
toil out of Saleh. He had not been uniformly successful, and there was little love lost between the two
men.

Saleh was never quite clear how it was that the mistake in his accounts originated. Persistent carelessness upon his own part, aided possibly by dishonesty
on that of one or more of his Malay clerks, was probably responsible; but upon a certain day he made the
discovery that he was some five hundred dollars short
in his cash.

He had just concluded the annual collection of land
rents in his district, and there were nearly six thousand dollars in the safe. He had already anticipated
the greater portion of his next month's allowance—in
itself a serious irregularity—and he had no means of
making good the deficiency. The visit of an audit
clerk was to be expected at any moment.

At first Saleh was in despair. Once more he had
failed, and had failed hideously. The thought of the
open shame to which the incident would expose him

made him wince and tingle. The prospect of the sort
of interviews which awaited him with Wilson and
with the Resident made him squirm and fume in anticipation. And then anger, the fierce, unreasoning anger
of the Malay, and the old hatred of a manifest injustice, the keenness of which was due to his English
upbringing, came to his aid. After all, was not this
missing money the property of the rightful rulers of
Pĕlĕsu? Was it not his, *his*, to have to hold, to do
with as he chose? What claim had the white men to
it, the white men who would presently call him to
account because of its loss? In imagination he saw
himself publicly disgraced by those same white men,
spoken to, in the presence of his people, it might be,
in language which hot, royal blood could ill brook.
relegated thereafter to contemptible obscurity as a
tool which had been tried and found worthless. Once
before, in a Richmond ballroom, when the conversation of a pair of lovers, overheard by chance, had
seemed to knock the bottom out of his world, Saleh
had had his soul whipped into that turmoil of excitement which, among men of his race, produces the
âmok-runner: once again this inherited madness
gripped him, but this time there was no Jack Norris
at hand to exorcise the demon by the force of his
strong, calm presence. Instead, at his very elbow was
Râja Pahlâwan Indut, a warrior whom experience had
made expert in the morbid psychology of his kind, to
play upon his emotions and his passions, upon the
angry, tortured soul of the lad, as a skilled musician
plays upon his chosen instrument. The two sat com-
muning together far into the night. Wild words were
spoken, wild counsel was given and taken, wild
schemes were framed, wild plans were laid. Then, a

little before the dawn was due, Râja Pahlâwan arose and presently melted away into the district.

Thereafter Saleh spent a miserable ten days. He watched the bend in the bank downriver, expecting every moment to see a boat bearing either Wilson or the dreaded audit clerk loom into view. He was torn by agonizing vacillation. At one moment he was for surrender, for making a clean breast of everything to Wilson, and for accepting the consequences of what had occurred, let them be never so unpalatable. At others he was goaded to fury by the thought of the unmerited injustice of which he was the victim; and then again he would recall the fact that Râja Pahlâwan had gone forth upon a mission which had for its object the raising of the green flag of the Prophet in the land of Pělĕsu, and that he, Saleh, could not now withdraw without betraying his friend. His brain, his whole being, were in a turmoil; he could neither eat nor sleep. His moods varied hourly, now plunging him into depths of despair, now elating him with a wild, savage joy at the prospect of battle to be done for the rights of which the white men had robbed him, now reducing him to a sullen torpor, again goading him to the manifestation of a half-delirious hilarity.

Upon the tenth night, as he lay wide-eyed upon his sleeping-mat, he was startled by the sound of a sudden, fierce outbreak of rifle-fire. Tingling from head to foot, and anticipating he knew not what, he leaped to his feet, seized a native broadsword in his hand, and, followed by half a dozen of his people, plunged out into the darkness. Loud cries and an occasional shot sounded from the direction of the police station; in the Chinese shops of the long street bordering the river bank he could see lights passing to and fro, could hear the noise made by the inmates as they hastily fortified the doors, and the keening of frightened women. As he ran, he saw a great, crimson tongue of flame leap upward into the night, licking hungrily at the darkness.

The police station was distant half a mile from the bungalow and by the time Saleh arrived upon the scene the building was a roaring bonfire, round which danced a host of armed Malays waving their weapons aloft, yelling their battle cry, their faces seen in the red fire-glare strained and savage with excitement, their figures eloquent of the mad lust of fighting whereby they were possessed.

Râja Pahlâwan Indut, who entertained certain doubts as to whether, at the last moment, Saleh would nerve himself to break finally with the old life, had taken it upon himself to go a step beyond the plan prearranged between them. He had delivered a successful night attack upon the police station, whose occupants, grown careless through long immunity, had not the faintest notion that any danger threatened them; had butchered the garrison of five-and-twenty Sikhs before they could wake from their sleep or reach for their weapons; had removed all the arms and ammunition which the place contained; and then had set the building in a blaze. All had been done in the name of Râja Muhammad Saleh, the leader of Young Pĕlĕsu, the Champion of Islâm, the Scourge of the Infidel, the Pretender to the throne of his Forbears! Râja Pahlâwan, as he knew full well, had not only burned the police station, for Saleh's boats had gone up to the angry heavens also on that tongue of flame!

Chapter Twenty-two

AND now the men of the war party were possessed by demons. Those among them who in the
old days had "bathed them in the bullets and the
smoke"—as the Malay phrase has it—felt youth, fierce
and reckless, revive within them, the youth which they
had thought had been forever taken from them. The
young men saw in the bloody doing of this night a
materialization of a thousand dreams. One and all
were beside themselves with an intoxication of excitement, so masterless and savage that its effects resembled those of a demoniacal possession.

A group of youngsters, close to Saleh, were dancing and yelling around the bodies of three half-naked
Sikhs, plunging their daggers into them near the
region of the heart, and licking the blades with howls
and outcries. This, which is the last trace of prehis-
toric cannibalism that still lingers among the Malays,
is analogous to the practice of blooding a boy at the
death of his first fox; but the sight caused in Saleh a
keen revulsion of feeling. What were the unknown,
savage forces which he had unwittingly let loose?
How should he curb them? Whither would they lead
him?

There was no question of governing them now, for
the war party was beyond all human power of control.
Half a dozen of the older and saner men grouped themselves about Saleh, at the bidding of Râja Pahlâwan,
for a Malayan râja of his rank is not suffered to take
a personal part in battle, and then the mob of scally-
wags rushed headlong down the village street. Saleh
stormed and shouted, commanded them to hold their

hands, would have thrown himself before them in his impotent desire to restrain them, but those about him clung to him with respectful vigor and would not let him go. For the rest, he spoke and shouted to deaf ears.

In a moment the hounds of war, which so long had slept in Pĕlĕsu, were let loose upon the Chinese shops. The gambling and opium farm, the biggest building in the place, was stormed and looted in an instant; the other shops were pillaged and plundered without mercy; Saleh saw men, ay, and even little male children, struck down ruthlessly while they pleaded and groveled for mercy. They were infidels, these Chinese, and this was a *jehad*, a holy war, in which infidel women might be carried away into bondage, but the males of the accursed people must be exterminated with a biblical completeness. In an hour the prosperous little settlement was a ruin; in an hour and a half it was a bonfire; before the dawn it was an unsightly cinder. The money in the Government treasury was secured by Râja Pahlâwan, who knew that the sinews of war would be required; and an hour after daybreak the war party, its numbers swelling every moment by young recruits from the neighboring villages, melted once more into the forest.

Saleh knew that his boats had been burned. He was the nominal leader of this band of outlaws, and he had no alternative but to go with them. For the future, he realized, his lot must be shared with them, but once again there was a bitter disillusionment in his heart. It had all been so different from anything which he had conceived, imagined. From the point of view of Râja Pahlâwan the attack had been most eminently successful. There had been some slaughter and much loot;

the young men had been blooded; the whole force would derive a fortifying confidence from that night's work; it was a fateful beginning of an epoch-making war, such as proved that Allah and his Prophet were on the side of the children of Islâm. But to Saleh, this, his latest experience, was fraught with woeful disappointment. It had held nothing that was uplifting or inspiring; it had called for the display of no valor; it had excited no emotions that were not mean, squalid, and brutal. It had not been *fighting*, as he had pictured it to himself in imagination. It had begun with the treacherous murder of five-and-twenty Sikhs, which had been followed by unspeakable rites performed over their corpses; by the indiscriminate and cowardly slaughter of a hundred defenseless Chinese; by the lawless looting of private and public property; and now the assailants were sneaking off into the forest like the blood-stained thieves they were. The Past, looked at through the glamour of romance—the fierce unfettered Past of a thousand stories—had appealed to him with a wonderful force; now that it had been revived and had been made actual in the Present, it filled him with horror, disgust, and shame. Indeed, indeed the English had robbed him of many things.

Chapter Twenty-three

NOW it so happens to my countrymen, in the East and out of it, that the very last thing they expect is ordinarily the thing that happens. The holy war, led by Tŭngku Muhammad Saleh, was one of these things. This meant that the Government in Pĕlĕsu was not in a position to take the offensive until several weeks had elapsed, and that the insurgents were given more law than was useful to anybody. Wilson came up river in his boat, practically without escort, as soon as news of the occurrence reached him; but he was fired upon from the jungle on the banks, two or three of his boatmen were injured, and he himself had no alternative but to beat a hasty retreat. He tried to open up communication with Saleh by letter, but in this he failed. Râja Pahlâwan Indut made it his business to prevent any outside influences being brought to bear upon his reputed leader. Then Wilson stockaded his own station and waited for reinforcements from Kuâla Pĕkâra.

Meanwhile the insurgents were in undisturbed possession of the Pûlas Valley, the valley which had been Saleh's administrative district, and the ignorant peasants, mindful of the welfare of their kindred and their property, and persuaded that the rule of a Râja of the royal house had come again, flocked to the green standard with the docility of sheep. And, indeed, for a space the old days *had* returned. For the insurgents the hitherto omnipotent white men had ceased to exist, save as enemies who were in a fair way to be severely drubbed; the peasants were once more as driven cattle before the followers of a prince;

the old lawlessness, the old carelessness of the rights of the weaker, revived with a new strength due to the reaction consequent upon long suppression. The hatred of injustice, which the white men had implanted in Saleh, blazed up daily, almost hourly, at some act of his followers, but he was powerless to control them. He began to understand, as he never before had understood, why native rule, as it of old existed, had been a thing intolerable in the eyes of the English. Too late he was realizing the nature of the justification upon which is based the usurpation of authority by the white men in Malayan lands. Also, when he thought upon the might of England despair would seize him. At the best, it seemed to him now, he was leading a forlorn hope. Yet he felt no desire to withdraw. The hatred of life, which in his people leads not to suicide, but to *amôk*-running, possessed him. He had no wish to live, but he was passionately determined to sell his life as dearly as he might.

Messages had been sent to chiefs all over the country calling upon them in Saleh's name to rise against the white men, but the response made had been feeble. The chiefs preferred to await events, to see how the cat would jump, and once more the paralyzing want of cohesion, which always frustrates attempts at concerted action among Malays, foredoomed the outbreak to early failure. But though there was no general rising in Saleh's favor throughout the state, a wide sympathy was felt for him by men who recalled that he was his father's son, a prince to whom they were bound by ties of hereditary loyalty. For their own well-being they hesitated to throw in their lot with him; but the memory of a decade and a half of peace enjoyed and benefits reaped under British rule did not

suffice to induce the natives to show themselves active
supporters of the representatives of the new *régime*.
Here and there a youngster, more hot-blooded than his
fellows, slipped away to join the insurgents, and the
good wishes of his friends and relatives went with
him; but for the rest, Saleh's people were prepared to
afford him none save negative assistance. They would
not help the white men, they would even go the length
of delaying their preparations and of putting obstacles
secretly in their way, but that was the limit of the personal risk which they were willing to incur. Even the
call of Muhammadan to Muhammadan, of folk of the
As-Sanusi Brotherhood to their brethren, fell on deaf
ears. It was well known that this *jehad* was not the
holy war which the saiyid had foretold, that Saleh
and Râja Pahlâwan Indut had raised the green standard prematurely, of their own motion, without orders
from the head of the Brotherhood. If victory lay for
a space with them, then the wild fire of a holy war
might perhaps spread throughout the state; but for
the present Pĕlĕsu was content to wait. Even the
young men who had dreamed of the old days and had
thought that they longed mightily for their return
when that return seemed to be impossible, began of a
sudden to count up the cost of unsuccessful rebellion.
Râja Pahlâwan Indut appealed to their imaginations,
and Saleh was the scion of their royal house. Young
blood and their Malayan hearts urged them to join in
the struggle; but the large measure of material pros-
perity which they had gotten furnished a ballast of
saner counsels. The vast majority saw wisdom in a
prudent waiting upon events.

Meanwhile, Saleh was finding himself once more the
Merovingian king, with Râja Pahlâwan as his Mayor

of the Palace, as completely under tutelage as ever
was a Malayan râja to the British Resident appointed
to the charge of his state. Everything was done in his
name, for that name lent force to the cause, but often
enough even the formality of consulting him had not
previously been observed; almost as often the thing
done was to him an abomination. In warfare Râja
Pahlâwan Indut was an expert; his reputation for
valor and strategy stood high in the land; his word
carried weight and authority with his fellows; Saleh
was required to be present as a symbol of Malayan
royalty, to do what he was advised, and to keep out of
personal danger. His life, not his individual leadership, was precious to the cause.

After a fortnight spent—Saleh would have said
"wasted"—in preparations, the mustering of the cowed
peasants of the valley, the building of a large stockade in the center of a rice swamp at a place called
Ulu Pĕnyûdah, where Saleh's headquarters were established, and the collection of mountains of supplies,
Râja Pahlâwan Indut led off a rabble of some five hundred men to make an attack upon Wilson's fortified
post at Kuâla Pûlas. Saleh pleaded hard to be allowed
to go with the war party, but the old men who now
formed his council would not hear of it. Accordingly,
he remained behind with the women and children, the
impedimenta, and a strong force to guard him. He
felt like a prisoner, as though he had lost, not recovered, his liberty; his position was to him at once
ignominious and shameful, and he was rent by an
agony of suspense.

The attack failed badly. Wilson had had ample time
in which to strengthen his defenses and to complete
his arrangements; the surprise, so successful in the

night assault on the police station, could not be repeated; the charge of fifty youths, intoxicated by
excitement, enthusiasm, and fanaticism, and led in
person by Râja Pahlâwan, was met by a withering fire
from behind the government stockade, and an attempted siege was put an end to by the arrival of
large reinforcements from Kuâla Pĕkâra. With those
reinforcements came Saleh's old friend Jack Norris,
who, on account of his intimate knowledge of Pĕlĕsu
and its people, had been sent to take charge of the state
in this hour of stress—Craster, the Resident, being
absent on leave, and his *locum tenens* being considered
too inexperienced to grapple successfully with the
emergency.

It was a disorderly and woebegone-looking mob that
straggled into Saleh's stockade when the retreat from
Kuâla Pûlas had been made, and the tale they had to
tell was a sorry story. These men, who had been so
intoxicated and uplifted by a facile victory, were cast
into the depths of despondency by the first check.
The sight of them filled Saleh with an angry disgust
and contempt.

But the news which touched him most closely was
the coming of Jack Norris. Mentally he contrasted
the grip and the grit, the calm, keen force of the man,
with the feeble qualities of the men about him. What
chance had any of them, he thought, against him?
Also the re-entry of Jack Norris into his life made
him plumb suddenly with an intense self-hatred the
depths to which he had fallen since that day so long
ago on board the P. & O. steamer at the Albert Docks.
Old memories crowded upon him and set him to the
weary task of reliving in imagination the past five
years, noting each failure that marked, as it were with

a tombstone on the grave of dead hopes, every stage
of that woeful progress. And yet, looking back with
the clear eyes of one who believes himself to be very
near to death, Saleh could not see how events could
have been shaped by him into a mold other than that
which they had taken. From first to last circumstances had been against him. At one time it was the
part of him which had been developed by his training
in England that had led to his undoing; at another it
was the Malay in him that had betrayed him into paths
whence there was no return. He had never had a
chance, never had a chance! He had been handicapped
from the outset by his birth and breeding, handicapped
yet more cruelly, because wantonly, needlessly, fruit-
lessly, by the folly which had tried so vainly to turn
him into the likeness of an Englishman. He saw himself, like Muhammad's coffin, suspended betwixt earth
and heaven—unfitted by training to be a Malay râja,
unsuited by nature to be an Englishman—a hybrid, a
waif, an outcast, and now, alas, an outlaw! For it was
to this that the long tale of mistakes had brought
him—to be the leader of a band of ragamuffins, whose
savagery sickened and appalled him, and to be fighting a futile fight against the man who had been to him
his best friend.

Chapter Twenty-four

NORRIS did not allow any grass to grow under
his feet. He knew with what rapidity the flame
of insurrection can spread at times in Oriental lands;
he remembered the reputation for pugnacity and lawlessness which the people of Pĕlĕsu had borne twenty
years earlier, when he had filled the post of political
agent at the king's court; he was watching the growth
of the As-Sanusi Brotherhood throughout Malaya
with keen anxiety, recognizing in it a new force, the
effect of whose operation remained yet to be determined. All things combined to make delay fatal.
From the first, too, he had excellent information. Of
old he had known, or had been known by, every man,
woman, and child in the state, and had won for himself
a name among the natives as a good man to deal with
and a bad man to cross. Now old acquaintances seemed
to spring out of the ground on every side, ready to aid
him with news, with transport, with men. Wilson
could not understand the sudden transformation
wrought in his people, who, a few days earlier, had
been such sluggards in the white man's cause, but in
truth the reasons were simple enough. The abortive
attack on Kuâla Pûlas had dealt a severe blow to the
prestige of Râja Pahlâwan Indut and had shown the
natives that Saleh's was, from the outset, a lost cause.
Now the rail-sitters were scrambling down hastily
upon the Government side of the fence, and were eager
to obliterate the memory of past lukewarmness by
present zeal. Also the coming of Jack Norris had
impressed the popular mind with the notion that the

Government meant business and that that business would now be done with thoroughness.

Norris's force moved swiftly up the Pûlas Valley, partly by river, partly by land, sweeping all before it, meeting with only a fitful and sporadic resistance, losing a considerable number of men in ambushes, but suffering nothing to check its steady advance. The villages were mostly deserted, and showed signs of the evil things which they had suffered during the six weeks that had seen the resurrection of native rule. At every stage of the journey fugitives joined them in shoals, for Saleh's supporters were melting away like snow under a strong sun. It was nearing crop time and the peasants were anxious to get back to their fields; the month and a half during which they had once more been at the mercy of a Malayan râja and his followers had caused them to accumulate a number of unenviable experiences; moreover Saleh's cause was now, in the eyes of the blindest, a forlorn hope.

Saleh witnessed the defection of his people with a species of cold despair. Their fickleness, their lack of continuity of purpose, their inability to fight an uphill fight sturdily and with constant hearts, the speed with which adversity cooled their fiery enthusiasm, all filled him with disgust. These things seemed to seal the race to which he belonged with the curse of Reuben: "Unstable as water, thou shalt not excel."

In Râja Pahlâwan Indut (Râja Haji Abdullah, prudent soul, had decided not to join the force until the turn events were likely to take was more clearly indicated) the wholesale desertion roused fury and rage which seemed to threaten apoplexy. He raved through the camp like one possessed by devils, cursing, exhorting, trying to shame his followers into fidelity, seeking, in vain, to inspire them with courage and constancy; but all his efforts were fruitless. Every hour saw the number of the insurgents dwindling apace. At last, even he was forced to admit that the game was lost. Norris's force was distant barely half a dozen miles from Saleh's stockade at Ulu Pĕnyûdah; the bulk of several of the parties sent out to lay ambushes and arrest his progress had deserted incontinently to the white men. On the morrow he would be at the doors of the stockade, and only a handful of Saleh's adherents remained to man the defenses.

Râja Pahlâwan, glowering and fuming, explained these things to Saleh and pointed with his chin, Malay fashion, in the direction of the forest, which rose in a vast, somber wall half a mile across the grazing-grounds.

"When the big house is untenable, the little house avails: when the house prop snaps, one must be content to substitute a rough-hewn pole," he said, quoting a proverb of his people. "We must get us to the jungle yonder. There alone lieth safety. The white men will follow, but they will never catch us. These rotten-livered folk who will not stand by us will yet aid us to hide and to escape. In the end, Allah being willing, we shall win free of this land of Pĕlĕsu and in exile find safety."

But Saleh would have naught of such counsel. This futile attempt to raise the green standard of the Prophet, and, rallying the warriors of Pĕlĕsu about it, to drive the white folk from the land, had been yet another, and his greatest, failure; but it should be his last. The crowning ignominy, he felt, would be to seek safety in flight ere he had struck so much as a blow with his own hand in the war which was of his making. Also, he had no further use for life. He had no place amid either the new conditions or the old. It remained only to ring down the curtain.

Finding him fixed in his resolve, Râja Pahlâwan, albeit cursing, not for the first time, the teaching of the devils by which the white men had caused his prince to be possessed, decided on his part to make a virtue of necessity. His code of chivalry forbade the idea of desertion. He would stand by Saleh, and perhaps a score of his followers would do the like. Those who desired to depart were set free to follow their inclination; the men who remained swore on the Kurân to abide with Saleh while life still was in him.

Then grimly they set about preparing for the fight which, they felt, was to be the last that many of them would ever see.

Chapter Twenty-five

ULU PENYUDAH is a compact village, situated
in the heart of a valley shaped like a horse-shoe,
inclosed by jungle-covered hills. The Pěnyûdah, a
little sparkling stream, barely two feet in depth,
tumbles out of the forest and chatters down the valley,
tossing a glistening mane of splashing, broken water.
To the right and the left rice fields and grazing-
grounds, dotted sparsely with tiny villages set upon
little hills under the shade of cocoanut palms, spread
away to the edge of the lowering forest. The place is,
as it were, a green oasis of cultivation and clearing in
the broad desert of woodland. It was in the village of
Ulu Pěnyûdah, on the right bank of the stream, and
surrounded by wide rice swamps, that Saleh had his
stockade.

Much labor had gone to the strengthening of that
place. The earthworks were from fifteen to twenty
feet in thickness, faced and surmounted by a high
wooden stockade, cunningly loopholed. Flanking
caponiers abutted at each angle and commanded each
wall; two strong fences had been raised without the
stockade at distances of fifteen and twenty-five feet,
respectively, encircling the whole, and the intervening
spaces were sown thickly with calthrops, and mined
with pitfalls, each harboring a murderously sharpened
stake. The deep mud of the rice swamps formed an
outer and final line of defense. It was, Norris saw at
a glance, a villainous place to attempt to rush.

He had three six-pounder guns with him, and these
he posted on low hills on three sides of the stockade.
He also, during the night of his arrival, threw up a

dozen small earthworks to protect the pickets which he placed at the edge of the rice swamp in such a manner as to cut off all means of retreat for those within the defenses. Then, these preparations completed, he wrote to Saleh explaining that the latter was hopelessly surrounded and out-numbered, advising surrender, promising an amnesty, and winding up with a personal appeal in the name of old times in England and the friendship which had subsisted between them. He also begged Saleh, for old sake's sake, to agree to meet him and to talk things over, giving his word of honor that no unfair advantage should be taken of him if he should consent.

Saleh pondered over that note with tears in his eyes. The references to the old life in England and the memories which he and Norris shared in common, touched him nearly, but they awoke in him a passionate self-pity, blended with a deep self-hatred that only served to put the seal upon his resolve. The note which he returned—surely the queerest document that ever found its way out of an insurgent stockade in Asia—was scrawled with ink made from lamp-black and a pen improvised from a reed. It ran as follows:

"DEAR MR. NORRIS,—Thank you for your kind letter. I am sorry to give so much trouble, but I cannot accept your terms. I often remember the old times you write of and I think my heart is broken. I will come and see you to-night. Good-by, and you must say good-by to everybody for me. It really has not all been my fault, though all this fighting is all my doing and nobody else's. You must tell Mrs. Le Mesurier and the others that I was not all bad, not really, I don't think sending me to England to be

educated was a good plan.   Good-by again.
"Yours,
MUHAMMAD SALEH."

"Poor little beggar," said Norris, as he read these lines, and there was something like a lump in his throat. "More sinned against than sinning, of course, but I wish I knew what he means. He declines to accept my terms, but says he will see me to-night. I wonder when and how he will come."

Chapter Twenty-six

AND this was the manner of Saleh's coming.
The Malayan night had shut down and from a velvet heaven the stars blinked sleepily. The forest half a mile distant across the grazing-grounds sent out its dropping chorus of night-song—the hum of insects, the gurgling call of tree-frogs, the occasional strident cry of an agrus pheasant, the hoot of an owl, and once in a while the grumpy trumpeting of an elephant or the startled bark of a deer. Coolness had come with the darkness, a coolness that wooed to slumber, and the very earth, rustling ever so faintly under the slow-moving breezes, seemed to be stretching itself in its sleep. To keep awake amid such universal somnolence was a veritable outrage upon the intentions of nature.

So thought Ram Singh, the Sikh sentry at the entrance to Norris's camp, as, half dozing, he leaned upon his rifle and listened to the soft splashing of the frogs in the neighboring swamp. They were very active of a sudden, those frogs, but he was too weary, too drowsy, too inert to take much note of them. Presently he caught himself up into painful wakefulness. His rifle had nearly fallen from his hands, and, as in a vision, he had seemed to see a dim figure draw itself out of the rice swamp just ahead of him and creep into the bushes on his right. Was it really something, or merely a figment of a dream? Stepping clumsily, after the manner of his kind, he tramped along his beat in the direction of the bushes. Something moved in the scrub, and "Who goes dar?" cried Ram Singh.

"Friend!" came the prompt reply in an English voice, and as the sentry, reassured, lowered the muzzle of his rifle, something wet and warm leaped suddenly upon him and a *kris* was plunged into his heart. Ram Singh fell to the ground in a limp heap, with a thud and a rattle of his accouterments, and at once the peace of the night was broken by the ear-piercing Malayan yell, *"Amok! Amok! Amok!"*

A lithe yet thickset figure stooped above the fallen Sikh, withdrew the dagger which had done its work, and flitted like a bat into the sleeping camp, and again the stillness was broken stridently by that fierce out-cry, *"Amok! Amok! Amok!"*

The camp, rudely awakened, was humming like a disturbed hive of bees. Men reaching hurriedly for their weapons were struggling to their feet and tumbling from under the lean-to sheds beneath which they had been lying—bearded Sikhs, brawny Pathans, angry little Malays, and alert white men. That shadow, carrying death in its hand and still pealing its war-cry, flung out of the gloom and precipitated itself upon a knot of Sikhs who, crawling clumsily from below a palm-leaf shelter, were hopelessly entangled with one another. Swiftly the knife rose and fell, doing its work with rending wounds, and its bearer, rushing onward like a mad dog, paused not to examine his handiwork, but plunged deeper and deeper into the camp.

As Norris leaped out of his hut, a pistol in his hand, a star-shell burst overhead and the earth for a minute was illuminated wonderfully. Jack saw the *âmok*-runner, his head thrown back, his face, livid in the bluish glare, strained heavenward, his right arm, blood-stained to the elbow, rising and falling, the whole figure a picture of the delirium of savage wrath, of the intoxication of that excitement to which the Malays, beyond all other people, are subject. A pair of short fighting drawers clothed the lower limbs, a sleeveless linen jacket fitted the bust closely, there was a huddle of *sârong* about the waist, and a headkerchief was knotted round the head, shaggy black locks escaping from it and streaming behind as the man ran headlong. A little Malay, weaponless and an incarnation of panic, ran from his pursuit, squealing with terror. All this Norris saw in a flash. Then three rifles spoke at once. The *âmok*-runner was suddenly arrested in mid-career; shuddered, as a steam-launch shudders through all its length when brought to a standstill by collision with a hidden rock; the *kris* fell from the nerveless hand; and the figure pitched forward on to its right shoulder. As it fell, the star-shell aloft was extinguished.

"Bring a light!" cried Norris, and his voice was vibrating with emotion. The face of the *âmok*-runner had been strange to him, but in his heart there was a haunting fear. Had not Saleh said that he would visit him that night?

A hurricane lamp was speedily produced, and by its light Jack Norris gazed down upon the still form of the thing which had once been Saleh. Fixed upon the face was the expression which it had worn at the moment of death. The lips were drawn back over the gums, exposing the locked teeth, the facial muscles were taut and strained, the cheekbones stood out prominently, but in the glazed eyes there was still a light of fierce joy. The gay garments in which the lad was clothed were drenched with swamp water and stained with the slime through which he had crawled.

"It's Saleh, poor little wretch!" cried Jack, and there was a catch in his voice. "May God forgive us for our sorry deeds and for our glorious intentions!"

To which I say, "Amen!"

THE END

Some other Oxford Paperbacks for readers interested in Central Asia,
China and South-East Asia, past and present

CAMBODIA

GEORGE COEDES
Angkor

MALCOLM MacDONALD
Angkor and the Khmers*

CENTRAL ASIA

PETER FLEMING
Bayonets to Lhasa

ANDRE GUIBAUT
Tibetan Venture

LADY MACARTNEY
An English Lady in Chinese
Turkestan

DIANA SHIPTON
The Antique Land

C.P. SKRINE AND
PAMELA NIGHTINGALE
Macartney at Kashgar*

ERIC TEICHMAN
Journey to Turkistan

ALBERT VON LE COQ
Buried Treasures of Chinese
Turkestan

AITCHEN K. WU
Turkistan Tumult

CHINA

All About Shanghai: A Standard
Guide

HAROLD ACTON
Peonies and Ponies

VICKI BAUM
Shanghai '37

ERNEST BRAMAH
Kai Lung's Golden Hours*

ERNEST BRAMAH
The Wallet of Kai Lung*

ANN BRIDGE
The Ginger Griffin

CHANG HSIN-HAI
The Fabulous Concubine*

CARL CROW
Handbook for China

PETER FLEMING
The Siege at Peking

MARY HOOKER
Behind the Scenes in Peking

NEALE HUNTER
Shanghai Journal*

REGINALD F. JOHNSTON
Twilight in the Forbidden City

GEORGE N. KATES
The Years that Were Fat

CORRINNE LAMB
The Chinese Festive Board

W. SOMERSET
MAUGHAM
On a Chinese Screen*

G.E. MORRISON
An Australian in China

DESMOND NEILL
Elegant Flower

PETER QUENNELL
Superficial Journey through
Tokyo and Peking

OSBERT SITWELL
Escape with Me! An Oriental
Sketch-book

J.A. TURNER
Kwang Tung or Five Years in
South China

HONG KONG AND
MACAU

AUSTIN COATES
City of Broken Promises

AUSTIN COATES
A Macao Narrative

AUSTIN COATES
Macao and the British, 1637–1842

AUSTIN COATES
Myself a Mandarin

AUSTIN COATES
The Road

The Hong Kong Guide 1893

INDONESIA

DAVID ATTENBOROUGH
Zoo Quest for a Dragon*

VICKI BAUM
A Tale from Bali*

'BENGAL CIVILIAN'
Rambles in Java and the Straits
in 1852

MIGUEL COVARRUBIAS
Island of Bali*

AUGUSTA DE WIT
Java: Facts and Fancies

JACQUES DUMARÇAY
Borobudur

JACQUES DUMARÇAY
The Temples of Java

ANNA FORBES
Unbeaten Tracks in Islands of the
Far East

GEOFFREY GORER
Bali and Angkor

JENNIFER LINDSAY
Javanese Gamelan

EDWIN M. LOEB
Sumatra: Its History and People

MOCHTAR LUBIS
The Outlaw and Other Stories

MOCHTAR LUBIS
Twilight in Djakarta

MADELON H. LULOFS
Coolie*

MADELON H. LULOFS
Rubber

COLIN McPHEE
A House in Bali*

ERIC MJÖBERG
Forest Life and Adventures in the
Malay Archipelago

H.W. PONDER
Java Pageant

HICKMAN POWELL
The Last Paradise

F.M. SCHNITGER
Forgotten Kingdoms in Sumatra

E.R. SCIDMORE
Java, The Garden of the East

MICHAEL SMITHIES
Yogyakarta: Cultural Heart of
Indonesia

LADISLAO SZÉKELY
Tropic Fever: The Adventures of
a Planter in Sumatra

EDWARD C. VAN NESS
AND SHITA
PRAWIROHARDJO
Javanese Wayang Kulit

HARRY WILCOX
Six Moons in Sulawesi

MALAYSIA

ODOARDO BECCARI
Wanderings in the Great
Forests of Borneo

ISABELLA L. BIRD
The Golden Chersonese: Travels
in Malaya in 1879

MARGARET BROOKE
THE RANEE OF
SARAWAK
My Life in Sarawak

SIR HUGH CLIFFORD
Saleh: A Prince of Malaya

HENRI FAUCONNIER
The Soul of Malaya

W.R. GEDDES
Nine Dayak Nights

C.W. HARRISON
Illustrated Guide to the Federated
Malay States (1923)

BARBARA HARRISSON
Orang-Utan

TOM HARRISSON
Borneo Jungle

TOM HARRISSON
World Within: A Borneo Story

CHARLES HOSE
The Field-Book of a Jungle-Wallah

CHARLES HOSE
Natural Man

W. SOMERSET
MAUGHAM
Ah King and Other Stories*

W. SOMERSET
MAUGHAM
The Casuarina Tree*

MARY McMINNIES
The Flying Fox*

ROBERT PAYNE
The White Rajahs of Sarawak

CARVETH WELLS
Six Years in the Malay Jungle

SINGAPORE

RUSSELL GRENFELL
Main Fleet to Singapore

R.W.E. HARPER AND
HARRY MILLER
Singapore Mutiny

MASANOBU TSUJI
Singapore 1941–1942

G.M. REITH
Handbook to Singapore (1907)

C.E. WURTZBURG
Raffles of the Eastern Isles

THAILAND

CARL BOCK
Temples and Elephants

REGINALD CAMPBELL
Teak-Wallah

ANNA LEONOWENS
The English Governess at the
Siamese Court

MALCOLM SMITH
A Physician at the Court of Siam

ERNEST YOUNG
The Kingdom of the Yellow Robe

* Titles marked with an asterisk have restricted rights.